Praise for Nell Pattison

'Tense, twisty and full of toxic secrets – a chilly fight for survival guaranteed to give you shivers'
T.M. Logan

'Holy. Hell. I haven't finished a thriller this fast since *Gone Girl*'
Reader Review ★★★★★

'A **superb innovation** for the crime genre . . . a brilliantly terrifying premise'
Philippa East

'I am **freaking out!** Boy – did I not see that coming!'
Reader Review ★★★★★

'Sinister, layered, atmospheric . . . I couldn't turn the pages quickly enough'
Debbie Howells

'A fun, wild, suspense book that I **couldn't get enough of**'
Reader Review ★★★★★

'A **nail-biting page-turner** of a thriller [with] satisfying layers of complexity'
James Oswald

'You'll definitely be left with your **jaw on the floor** and your head spinning'
Reader Review ★★★★★

D0726736

After studying English at university, Nell Pattison became a teacher and specialised in Deaf education. She has been teaching in the Deaf community for fifteen years in both England and Scotland, working with students who use BSL, and began losing her hearing in her twenties. She lives in North Lincolnshire with her husband and children. Nell's first novel, *The Silent House*, was a *USA Today* bestseller.

Also by Nell Pattison:

The Silent House
Silent Night
The Silent Suspect
Hide

FRIENDS DON'T LIE

NELL PATTISON

Published by AVON
A division of HarperCollins*Publishers* Ltd
1 London Bridge Street
London SE1 9GF

www.harpercollins.co.uk

HarperCollins*Publishers*
1st Floor, Watermarque Building, Ringsend Road
Dublin 4, Ireland

A Paperback Original 2022

First published in Great Britain by HarperCollins*Publishers* 2022

Copyright © Nell Pattison 2022

Nell Pattison asserts the moral right to be identified as the author of this work.

A catalogue copy of this book is available from the British Library.

ISBN: 9780008468057

This novel is entirely a work of fiction. The names, characters
and incidents portrayed in it are the work of the author's imagination.
Any resemblance to actual persons, living or dead, events or
localities is entirely coincidental.

Typeset in Sabon LT Std by Palimpsest Book Production Limited,
Falkirk, Stirlingshire
Printed and bound in the UK using 100% renewable electricity
at CPI Group (UK) Ltd

All rights reserved. No part of this text may be reproduced,
transmitted, down-loaded, decompiled, reverse engineered, or stored in
or introduced into any information storage and retrieval system, in
any form or by any means, whether electronic or mechanical,
without the express written permission of the publishers.

MIX
Paper | Supporting
responsible forestry
FSC™ C007454

This book is produced from independently certified FSC™ paper
to ensure responsible forest management.

For more information visit: www.harpercollins.co.uk/green

For Beatrice

Prologue

Two women look at each other across the table. The furniture is sparse and bolted to the floor, forming an uncomfortable distance between the seat and the tabletop if either of them want to lean forward on their elbows.

'Isabella,' the first woman says, eyeing her companion warily.

'Isabella,' the other responds with a nod. Her lip curls up at the side, but it's certainly not a smile.

There's a long pause. The second woman won't take her eyes off the first, no matter how uncomfortable it makes her.

'Why are you here?'

'I wanted to see how you're doing,' the first woman replies. The fingers on her right hand worry at the nail of her left thumb, and she looks down at the table.

The second woman sighs and sits back, folding her arms. Her clothes are rumpled; she's clean, but her skin has the telltale pallor of someone who has been indoors for too long without adequate nutrition.

'What the hell do you expect me to say? Everything's wonderful, I've never been happier?'

The first woman doesn't respond, and the silence stretches on. Craning her head around, the second woman looks for one of the guards to tell them she's had enough of her time with this visitor.

'Wait.' The first woman leans forward, stretching her hand out to take that of the woman opposite, who recoils.

'No physical contact,' she snaps. 'Look, just say what you want to say then get out. I don't want to see you.'

A sigh. 'I don't know. I don't know what I wanted to say.'

The second woman shakes her head and makes a disgusted noise. 'Leave.'

'I'm sorry. I know you probably never want to see me again.'

'Oh, I'll see you again. Don't worry about that.' Her face is drawn into a snarl as she signals to a guard, and the first woman stands up hastily.

'I never meant . . .' she begins, but she's silenced by a glare.

She watches the other woman being led away before turning and leaving as well.

IZZY

Chapter 1

From: kelly@photosfromthehart.org
To: isabellabutterworth@mymail.com

Dear Mrs Butterworth,

We loved having you and your family in the studio
for a photoshoot the other week, and I'm pleased to
attach proof copies for you to see. When you've
selected the images you like best, drop me a line and
we can discuss print sizes. For a full range of the
products we offer, please go to our website.

Looking forward to hearing from you soon,
Kelly Hart
Photos From the Hart

I hit the delete icon as soon as I realise the email is
not intended for me. Is this woman – the other Isabella
Butterworth – incapable of typing her own email address

correctly? Feeling an irrational spurt of annoyance that she's interrupted my concentration yet again, I go back to what I've been working on.

I'm a virtual assistant, and this particular client has sent me a list of social media posts to write and schedule, which have taken longer than I expected. It's not too much of a problem, because I bill my clients for the hours I work, but it's dull. I have no interest in this particular brand of pithy motivational posts, and the fact that so many of them are scheduled in advance only adds to their fakeness, in my opinion. But I do what I'm paid to.

After another fifteen minutes, I know I need a break, so I save what I've been doing, grab my purse and get ready to go for a walk to the corner shop. Frost is creeping across the edges of the window panes, so I layer up, shoving my hat down firmly to hide the fact that I haven't washed my hair for a few days. Before I leave the flat I hesitate; my hearing aids are sitting on the coffee table, unused since the last time I went out. I know if I wear them more often I'll get used to them, but I hate them so much I rarely put them in. This, however, is an occasion when I'm going to need them. I hook the devices over my ears and slide the slim tubes into place, grimacing as they pinch the tops of my ears. They play a jaunty tune when I switch them on, but that doesn't detract from my discomfort.

Leaving my flat, I walk slowly, nosying into other people's windows as I go. It's dark, but early enough that people haven't yet drawn their curtains, my favourite time of day. Through each window I can see something festive,

6

be it a lavishly decorated tree, or a tacky flashing reindeer. An elderly couple in one house proudly display the cards they've received around the mantelpiece, fastened onto cardboard hangers that seem like they're nearly as old as the couple themselves. I stop outside their window, pretending to tie my shoelace in order to justify lingering. I think there are fewer cards than there were last year, but that doesn't surprise me. Nobody my age sends cards any more.

I'm fascinated by the way other people live their lives, and I've learnt so much about the people who live on my street simply from looking through their windows. I know my life is hardly something to shout about, dull as it is, but at least I don't sit in my window in my underwear at all hours of the day, like the man at number forty-five. And if I ever feel my life is hard I just have to take a look at the family in seventy-eight with their bare floor-boards, one sofa for a family of six, and no curtains. I sometimes wonder if there's something I could do to help them, but the one time I tried to approach the woman who lives there she glared at me so fiercely I chickened out. Still, I dropped off a couple of bits for the kids near Christmas last year, so I hope they were well received.

That time of year has come round again so quickly, and I feel a pang of guilt about not repeating my act of generosity, but I've had so much on my mind recently. I haven't even decorated the flat; it feels a bit pointless when I'm the only one there, and I doubt anyone will be getting me any presents to put under a tree.

Stopping in the middle of the pavement, I feel my

breath catch in my chest as I think about childhood Christmases, Tony and I racing to be the first to get downstairs and see if Santa had been. I could really do with some of that magic right now. Blinking back tears, I find a tissue in my pocket and blow my nose, hoping that anyone who sees my distress mistakes it for the symptoms of a winter cold.

The bell above the door jingles tiredly as I go into the shop, the pitch of it distorting slightly through my hearing aids. I have to put my shoulder to the door to get it fully open. It sticks on a bit of floor tile that's rucked up, but nobody has got around to fixing it in months.

'Izzy,' comes a voice from the back of the shop. 'How are you?'

I look up and flush slightly. 'Hi, Adam. I'm okay, how are you?'

He flashes me his most charming grin. 'I'm well, thanks. Just here to help my uncle out.'

I nod at the door. 'You could help him out by fixing that floor tile.'

'It's on my list, don't worry.'

I sidle past a stack of boxes containing brands of crisps I've never heard of, probably all approaching their sell-by date, and go toward the wall of chiller cabinets at the far side of the shop. Just my luck that Adam's here. He's married, but that doesn't stop him flirting with every woman who comes into the shop, and like the fool that I am I always fall for it.

I wasn't always like this. There was a time when I would have flirted back, given as good as I got, but my confidence and self-esteem have started to dissipate along with my hearing. Now I just find myself getting embarrassed. The rational part of me wants at least to scowl at him and tell him to piss off, but unfortunately the more primal part of my brain always takes over and I end up simpering and laughing at every word he says.

I'm the first to admit there's nothing about me that's particularly special. I'm average height, average weight, my eyes are a boring shade of brown and my hair is lighter but equally dull. This used to bother me; I would spend hours finding the best way to dress to make myself stand out and watch countless online tutorials to learn the latest make-up techniques. Now, I feel like I can use it to my advantage and enjoy the anonymity of being forgettable, but there's still a part of me that longs to be flirted with.

There's a mound of Christmas chocolate at the end of the aisle, and I linger by it for a moment. I know I eat too much junk, but I'm tempted to get some in for all the evenings when I'm alone in front of the TV. I'm contemplating what to get when I hear his voice again.

'Work your hips.'

I turn and stare at Adam, wondering what the hell happened to push his flirting up a gear. Heat rises in my face and I know I've turned bright red. It's not even like I'm wearing anything that allows him to see my figure – jeans and a jumper under my thick winter coat, the padded rolls of which make me look like I'm at least part marshmallow.

For a moment my mouth gapes as I wonder what I'm

supposed to say in response. Back in the day, if a bloke had said that to me in a club I would have had the perfect witty response, depending on whether or not I wanted to encourage him, but now my mind is blank. Then, I remember his wife and frown.

'Aren't you married?' The words are out of my mouth before I can think about how they sound. I expect Adam to either get defensive or laugh it off, but a puzzled frown crosses his face.

'Huh? What's that got to do with it?'

I've done it again, I realise with a sinking feeling.

'Nothing,' I mumble, shaking my head. Now would be a good time for the floor to swallow me up.

'I said I work for tips. I meant I'd fix the floor for my uncle if he makes it worth my while. What did you think I said?'

Squeezing my eyes shut, I try to control my embarrassment. It's all I can do to stop myself bolting from the shop then and there, but if I do that I'll never be able to come back.

Forcing a laugh, I shake my head. 'Sorry, must have misheard you.' One of my stock phrases. If I laugh when I say it, it won't be obvious how disorientated it makes me feel.

He grins at me. 'Go on, what did you think I'd said?'

I shake my head, not willing to admit the full extent of my mistake. He doesn't need to know how mortified I'm feeling, thinking he was coming on to me.

'Tease,' he says, following it up with a wink.

Desperate to get out of there before I make even more

of a fool of myself, I grab a bottle of wine, a frozen pizza, and a multipack of chocolate bars before paying and scuttling out onto the street again. One day I might actually meet a man who's perfect for me, but I think by then I'll be so used to running away from conversations like this that I'll miss my chance.

I walk much faster on my way home, no longer entranced by other people's Christmas decorations. Most of the windows have their curtains closed now, nothing showing but a chink of light around the edge. It doesn't bother me now; I want to get back into my safe space and try to forget about how lonely I feel.

When I get back to my desk, I click onto my emails to check nothing has come in while I was out. There's nothing that can't wait, so I spend a few minutes scrolling through my social media feeds, trying desperately to forget my deep embarrassment in the shop. Some photos catch my eye – a group of my friends, three of them having a Christmas cocktail-making session at one of the bars in town. I read the caption; this was Saturday, two nights ago. In contrast, I was home alone, watching *Star Trek* on Netflix and drinking a bit more than was good for me. A standard Saturday night.

What hurts is that these gatherings always used to be the four of us. Ever since we met at college when we were seventeen, we'd been a little, close-knit gang, and we always went everywhere together. We even went on holiday a few times. Not any more, though. The nights in clubs were becoming exhausting, trying to keep up with the conversation, pretending I got the others' jokes even though I hadn't heard the punchline correctly. Even when we just went to the pub, I found it difficult, so it was easier not to join in with what they were saying, or not to go out with them in the first place. At some point they stopped inviting me.

I take a deep, shuddering breath, wishing I could speak to Tony, but I know I have to wait for him to call me. He usually calls a couple of times a week, so I'll just have to muddle through until then. Closing the app, I push my phone across the desk, as if this action will erase the memory of those photos, of my friends having fun without me. I've considered trying to talk to them about why I started to pull away, but I'm too scared they won't care.

There's no way I want to do any more work today, so I shut down my computer and cross over to the window, staring out at the park opposite for a few moments. I see a figure standing just outside of the light from a lamppost, and I wonder what they're doing there. Probably waiting for a date, or finding somewhere for a cigarette while they text a friend. I expect this random stranger has someone important in their life, which is more than I have.

With the new year approaching, I know I need to do something to change my lifestyle, because my world is shrinking rapidly. I think Tony is the only person who would notice if I disappeared.

Chapter 2

People think that when you start losing your hearing everything just begins to get quieter, but that's not how it works. It starts out so insignificantly that you don't even realise it's happening. You mishear a couple of things and put it down to tiredness, or the acoustics in whatever room you're in. Eventually, you notice that the mishearing is becoming more frequent, having to ask people to repeat themselves, or pause in the middle of a conversation to ask yourself if you heard that correctly.

When I finally went to have my hearing tested, they explained it to me. Some speech sounds are easier to hear than others, so you get to the stage where you can only hear half a word. The person you're talking to might say the word 'mass', but you can't hear the end of it, so you're stuck wondering if they might have said 'mast', or maybe 'mask'. Your brain often fills in the gaps, especially if you know the context of what the other person is talking about, but when it guesses incorrectly it can lead to some really strange misunderstandings.

My friends noticed that I was becoming increasingly withdrawn when we went out. I couldn't stand it, suddenly not being able to keep up with them, but I didn't want to tell them the truth. What would they have done? Probably just given me sympathetic looks and carried on as usual. I couldn't bear the idea of them not caring, not bothering to do anything to include me, so I didn't give them the opportunity. Of course, I might have been wrong – might have been too hasty in my choice – but now I'll never know.

I crawled into bed quite early last night, because sleep was the one thing I knew would detract from the misery of seeing the photos of my friends having fun without me. These days I seem to spend a lot more time in bed, even more than I did as a teenager. I'm glad I've always been strict with myself about working at my desk and never from my bed, because that could be a slippery slope.

My morning routine is a bit slow today, I'm feeling sluggish. There's something niggling at me and I can't figure out what it is. I miss my brother, although I know I probably won't tell him how I'm feeling, at least not to the full extent. He'll only worry about me, and there's nothing he can do to help right now, so that will make him feel worse. I don't want to be the cause of any extra suffering for Tony, not on top of what he's already experiencing.

I settle myself at my desk, looking through the list of tasks that I've set myself for the day. When I started losing my hearing, I was working in a call centre for an insurance company. At first it didn't impact my work, but I noticed I was more tired when I got home every day, unable to do much other than collapse in front of the TV. Later, I discovered that's called 'concentration fatigue', because it was taking me more effort to listen to the people on the other end of the phone. After a few months, however, I started making mistakes, writing postcodes incorrectly or getting crucial values wrong. My boss gave me a warning, which Tony insisted was discrimination, but instead of trying to fight, I decided to quit. It was around the time everything blew up for Tony, too, and I couldn't handle the stress from both sides.

I've always been sensible with money and I had enough saved to see me through a few months. In the meantime, I found a way to earn some money from home. I've always been good at admin tasks, the boring things people would rather farm out to someone else, so I thought I could take advantage of that by becoming a virtual assistant. Now my job is a real mixture, from website copywriting and social media, to data entry and managing email queries. I love being able to work from home, to set my own schedule, negotiating my own terms of employment for each client, but I've become more and more isolated as time has gone on, without even realising it.

My inbox pops up, and after I've dealt with a few junk items and filed a couple of enquiries about my services, I find myself thinking about the email I received yesterday. The cursor hovers over the deleted folder for a moment before I open it and retrieve the email.

I don't know why I do it. Over the last couple of years

I've received quite a few of these emails intended for someone else with the same name. Before now, I've just deleted them and moved on, but for once I'm tempted to have another look. Maybe it's because I've finally accepted that I've drifted away from my friends, and I'm feeling lonely. Maybe it's because there are photos attached to this email, and the nosy part of me can't resist having a look. Whatever it is, my curiosity gets the better of me and I find myself wondering what this other Isabella Butterworth looks like.

I click on the email attachments, not realising I have been holding my breath. I don't know what I was expecting – maybe for her to look similar to me – but she doesn't, at all. The other Isabella is beautiful, not in a carefully posed Instagram sort of way, but with an effortless, natural grace that makes me feel like a baby elephant in comparison. Her hair is a rich, dark brown, contrasting with mine, which resembles straw in both colour and texture. In the first picture, she just has a hint of a smile, but in the second it's much broader, as if she's about to burst out laughing. She has the sort of figure I would kill for, although I bet she's been conditioned to hate her curves.

Turning my attention to the other three people in the picture, I can see that the two daughters have their mum's colouring, though their face shapes are quite different. I'm not much good at judging kids' ages, but they're quite young – I'd say maybe between five and nine, something like that. For the photo shoot they're wearing matching pink dresses with flowers on, which I wouldn't have picked for my worst enemy, so clearly this other Isabella doesn't share my taste. The girls are posing nicely in the first few pictures I open, though there are some later on with them messing about, tickling each other and pulling silly faces. If this were my family, those are the photos I would keep.

But it's the fourth person in the photos who draws my attention the most. Isabella's husband, I assume. Something about his smile makes me uneasy, almost as if he's gloating. It's the sort of look I associate with men who are over-confident, who don't care about other people as long as they get what they want. Maybe he reminds me of someone . . . It seems a little unfair of me to assume he's that sort of man, but I can't shake that first impression. Still, he's pretty good-looking, and some of the photos leave me with a flutter in my belly just looking at him.

What would my friends say if I was seeing a man like him? I can just picture their faces. My love life always seems to come up in conversation every time we meet, even when I have nothing to tell them. It's just a big joke to them, all happily paired off and doing couples things together. Imagine if I ended up with the best-looking man of the lot of us; I think I'd be entitled to be a bit smug.

I can picture us sitting round drinking cocktails. They'd all be talking about promotions or mortgages or babies, and I wouldn't be able to hold it in. 'I've started seeing someone,' I would blurt out, taking a big gulp of my espresso martini as soon as the words were out of my mouth. The look on my friends' faces would be priceless, something I'd want to remember for a long time.

'Really? Why didn't you say! Tell us all about him.' They'd sit forward eagerly, clutching their sickly-sweet drinks, dying to know more. One of them would clap her hands together softly in a gesture of excitement, as she always does when there's new gossip of any kind.

I know it's just a fantasy, but I'm actually enjoying this imagined conversation. How nice it would be to meet a bloke I'd feel excited to tell my friends about. The last guy I went on a date with was an arsehole whose profile hadn't given away that he was a right-wing racist anti-abortionist. He talked down to me the whole time we were out, and I seriously contemplated getting up and walking out several times. I can't imagine that the sort of man the other Isabella would marry would be anything like that. I'm sure he'd be utterly charming on a first date, and leave you wondering how you'd been so lucky.

'He's called James.' I continue my imaginary conversation with my friends, making up my own name for the other woman's ruggedly handsome husband. 'He works in property.'

'Ooh, nice. How old is he?'

'He's thirty-eight,' I'd reply smoothly. 'It's his birthday in a couple of weeks, actually.'

Their eyes would light up. 'Are you doing anything special? When can we meet him?'

I'd be coy though, not wanting to give too much away at this stage. 'Don't get ahead of yourselves. It might be a while until we meet friends and families. We're taking things steady,' I tell them in my head, making it up as I go along. 'He's got kids, so obviously things need to be settled and stable for them.'

'Kids?' At least one of my friends would open her eyes wide. 'Oh, is he divorced, then?'

I know that aspect would disappoint them, and I sigh inwardly. Sometimes my friends could be such snobs.

'No, he's widowed,' I'd reply, mentally apologising to the other Isabella for killing her off. 'His wife died of cancer a couple of years ago. So you can understand that he doesn't want to disrupt anything for his girls, they might not be ready to accept their dad having a new love interest just yet.'

What the hell am I doing? I sit back in my chair and shake my head. Not only have I conjured up a completely fictitious relationship with a man whose name I don't even know, I've just had a ten-minute imaginary conversation with my friends about him. Pushing myself sharply away from my desk, I go through to the kitchen to pour myself a strong drink, wondering if I've been working too hard. I definitely need to spend some more time outside, seeing real people, instead of in front of my computer screen. But the more time I spend at home, the more comfortable I get here.

I don't think there's anything wrong with me having my little fantasy about the man in the photos, really. He is, after all, very good-looking, and in the outfit he was wearing for the shoot it's clear that he's no stranger at the gym. I like an active man, and for a moment I even kid myself that that's the sort of man I want to be with. In truth, I'm definitely not an outdoorsy or a gym person, and no man would ever be able to change that aspect of me, but we can be who we want in our heads. That's the beauty of the imagination.

Coming back to my computer, I pull up the photos once again, intending to delete them, but I find myself looking through them one more time. Her life looks so different from mine, and I feel a stab of envy. My friends assume I don't want a partner, a family, a nice house, but that's because I don't talk about any of those things. I've given up on having them for myself, but now I look at these photos and think why? Why does she get all of this, and I don't?

Chapter 3

A hand grabs my shoulder and pulls me roughly back towards the bush. The light outside my building casts only a weak glow onto the path, and at this time of night it's easy for someone to hide just beyond, in the shadows.

'Don't scream.'

There's a slight whine of feedback in my hearing aid as someone presses their face to my ear. Without pausing to think, I slam my elbow backwards and I'm rewarded with a grunt as it makes contact with the person behind me. Their grip loosens, allowing me to wheel around and step back.

'Who the fuck are you?'

The adrenaline coursing through me has made me braver than I might normally have been, though I can feel the fear jangling every nerve. As soon as I've spoken I think I should have just run, but I'm frozen to the spot. I've been working all day, and I thought I'd pop out to get something to eat then curl up on the sofa with that and some Netflix sci-fi, but this man grabbed me as soon as I stepped out of the door.

He doesn't look familiar. He's breathing heavily and scowling at me, but he doesn't make another attempt to touch me. His breath fogs in the cold night air as he exhales. I can't have hurt him. I didn't strike him that hard, but he looks wary. Perhaps he's not sure what I'm going to do next. That makes two of us.

'You can start by telling me why the hell you're lurking outside my front door,' I growl. It's only once the words are out of my mouth that I think I shouldn't have confirmed that I lived there. Still, he's just seen me coming out of the front door, so it's probably no surprise . . .

'Where is she?' he asks, the threatening undertone in his voice still there. I'm glad there's a light out here, so I can get a good look at his face but also so I can understand what he's saying to me.

'Who?' I don't have to fake the confusion I know must be showing on my face.

'Butterworth.' He spits the name, jabbing his finger at the door buzzer, with my surname written on a little card next to my flat number. 'I know that's her flat, but you're living in it. I've seen you through the window, the top floor belongs to her. Where is she?'

I shake my head. 'I don't understand. What do you want?' I don't know who the hell this man is, but it sounds like he's been looking for me. My bravery from earlier has faded and I have to fight to control my breathing.

'Isabella fucking Butterworth.' He's almost shouting now, and I glance at the windows closest to us. I live in an old Victorian house that's divided into five flats, and the whole of the top floor is mine. Well, mine and Tony's, technically. My two neighbours on the ground floor are reasonably friendly, but it's gone ten at night and I don't want them thinking I'm having some sort of domestic situation right outside their flats.

A split second later, I remember that strange feeling I had the other night, when I thought I'd seen someone watching me from over the road. Without thinking, I glance over there, and when he follows my gaze I see his nostrils flare. It must have been him, standing there, watching me as I looked out. A shiver runs through me that's nothing to do with the low temperature out here, and I wonder how many times he has stood there. I'm careful to close my curtains every evening, but I also like to look out of the window while I'm thinking, so it wouldn't be hard for someone to keep an eye on me.

Whoever he is, I need to know why he was lying in wait to grab me outside my house.

'You've been following me,' I say, reaching into my pocket for my phone. Why the hell didn't I call the police the moment I got away from him after he grabbed me? 'I don't know you. Who are you?' I read that you should always say this if you're confronted by someone aggressive, then any passers-by know you need help, instead of thinking you're having a row with a partner.

He shakes his head. 'I need to know where she is. Tell me, and I'll leave you alone.'

What the hell am I supposed to tell him? If I tell him the truth, that that's my name, what will he do to me? I don't know who he is, so maybe he has the wrong person and isn't looking for me at all, so if I tell him he'll leave me alone. But what if he doesn't? What if confirming my identity makes him hurt me?

'Why do you want to know?' I ask, trying to keep my voice from shaking with fear as I speak.

He takes a step closer to me and I flinch, gripping my phone tighter. My thumb hovers over the icon marked 'emergency call'. Part of me thinks if he was going to do something to me, he would have done it already, but do I really want to test that theory?

'When I find that woman, I'm going to fucking kill her,' he tells me, his voice quieter now. 'So tell me where I can find her, and then you won't see me again.'

'I'm calling the police,' I say, my voice cracking. He's backed me up against a fence, and I quickly glance to each side. Should I run back to the front door of the building, and hope I can get through it before he catches me? If he gets through the door, can one of my neighbours help, or will he be put off by the presence of other people? My other option is to run out onto the street and towards the nearest shop, but that tactic relies on me being faster than him. I'm not particularly athletic, beyond some half-hearted yoga most mornings, so I don't think it's worth the risk.

He's in my face now, back to breathing heavily, but I can see panic in his eyes. His glance darts to the phone in my hand and he backs off.

'Fine, you keep your fucking secrets. But tell her from me, I'm coming for her. She can't hide from me forever.'

With that, he turns and runs up the street, glancing back over his shoulder once before crossing the road and disappearing into the darkness. I stand there for a moment, frozen to the spot by the encounter, before I remember what I'm doing. Yes, I'm hungry, but I can order in. There's no way I'm going out in the dark now, not after what just happened.

I slip back inside the house and push the door closed behind me, leaning on it for a moment after I hear the latch click. There's a rustle upstairs, as if one of my neighbours has just ducked out of the hallway, but I ignore it. The stairs light is turned on, which is a relief, so I quickly ascend the two flights to my own little penthouse.

Calling it that is my idea of a joke – it's tiny, but I have the top floor to myself while Tony isn't here. Unlocking my door, I turn to the left and go into my narrow kitchen, grabbing a glass and pouring myself a healthy slug of vodka. I drink it in one, standing in front of the sink, then pour another. This one I take through to the other room, crossing the narrow strip of carpet at the top of the stairs to my living room slash home office, the two tiny bedrooms accessed from there. I sink down onto the sofa and put my glass on the table, then rub my face with both hands, trying to work out what the hell that guy was talking about.

At this point, I have no idea if I should call the police. I don't know who he was, or even what he wanted. He didn't hurt me, and though he made threats he didn't carry any of them out. Then I remember what he said about having seen me through the window, which means he's been watching the building, and me, for at least a few days, if not a couple of weeks. The thought makes me shiver, and with that I've made up my mind. I need to tell the police.

There's a notepad and pen on the low coffee table in front of me, so I pick them up and start writing down everything I remember about him. White male, maybe about 5'9? He wasn't that tall, anyway. Nondescript features, mousy brown hair that needed a trim, and a scrubby beard he probably thought made him look edgy. What was he wearing? I stop and try to think, doing my best to conjure up an image of him in my mind, but I have no idea. He was wrapped up against the cold, as everyone is at the moment, but that won't help the police find him. No wonder they say eyewitness accounts of anything are never reliable.

Next, I try to write down exactly what happened. It's gone nine in the evening: I work online and flexibly to suit myself, so I sometimes work quite late, which can be useful if I've got a client in a different time zone. When I finished my tasks for the day, I locked my door and left the flat, intending to get something to eat. My stomach rumbles to remind me that I still haven't eaten, and I've had quite a bit of vodka on an empty stomach. I quickly open a delivery app and click on the first option that's available – right now I just need to find something that's open and that someone can bring to me. That done, I go back to my notepad.

Even after only a short time I can't quite remember the order everything happened, or exactly what he said, but I do my best. I know I need to report this to the police, so I want to get my story written down now, before I forget it all in a vodka haze.

When I've finished, I read it through and make a couple of notes at the side, then put the notebook down. I can't keep going over it, because I'll end up exaggerating, or adding in details that didn't happen. Anyway, I want to forget about it now.

I sit back on the sofa and look around my small living space. I've done my best to separate off the three areas I use on a daily basis. My sofa is in the corner, with its brightly-patterned throw and the coffee table piled high with copies of SFX magazine, and the television opposite. Then I have a bookcase sticking out into the room, creating a makeshift wall between the areas where I relax and where I work. My desk and workspace are a complete contrast to the sitting area: everything is white: furniture, laptop and accessories, and it's spotlessly tidy. I need order and neatness if I want to work well, and I also like to have a clean backdrop when I'm on video calls. Even the clients that I've worked with since I started are still clients, not friends, and I don't want to give away any clues to my personal life if they start nosying while we're having a meeting.

On the other side of my desk is a door with a glass panel in it, covered by a white mesh curtain, which leads to my bedroom. Here I'm back to bright colours and clutter that's only just on the right side of chaotic. Tony's

27

room is on the other side, the door closest to the sofa, but I haven't been in there since the day he left, except to check for plates and cups that needed to be cleaned. I'll go in and clean it at some point, but for now I try to forget how alone I feel without my brother here.

I know a lot of people would hate the idea of spending so much of their life in such a small space, but it suits me. In only a couple of years I've built up a thriving business and a strong reputation, and I no longer have to worry about struggling in an office environment.

The idea that someone has been watching me fills me with unease; this flat is my sanctuary, and I can't allow anything to disturb that. I don't know if he'll be back, but he didn't sound like he was going to give up. The thing is, I don't have a clue what he was talking about. He said he was looking for Isabella Butterworth and wanted to know why I'm living in her flat – but I AM Isabella Butterworth. If he was looking for me, he didn't recognise me, which makes me think he has the wrong name. It can't have been me he was looking for, because I haven't done anything that I need to hide. Have I?

Chapter 4

I stifle a yawn with the back of my hand as I sit on the hard plastic chairs in the police station lobby. Why didn't I just call the non-emergency number and report it? There was no need for me to come here in person. Part of me knew, however, that it was important for me to get out of the house this morning, to get over the fear that someone would be lurking outside the door again.

I didn't sleep well. Every time I started to drop off, I heard a thump or a creak from somewhere inside the building, and my imagination went into overdrive. Was the man creeping up the stairs, waiting until I was asleep to break in and finish the job? It doesn't help that I find it harder to identify environmental sounds now my hearing is deteriorating.

My door was locked and I'd put the chain across, but that didn't really mean anything. It's a cheap plywood internal door that was fitted about ten years earlier when the house was converted into flats. It was never designed to withstand any sort of force, and if someone was determined enough I doubt it would stop them for long. The locks are pretty flimsy, too. The only reason I feel secure in there is because it's at the top of the house, so anyone breaking in would be unlikely to make their way all the way up to the attic conversion. Ground floor flats are tempting for opportunistic thieves, but not mine.

Taking some deep breaths, I try to clear my mind while I wait for someone to get to me. I told the woman on the desk that I wanted to report an assault, so they know I'm here for something more serious than a lost pet, for example. There are probably plenty more serious crimes out there that will take priority, I remind myself. Still, I can't sit here all day. Even working flexibly on a freelance basis doesn't mean I can take time off whenever I feel like it.

Just when I'm considering giving up and calling to make my report instead, a uniformed PC sticks her head out of a door and calls my name. She greets me with a fleeting smile and I can see she's probably more tired than I am, then she leads me through to another room.

'I understand you're here to make a report,' she says.

'Er, yes. I was assaulted.' My voice is shaking, and I wish I sounded more confident. What if they don't believe me? I have no reason to think they won't, but I'm one of those people who always expects to be disbelieved. At school, even when I told the truth I shook as if I were lying, and that never went too well for me.

The PC gives me what's probably a well-rehearsed professional yet sympathetic look, then takes down my name, address, and phone number. At first I'm hesitant, natural wariness appearing again, but I give her everything she asks for.

'Can you give me some details? Tell me what happened?'

I take another deep breath then think back to last night, wondering where to start.

'I finished work for the evening, and I was going out to get something to eat . . .'

'What time was this?'

The interruption throws me, but of course, I know I need to be specific.

'Er, around nine.'

It takes longer than I expected, but eventually I've given her my account of what happened. She takes some notes and checks a few details with me along the way, but mostly she lets me talk. At the end, she asks me for as full a description of him as I can manage, and I'm thankful that I took the time to write something down last night, because by now my memory is throwing up all sorts of extra details that I can't be certain are accurate.

'And you don't know this man?' she asks, giving me a look that I can't decipher.

I shake my head. 'No, and that's what's really strange. He knew my name, but he didn't think I was the person he was looking for. I mean, he was looking for Isabella Butterworth, and that's me, but he kept asking me where she was . . .' I tail off, unsure if I'm making any sense.

The PC frowns. 'That is strange. Did he give you any other information that might suggest why he was looking for you? Or her?' she adds.

'No, nothing.' I pause, before voicing something that has been going round in my mind since it happened. 'Do you think he'll come back?'

The PC's expression is one of bland reassurance. 'From what you've told me, it sounds like you're not the person he was looking for. Of course, it's natural to be concerned.'

'I just thought, what if he finds out that my name *is* Isabella Butterworth? Maybe he'll come back and hurt me, like he was threatening to do?'

There's a pause that goes on a little too long. 'I can give you a leaflet on personal safety, and there's a website that will show you how to make sure your home is secure.'

I nod politely. That's not any use to me, but now I think about it I don't know what I want from her. I know I'm not exactly going to get police protection, but isn't there anything else they can do?

I don't say any of this, however. It's bad enough being here, having drawn this much attention to myself, and I really just want to get home and get on with some work. A few minutes later I've signed my statement and have been bundled out of the door with the information the PC offered, along with a couple of leaflets detailing where I can get support following my assault, and who to call if I see the man again.

While walking home, I don't look at my phone, or listen to music. I'm hyperaware of the people around me, and I find myself glancing at every face I pass, trying to commit them to memory in case someone else might be following me. By the time I get back to my flat, I'm exhausted from the mental effort. The sofa looks incredibly inviting, but

I resist its siren call and settle myself at my desk straight away. I know if I don't get on with some work immediately then I'll end up making excuses to myself and take the whole day off, which I can't afford right now. Building up a solid reputation is important when you work freelance, and the smallest thing can destroy that reputation. Missing a deadline would be career kryptonite for me, and I'm not willing to risk it, despite the fact that I just want to rest.

Half an hour later, my mobile rings. My heart leaps when I see who it is; in all of the drama I'd completely forgotten he was due to call.

'Hi, Tony,' I say, feeling better than I have since last night, knowing I can talk to him about what happened and hopefully get some decent advice.

'Hiya.' In the background I can hear a low rumble of male voices, and the occasional clatter that I can't identify.

'How are you?'

He lets out a bitter laugh, which deflates my mood a little. Most of the time he's quite relaxed, but he has his bad days, and I get the feeling today is one of them. At least I know which version of my brother I'm getting today. 'Absolutely peachy. How about you?'

The sarcasm in his words cuts through my relief at being able to speak to him. I hesitate, wanting to tell him about the strange man from last night and his threats, but now I'm wondering if it's a good idea. Before, I would have called him right after it happened, wanting my big brother to protect me and defend me from everything that's bad in this world. Now, though, he can't rush to my aid and I don't know if he has the headspace for anyone else's problems.

'I'm okay,' I tell him, but I don't get the tone right.

'You sure?'

'Yeah. Just had some hassle from a random guy last night. It's nothing.'

He seems to take my word for it, because he's already moving on. That's a bad sign, too. Tony is one of the most selfless people I've ever known, and only a scary level of depression would stop him from asking more.

'Have you had any luck yet?'

I wince when I remember our conversation from last week, and what he asked me to do. I've been really busy and I completely forgot, but I can't tell him that. Either I'll hurt his feelings, and leave him thinking I don't care about trying to help him, or I could risk pushing him further into his depression. This is my fault, though. I agreed to help him, so I press my phone to my ear with my shoulder, grab a pad of sticky notes and write myself a reminder, pulling it off and sticking it to the corner of my desk. It can stay there while I work, then once I've finished I can devote some time to helping my brother.

'Not yet,' I tell him now. 'It's a bit complicated, getting hold of the information you want. I need to try a couple of different avenues.'

He's silent for a moment, and I wonder if he's bought my lies. Well, not lies exactly. It will be complicated, when I get round to it, because I don't know if the information I want is in the public domain or not. And if it's not, then I need to figure out the best way of getting it without landing myself in the shit.

Tony sighs down the phone. 'Yeah, I know. Just keep trying, okay? And give Kane a call when you've got something.'

'Sure,' I tell him. I've got Kane's business card pinned to the corkboard next to the sofa, in case I need to contact him. I don't like Kane, Tony's lawyer; his suits are too shiny and he always looks hungry when he smiles at me, but Tony trusts him.

We make some small talk, but I can tell he's finding conversation difficult today, and he wants to get off the phone. There's very little that we can find to talk about these days, and I think he can't always cope with the details of my life. I understand that, but it makes it difficult to know what to say. Next time he calls, I need to have something to share with him, I think.

When he hangs up, I sit for a moment, willing myself not to turn and look at the door through to his room. I've got used to having the flat to myself now, but for a long time it was weird, as if I'd lost something. My heart aches for him, knowing there's nothing I can do to get him back, not just yet. Even when that day comes, I'm scared he won't be the person he used to be.

I glance at the time, then drag myself into my work. It's another couple of hours before I decide to take a break, and by then my head is starting to pound. I didn't even eat lunch, I realise, so I stand up and stretch before going through to the kitchen and rummaging in the cupboards. They're pretty bare, so it'll be another takeaway later, I think. I really should try to get to a supermarket, stock up on a few essentials, but it's a pain in the arse when you don't drive. I could always book a grocery delivery, I think, then all I'd need to do is carry it back up the stairs.

I ponder my options while I wait for the kettle to boil, then pour water into a plastic pot of processed noodles, watching the granules of nondescript flavouring dissolve and form a sauce. At some point I should really start paying attention to basic nutrition, I tell myself, though I know it's pointless. Convenience will always be my priority.

Chapter 5

Eight o'clock on a Friday evening, and Brayford Wharf is thronging with people. I totter along, past all the chain restaurants, secretly wishing I'd stayed in and ordered myself a Nando's. But here I am, out in town for the first time in ages, wearing boots with heels that I'm already starting to regret.

This spot is where several different aspects of Lincoln all merge – the inland harbour that was used by the Romans and then the Vikings, overlooked by the University of Lincoln, lined with hotels and restaurants with something to offer everyone. It's a popular spot with students and tourists, but I'm neither, and right now I'm feeling pretty overwhelmed. I love the history of Lincoln, but I know most of the people around me only care about the competitive prices of the drinks in whichever bar they're heading to.

I check my watch: I'm on time, and I feel a wave of

nervous energy surge through my stomach. Whenever I meet up with my friends, I'm always the first to arrive. You'd think I would have learnt by now that 'meet at eight' doesn't actually mean that. Punctuality has always been important to me, though, and I can't break the habit, even for a group of people I know will never be on time.

The venue I'm heading for isn't along the edge of the wharf, it's in it, or rather floating on top of it: a barge that's shed its last two letters to become a bar. I take a deep breath before stepping inside, knowing the others will expect me to find a table and claim it for the evening: that has become my role over the years, and if I step out of it now and stand outside to wait for one of them, there will be questions. When we were at college I was always the one who grabbed our usual lunch table, always the one who was first to class and collected handouts for the others, so I suppose I've brought this on myself.

Inside it's not as gloomy as I'm expecting it to be, and I'm thankful that I can easily spot a table within sight of the door. I choose the seat with the best view of anyone entering and slide into it, putting my bag on the table in front of me. I could be waiting for anywhere between ten minutes and half an hour, so I pull out my phone and scan the QR code on the table, bringing up the drinks menu on my phone. Should I order us cocktails? Our get-togethers have been sporadic in the last couple of years, so I don't know for certain what they'll be drinking. Kelly might still be breastfeeding, so does that mean she won't be having alcohol? I don't have a clue about any of that, so it's probably safest if I order my own drink, at least for now.

One dilemma out of the way, I order a gin and tonic and settle back to wait for one of my friends to arrive. When the others invited me out I was thrilled, but now I'm here I'm wondering if it wasn't such a good idea. What do I even have in common with them any more? I've seen plenty of photos online of Jess and Courtney out together, shopping trips and afternoon tea, stuff like that. They work together, and they've always been the closest of the four of us. Kelly had a baby earlier in the year – I can't remember exactly when – so she's been less available, but I've found that has meant I'm excluded from the invites too. I won't deny that it hurts, seeing photos of a friendship I'm being shut out of plastered all over my social media feed.

Three weeks have passed since that man was waiting for me outside my flat, and I haven't seen any sign of him since. This should be a relief, but part of me is always on edge, looking over my shoulder to check he's not watching me. I've barely left my home in that time, and it took a lot of courage to come out tonight. Christmas was lonely, but I spent it doing things I enjoy, with my favourite food and a lot of TV. Tony called, and we had quite a nice chat about our family Christmases when Mum was alive. Neither of our dads stuck around in our lives for long, but Mum was enough for us.

Now we're in that strange period between Christmas and New Year, when nobody really knows what day it is, and it's anyone's guess which shops will be open on which day. I've taken a bit of time off work, but it keeps my mind busy and stops me worrying about Tony, or about the man who attacked me, so after a couple of days of indulgence I got back to it again.

My thoughts are interrupted by Jess and Courtney arriving together, and I can tell from the in-depth conversation they're having that they haven't just bumped into each other in the doorway. It's too late for them to have come straight from work, but they definitely arrived together. I feel my face heat up as I realise I've been excluded from their little world once again.

'Hi, Izzy!' Jess trills when she sees me, giving me a broad smile that only lasts a fraction longer than is necessary to make it look genuine. 'I hope that's not lemonade you're on! Not got another baby coming, have we?'

She and Courtney both burst out laughing at this, and I join in, knowing it's either that or walk out. My single status always seems like something of a joke to them, and I'm sure at some point this evening they'll probe me about my dating life. I think of the imaginary conversation I had with them the other week and am almost tempted to try it out. They wouldn't have a clue if I was telling the truth or not, and it might be fun to string them along for a bit.

Both of them have been in stable relationships for several years, and Jess is getting married next year. Despite the fact that I haven't met a decent man in ages, I know if I were to get married I'd want a small intimate ceremony. Just a few close friends and family would be enough, because for me the marriage would be far more important than the big day. Not for Jess: she won't be content without at least two hundred and fifty people watching her swan around in ivory lace, a trail of adoring brides-maids behind her. I've been invited, though I noticed my invitation didn't come with a 'plus one'. I haven't RSVP'd yet. I think I might be busy that day.

'Come on. Cocktails,' Courtney says, opening the drinks menu. 'I'll get a round in, Kelly should be here soon.'

'I suppose it's harder to get out for an evening,' I say, 'now she's got a baby.'

Courtney laughs, not looking up at me. 'Doesn't seem to have held her back much so far.'

So the three of them have been having regular nights out without me. This realisation doesn't actually hurt as much as I thought it would, now that I'm here with them. The last couple of years have driven a wedge in our friendship, a wedge that I created by withdrawing into myself as I lost my hearing, but now I'm feeling less and less inclined to try to remove it. Jess and Courtney are browsing the cocktail menu and occasionally ask for my input, but all I can think about is getting home and taking off these bloody uncomfortable boots.

The acoustics in the bar aren't too bad, surprisingly, but the combination of other people's conversations and background music are making it difficult for me to hear what my friends are talking about. I lean forward and concentrate, watching their faces to add in some lip-reading cues, which might help me to follow what they're saying. After a while, I wonder if it's worth the effort I'm putting in to listen to the story Jess is telling about a prank they pulled on one of their new coworkers.

'It sounds a bit cruel,' I say, the words out of my mouth

41

before I've had a chance to stop and think. Courtney raises her eyebrow at me and Jess snorts, trying to hold back her laughter.

'All right, fun police,' Courtney snaps, and I can tell my comment has got to her a bit. 'We were only having a laugh. It's just office banter, but I expect you've forgotten all about that, shut away on your own in your little bedsit.'

There's a flash of venom in her eyes as she says this, and I know she feels a sense of smugness at the comparison between the three-bedroom new-build house she owns with her boyfriend, and my little flat that I'd still be sharing with my brother if things had been different. At least where I live has some character, I want to say, but I keep my mouth shut.

'Yeah, it's just banter,' Jess echoes. I remember office banter, all too well. It's a word that bullies hide behind when they don't want to accept that the things they say and do might not be as funny as they think. As my hearing loss became more of a problem and my mistakes became noticeable, the 'banter' I received somehow increased, so I don't have much tolerance for their idea of a joke. I'm half considering walking out, when Kelly finally arrives.

'Ooh, cocktails,' she says with a big grin as the drinks arrive at the same time. 'Excellent way to start the evening!'

I don't think I'll be staying out too late. Picking up my drink, I give the others the brightest smile I can muster as Jess proposes a toast to friendship.

'So,' she says, 'now we're all here . . .' She glances at Courtney, handing over to her.

Courtney looks around at the three of us, her smile so smug I expect it hurts to maintain it. 'Callum and I are engaged!' She waves her left hand, which I only now realise she's been keeping hidden under the table.

Jess obviously already knew about Courtney's news, but she squeals just as loudly as Kelly as the two of them throw themselves onto Courtney. Thankfully, I'm sitting opposite her so I can't reach her, even if I wanted to join in the display.

'That's fantastic, congratulations!' I tell her, forcing as much jollity into my voice as I can. I'm not faking it; I am genuinely happy for her. She and Callum are very well suited – they both view possessions as status symbols, and I'm pretty sure they've cheated on each other an equal number of times. They're a perfect match.

Of course, the next hour is devoted to wedding talk, and I slowly sip the prosecco that we've moved onto, not wanting to get too drunk. I've barely eaten today, and I can feel the alcohol going to my head. It's difficult when I don't really have much to add to the conversation – I'm not married, have never been anywhere close, and I'm not the sort of person who has a Pinterest board set up with dozens of dress designs, ready and waiting for the right man to ask me. I'd rather spend the money on a nice holiday.

The bar is packed by ten, and I'm starting to find the atmosphere a bit oppressive. It's getting too loud for me to do much other than sit and look around me, and my so-called friends aren't missing my contribution to the conversation. Making the excuse that I need a bit of fresh air, I squeeze through the crowd and out of the door, walking a few feet away to lean on a low wall for a while.

What am I doing here? I wonder. The four of us were friends when we were seventeen, at college. Now, ten years later, I don't see what there is that still connects us. I know if I leave now, the three of them won't miss me. I'm just glad they didn't have the opportunity to start probing me about my dating life, because God knows what I would have ended up saying under pressure.

I take out my phone, wondering if I should text them and tell them I'm not feeling well, that I've decided to go home. To be honest, I think it would be the best move for all of us. What I need right now is to spend some time with the only person I feel I can be honest with. Turning my back on the bar, I weave through the crowds knowing nobody will notice me. It's like I'm invisible, even with the people who are supposed to be my friends, and I feel a sharp sting of pain as I think about them still sitting around the table. They won't be wondering where I am, I'm sure. Blinking rapidly to try to stop the tears, I look for a taxi to take me home.

Chapter 6

The next morning, my phone is still silent. None of my friends messaged to check I'd got home safely. That has always been part of our routine whenever we go out: make sure everyone is okay at the end of the night. Their lack of concern is all the confirmation I need that I'm not one of them any more.

Dragging myself out of bed, I push any thoughts of them to the back of my mind. It's too painful for me to linger too long on my own loneliness; I need to spend some time looking after myself, starting with getting over my fear of the man who attacked me. I get dressed in a hurry, rushing to catch the first of three buses I need in order to go and see Tony.

Much as I love my brother, I hate visiting him. The room I'm sitting in is soulless, with dull grey carpet and matching walls. It smells of institution food, that mass-produced, low-quality, low-cost kind of food that you get in schools and hospitals – and prisons, it seems. The chair I'm sitting on is the middle of a row of three, facing a little low table, with a single chair on the opposite side. At least it's not too uncomfortable, though someone has been picking away at the upholstery of the chair next to me, so some of the stuffing is spilling out, drawing my eye.

I jiggle my leg absentmindedly while I wait, trying not to make eye contact with any of the other visitors. It's weeks since I've been, and I do feel guilty for not seeing Tony sooner, but I can't say I've missed this. Everyone eyeing each other up surreptitiously, wondering who we're here to see, what they might have done and how we're related. Wondering if we're complicit in whatever it was. Wondering if we need to be scared of the other men in the room, the ones we don't know. Or maybe that's just me. Maybe I imagine the furtive glances, and maybe I'm projecting my fears.

Tony eventually appears, and I give him a huge smile. Standing up, I hug him, trying to ignore just how skinny he's become since he's been here. My big brother was always solid, mostly muscle but he was never a meathead, just well-built. Now he's gradually fading away, and I worry that by the time he gets out of here there'll be nothing left of him. His work as a paramedic always inspired him to keep fit, along with rugby at the weekend with his mates, but now he doesn't have any of that. When he gets out, I hope he's able to find that part of himself again.

'Hey,' he says, trying his best to return my smile. I can see it's taking him a lot of effort – it's not that he's

46

unhappy to see me, more that he can't bring himself to be happy about much at the moment.

'I wasn't expecting you today,' he tells me once he's settled in the chair opposite me. 'Is something wrong?'

He knows me too well. Of course I can plan a visit just because I miss him, but he's so used to me coming to him when I need help or advice, he can read it in my face.

'Something happened a few weeks ago,' I begin. 'I didn't tell you at the time because I didn't want to worry you, but it's getting to me.'

Tony leans in, and I tell him all about the man who was waiting outside my flat for me, including his threats, and my visit to the police station. When I've finished, he sits back in the chair and runs a hand over his stubble.

'You definitely didn't recognise him? Could he have been someone you've met in the past trying some sort of prank?'

'No, I'm sure I haven't seen him before. And he definitely wasn't acting, he was too angry to have been putting that on.'

'You'd be surprised what people can fake,' he says, and I see him cast a look over his shoulder. Is he having problems with some of the other inmates? I want to ask, but I know he won't give me a straight answer, especially after the story I've just told him. Making a mental note to ask him about it another time, I continue.

'I really don't think he knew that was my name.'

'So he was looking for someone else with the same name?'

I pause. I'm glad he's said this without me suggesting it, because it shows me it's not such a crazy idea, even though the police dismissed it. I'm convinced it's something I need to consider, especially as I already know there's another Isabella Butterworth out there. After all, I keep getting her emails.

'Why would he think I was someone else, though? Or rather, how would he get us mixed up? Has he just searched the country for someone with my name and picked the wrong one? It sounds like a bit of a shot in the dark.'

'Not if he's narrowed it down somehow,' Tony says, gesturing with a hand as if to say it's obvious. 'If you both live in Lincoln, for example, or you're both members of the same Facebook group.'

It has never occurred to me that the other Isabella could live in the same city as me. What are the chances? I imagine it's not unusual if your name is Sarah Brown or James Smith, but Butterworth isn't exactly a common surname.

'I hadn't thought of that,' I say, but don't elaborate any further. I want to do a bit of digging for myself first before I mention it to Tony.

We talk for a while about nothing in particular. I mention that I'm feeling a bit distant from my friends, but he's starting to seem distracted, so I leave it. There's only so much of my life Tony can help me with at the moment. I haven't been able to track down the person he wanted me to find, but at least he appreciates that I've been trying, when I get time. Eventually, we run out of conversation and say our goodbyes.

On the bus on my way home, I keep thinking about the possibility that the man who attacked me was actually looking for another Isabella Butterworth. If he was, what are the chances it's the same one whose emails I've been receiving occasionally for the last couple of years? I need to find out if we have anything in common other than our names.

When I'm home, however, I need to get on with some work. I've taken some time off over Christmas and now I have a looming deadline, which keeps me at my desk until quite late. By nine p.m. I'm ready to stretch out on the sofa with a pizza and a bit of *Star Trek*. It's an episode I've seen several times before, but I don't mind; it's my comfort zone, and I need a bit of that right now. While I eat, and the *Enterprise* sails through space, I open up my emails and perform a search. It's something I've been thinking of doing all afternoon, but until now I haven't allowed myself to check.

I'm not someone who automatically deletes emails I'm not interested in. I tend to read them and scroll quickly through my inbox, but without bothering to clear out any of the junk. This means I'm bound to still have a few of the emails I've received that haven't been meant for me – I will have scanned them quickly, realised they were intended for someone else, then moved on to the next email.

It's not an easy search, because I can't exactly use her name as a search term. I have to wrack my brains to try to remember what sort of emails I've received, and narrow my focus that way. There have been some from websites

I don't use, and I'm sure there was something from a restaurant I've never been to.

It takes a few hours, but by early morning I have a folder with several emails in it: a restaurant reservation confirmation; a voucher code for 15 per cent off in a fancy boutique up near the cathedral; the email from the photography studio; and an invitation to a PTA meeting. This exercise has shown me that Tony was on the right track. Somewhere in Lincoln is the other Isabella Butterworth.

I don't know why these errors keep happening. Perhaps her email address has a dot between her two names – something easily missed when someone is typing it out. Whatever the reason, I receive things intended for her, and I'm now wondering if she gets some of mine, too. Is she aware of my existence just as I'm aware of hers?

Until my recent look through her photos, I hadn't really thought about her or who she might be. The only time I've responded to one of the emails was when I was invited to a job interview. I emailed back to say they had the wrong person, and hopefully they had the candidate's phone number to inform her of the interview. Now, however, I can't stop thinking about her. Did she get to that interview? Did she get the job?

The restaurant and boutique are both high-end, so I'm assuming she earns quite a bit more than I do. I know she has two daughters from the photos, and she's obviously the sort of parent who gets involved in their school life if she's been attending the parents' and teachers' association. I don't recognise the name of the school at first, but I look it up, and it's a private school with no details of fees on the website – if you have to ask, you can't afford it. Whoever she is, this woman lives a very different life to mine.

The big question, of course, is why was that man looking for her? I have to assume that it was indeed a case of mistaken identity, that he was looking for an Isabella Butterworth in Lincoln and his search led him to my flat. The emails have got me this far, but no further.

I can't stop thinking about her. I open up the photos again and look at them, focusing only on her this time rather than her husband and children. The man who attacked me was boiling over with rage and hate, and with that much emotion compelling him I can't imagine he'll give up before he gets what he wants. Is this woman in danger? If so, I feel like it's my responsibility to try to warn her.

It's three in the morning, so I can hardly pick up the phone and call the police station right now, but I rummage through the information they gave me and find a card with an email address on. The PC told me to contact them if I remembered anything else about the man. I put an email together quickly, explaining my theory that he was actually looking for another woman with the same name, then pause to consider how much information I should include. I have photos of her, and I know where her children go to school. If I tell the police about this, will they believe that I got this information purely by accident? Or will they start to look at me suspiciously? I'm sure they could use this information to find her and warn her, but I don't want to turn the focus back onto me. The police should easily be able to find her using means I don't have, they don't need to know about the emails.

I send my message, then crawl into bed, but it takes a while for me to fall asleep. Every time I close my eyes, I see that man's face as he growled at me, telling me he was going to kill Isabella Butterworth when he found her.

Chapter 7

I spend the next morning in bed, flicking through TV channels but not settling on anything. My phone vibrates with a notification and I wonder if it's a reply to the email I sent to the police, but it's probably too soon for a response. Picking up my phone I see it's come from the dating app I occasionally use. At first, I think about ignoring it – I'm not really in the mood for dull chat, or photos of a stranger's genitalia, which is all I ever seem to receive – but I have nothing better to do so I have a look.

According to his profile, Harry is a thirty-three-year-old landscape gardener who's looking for someone to spend some quality time with. My experience of these apps could give a rather flexible definition of 'quality time', but I click on his photo to have a better look. It won't load, which makes me roll my eyes. I look at his message anyway: it's brief, but at least looks personal, as if he's

53

read my profile. He mentions a shared interest in sci-fi, and to my surprise ends his message asking if I want to meet up tonight. Tonight? That's a bit quick for my liking. Usually I end up exchanging messages with men for a couple of weeks before we either meet for a drink, or the conversation tails off. The drinks usually end in an awkward parting, or awkward sex followed by parting, if I'm in the mood for that sort of thing. Strangely enough, the occasional few I've met who I've actually liked are the ones I won't take home with me on a first date. We all have our standards, however nonsensical they might seem to other people, and that's one of mine.

My love life seems to consist of these sorts of dates now. I've had one relationship that lasted more than a couple of months, and even that one didn't make it to a year. When my friends were single, or at least only at the dating stage with their partners, it didn't really bother me. But then they moved in together and got engaged, progressing along the typical settling-down path, while I stayed exactly where I was, living with my brother and never quite meeting the right man. I don't have any relationship horror stories in my past, though the longer I'm single the less confidence I have that I'll ever meet anyone good.

My hearing loss affects how I behave on dates now, too. I don't mention it on my profile, not since I had a couple of blokes tell me they weren't interested because of it, so I wear my hair down and have to concentrate really hard in order to be able to hear them. It gets exhausting, and I often wonder if it's worth the effort.

Should I go and meet Harry tonight? I quite like the idea of it, if I'm honest, after my disappointing night out with my friends. If nothing else it'll get me out of the flat and I might get a couple of drinks out of it, but the fact that his profile picture won't load is ringing some loud alarm bells. Plenty of people use dating sites pretending to be someone they're not. But if we meet in a public place, what harm is there?

I reply to suggest a meeting place, and he's quick to respond.

Thot u cud come to mine.

Sighing, I type out a quick response telling him a firm no, then block him. How hard is it to meet someone who actually wants to get to know someone, form a relationship? Very, in my experience.

Closing the dating app, I scroll through my phone, scanning for other Isabella Butterworths on social media, to see if I can find the one whose emails I keep receiving. There are a couple who have open profiles, but when I have a look through their pictures and activity it's clear none of them are who I'm looking for. I can't find any sign of her, which is really frustrating. She might not have any social media accounts, but even if she does, her profiles are private or hidden. I hover over a couple of the locked accounts – either of them could be her, because they don't have a woman's face as the profile photo. I have no way of knowing, because I can't see their locations or any of their other photos.

I go back to the folder of emails I put together last night, of those intended for the other Isabella. There's one from a tennis club that arrived last summer, reminding her about their upcoming open day, and asking for members to volunteer some time in order to help out. At first, I think that going to the club could be a good opportunity for me to try to meet her in person, but it's not a great time of year to be starting up tennis. I could have a look online, find out if they have regular open days, but I feel a knot of anxiety forming at the idea of turning up at the club and trying to spot her in a crowd. If I did see her, what would I say? 'Excuse me, a man attacked me and I think he might have been looking for you'? Hardly the best way to break the ice with someone and get her to trust me.

Another idea occurs to me, a way I could use her membership of this tennis club to find her and get in touch. I search for the club on Facebook and find it has a public page and a members-only group. Is there a way I can get access to that group? I get out of bed, pull on some comfy clothes and move to the sofa with my laptop, my head full of ideas about how to try and track down the woman I've been thinking about.

It's not long before I've formulated a plan, and it involves finding out a bit more about this tennis club. One way I can find out which of these locked profiles belongs to the other Isabella is by joining a group I know she's likely to be in, so this seems to be a good place to start. However, I'm not going to be able to join the group with my own profile, because I'm not a member of the tennis club, so I decide to set up a fake profile in order to get in. I know it seems extreme, but I'm genuinely worried about her. This man could be tracking her down, and I want to warn her.

I spend the best part of an hour reading through stories on the club's own website and Facebook page, as well as stories reported in the local press. By the time I've finished I have a list of names that I could use – some of them are older women, some are teenagers. It's tricky to know who would be less likely to have a profile of their own, but I baulk at the idea of impersonating a child, so I select the name of a woman who crops up in a few stories as one of their longest-standing members. The next thing to do is to set up the fake profile, which isn't really that difficult – I don't intend to use any photos, so all I need is an email address, and that's a matter of minutes to set up.

Soon, 'Jean Willows' has her own Facebook profile, and I spend a bit of time finding a few local places and businesses to like. I even get a generic photo of a tennis court and set it as the header picture, with one of a cat as the main profile picture. The real Jean might not be an animal lover, but I think a pet picture looks less suspicious than the greyed-out silhouette placeholder. Once the profile has these few details, I ask to join the tennis club members' private group, then sit back and wait.

While I'm waiting, I decide to have another go at hunting down the man Tony has asked me to look for. Ever since my brother went to prison, he's been fixated on finding this person, and getting him to tell the truth about what happened. I've discouraged him, knowing it wouldn't help his position in the long run, but it's become an obsession for him. I'm worried that if I don't help, he'll start to distance himself from me, or try to find other ways of tracking this man down. He's not in a high security prison, but there will still be people in there who have committed far worse crimes than his, and I'm worried that my brother will get mixed up with the wrong people in order to get what he wants.

It's well into late afternoon, and I've done nothing but mess about on the internet all day, in one way or another. I feel like I should have a shower and go outside, but I don't really see the point of putting in the effort. Maybe I could do with getting some shopping, but I've got enough of the basics in to put it off for another day or even two. I go back to looking through all the information I've found about the other Isabella, as if that will magically help me to find her.

One thing I haven't thought about is what I'm going to say to her. If I received a message that told me someone wanted to hurt me, I would assume it was spam, like the ones you get that say, 'I think you're in this video!' followed by a dodgy link. Even if I didn't, and I took the threat seriously, I'd think it was the person sending me the message in the first place who was responsible for the threat. I haven't had a response from the police to my suggestion that the man was looking for another Isabella Butterworth, so I still think I need to warn her myself, but the wording is going to be tricky.

I sit in front of the TV and write draft after draft, constantly deleting and changing what I've composed. Nothing seems to put across the urgency without making me sound completely deranged. As time passes, I grab myself some food and put my laptop away for a while, hoping that something will come to me if I let my subconscious work on the problem.

My phone pings with a notification and I quickly open Facebook, hoping it's going to tell me that I've been accepted into the group, but it's just one of those useless reminders to look back on my memories. As if seeing photos of good times with friends is going to make me feel any better right now. It's gone midnight, so I'm not expecting anything else to happen now, but I'm frustrated anyway. Putting my plan into action has been exciting, and I want to continue with it, but I know I need to wait. Hopefully it won't take long for one of the admins to approve me, but until then there's nothing more I can do.

Realising my curtains are still open, I cross the room to close them, looking outside for a minute before I do. Was that movement in the bushes across the road? The room behind me is only dimly lit, so I have a fairly clear view outside, but it's dark and I could have been mistaken. Still, I close the curtains, then go and double-check the locks on my front door before I go to bed.

Chapter 8

My door buzzer wakes me, and I struggle to surface from a deep sleep. I'm glad it's loud enough to wake me even without my hearing aids in, but at some point I'm going to have to think about installing some other system that would alert me to the doorbell. Doing that would mean accepting the gradual loss of my hearing, though, and I know there's a part of me that's still in denial about that.

The buzzer goes again. I check my phone and see that it's gone nine, but I don't remember my alarm going off. Maybe I turned it off in my sleep. I used to do that when I was at college, so I took to setting a second alarm clock and putting it on the other side of the room, so I had to physically get up and out of bed in order to turn it off. I haven't needed to use that technique for a few years now, but clearly my body needed some extra sleep this morning.

It buzzes for a third time. I drag myself out of bed and

into the living room, pressing the button to allow me to speak to whoever is outside. On the way, I quickly stick my hearing aids in so I can make sense of their response.

'Hello?'

'Hello, we're looking for Isabella Butterworth.'

There's a churning sensation in my stomach that has nothing to do with last night's alcohol, and my mind suddenly comes into sharp focus.

'Who's we?'

'Police. We have ID, if you'd like to let us in, or come down and check.'

'Okay,' I reply, deciding to opt for the latter. I grab a sweatshirt and throw it on over my pyjamas, then peer out of the window. I can see two uniformed police officers standing outside the door, and I feel a flutter of emotion, anxiety mixed with curiosity. Are they here about the man who attacked me? Have they found him? Or has something happened to the other Isabella?

I move slowly down the stairs, too late realising that I fell into bed without cleaning my teeth last night and I probably stink. I'm not sure what impression that will give them.

When I open the front door, the two women give me quick smiles that are gone in a flash.

'Isabella Butterworth?'

I nod. 'What's this about?'

'Can we talk inside?'

I glance over my shoulder at the stairs. I don't really want to invite them in, but I also don't want to stand on the doorstep talking about what happened to me.

Eventually I give in and hold the door open for them, then lead the way back up to my flat. It's a bit cluttered, but not too bad, and I curl up on the sofa while they stand.

'What's happened?' I ask straight away, hoping to preempt the bad news. 'Have you found him?'

The two police officers look at each other, then back at me. 'Who are you talking about?'

'The man who attacked me. I assume that's why you're here.'

Again, a look passes between them.

'Do you know a man called Ryan Beckley?' the first officer asks. It's clear that one of them has been given the job of speaker, because I haven't heard anything from the second one yet.

I think for a minute, then shake my head. 'I don't think so. I knew a Ryan in my last job, but that wasn't his surname. Who is he?'

'Are you sure you don't know him?' she asks again, fixing me with a look that makes me want to shrink into the corner of the sofa. 'He seems to know you.'

The churning sensation in my stomach has returned, and before she places a photograph down on the coffee table in front of me, I know who I'm going to see. He looks different in the picture, because it's daylight and he's smiling, but it's definitely him.

'Why didn't you say you were here about him?' I asked, a bit cross at their secretive attitude. 'That's definitely him.'

'Sorry, definitely who? Ryan Beckley?'

'I don't know his name. Well, if you say that's his name I assume you're right. I mean that's the man who attacked me. Is that why you're here, because you've caught him?'

The first officer turns her back on me and mutters something into the ear of her colleague, but I don't catch it. When she turns back, I can't quite read her expression.

'I think we're talking at cross-purposes, here. You're telling us this man attacked you?'

I sigh, frustrated. 'Yes, last month. I reported it, but I couldn't give a lot of detail. I didn't know anything about him, he was just a random man who jumped me outside the house one night.' Something tells me it's not wise to repeat the exact conversation I had with this man, this Ryan Beckley, at least until I know exactly why they're here.

'Nobody passed that report on to us, I'm sorry. Would you mind telling us again what happened, just so we're up to speed?'

The two of them are still standing, and it's starting to make me nervous. Why don't they just sit down, then we're all on the same level?

'Can I make you a drink or something?' I ask, hoping to take some of the tension away that's settled over my little studio flat.

'No, thank you,' the first officer replies, and the second just shakes her head. So much for that approach.

Taking a deep breath I think back to that night, then tell them as much as I can remember. I still have the piece of paper where I made some notes, so I show them that, too.

'I wasn't sure how much I'd be able to remember the next day, so I wrote it down,' I tell them with a shrug.

They spend more time looking at my notes than I'm comfortable with, and make some notes of their own.

'Look, what's happened? When you showed me the photo I assumed you were coming to ask if he was the man who attacked me. But if that's not it, why are you here?'

The first officer clears her throat. 'I'm sorry, but we can't share details of an ongoing investigation with you. We wanted to establish if you knew Mr Beckley, and what the nature of your relationship was.'

'That's the only time I ever met him,' I snap, nerves getting the better of me now. 'Thinking back, I thought I might have seen him watching me, outside the flat, before he attacked me, but that might have been my imagination. I didn't know his name until now, and I have no idea why he targeted me. He knew my name, and which of these flats I lived in, but that's all.'

Of course, a little voice in my head pipes up, now I know his name, maybe I can find out more about him and why he was looking for the other Isabella. Though could that be why they're here? Has she been attacked?

'Look, I've been wondering,' I say, before I have a chance to think it through. 'Could he have been looking for someone else called Isabella Butterworth? I mean, when he attacked me, could it have been mistaken identity?'

There's a pause. 'Do you think that's likely?'

For a moment, I don't know what to say. Should I say

yes, there's another woman with the same name who lives in Lincoln, maybe he wanted to attack her? But wouldn't that make me look as bad as him, because I've been looking her up online?

In the end, I shrug. 'I thought it might be possible, because he didn't recognise me as the person he wanted to find.'

'We'll look into it,' she says, in a tone of voice that's clearly meant to appease me, while promising nothing. I sag, knowing they have absolutely no interest in what I think about it.

The two police officers are huddled together and muttering something to each other again. When they turn back, I can see the second one is looking around my flat very carefully, and I start to feel uncomfortable again.

'Can we ask where you were three days ago?'

I give them an account of my movements – mostly here in the flat, working, but I don't know how I'm supposed to verify that, then in the bar with my friends. Well, former friends, I think, considering none of them have contacted me since that night. The second officer writes everything down and takes my friends' names and numbers too, which leaves me completely mortified. I've resigned myself to the fact that we've drifted apart, but if I send the police to their doors to confirm they were with me, I don't know what they'll do. Anyway, why the hell do the police want to know this? What has this man done, and what has it got to do with me?

'Look, can you at least tell me why you're asking me where I was?' I try, hoping this will prise a bit more information out of them, but I'm met with stony expressions once again.

'I'm sorry but we can't share any more with you at this time. We hadn't been passed details of your assault, so we'll make sure it's added to the file, then we might be back to speak to you again in a couple of days. Do you have any plans to leave the area?'

I laugh at this. 'No, I'll be here,' I reply drily. 'I don't have anywhere else to be right now.'

The two of them turn to leave and I hold the door open for them, watching them descend the stairs, not retreating into my flat until I see them close the front door and hear it click. Then I lock my door, strip off and get into the shower, turning it up to the hottest setting I can stand. The ferocity of the water helps to convert my fear into anger. What is going on? First this man attacks me and leaves me jumpy every time I leave the building, then suddenly the police are at my door, showing me a photo of him, but they won't tell me why? I'm seething.

Once I've dried and dressed, my skin still glowing pink from the heat of the shower, I make some breakfast and check Facebook. Nothing yet from the tennis club, which is frustrating, but hopefully an admin will log on at some point. Unless I've been rumbled as a fake, in which case I'll never know if my request to join has been declined. I need another plan, but for now I want to try to find out more about Ryan Beckley.

I put his name into Google, along with the name of the city, but nothing jumps out at me as being particularly significant. There are a few social media profiles that I'll have to comb through, though they seem to be people from Lincoln, Nebraska, rather than the cathedral city in England where I live. I'm going to need more information in order to narrow down my search, but I don't have anything else to go on other than his picture and the memory of what he said to me that night. Closing my laptop in disgust, I decide to go out for a walk to try to clear my head. The visit from the police has given me a headache, which isn't helped by all this confusion about what the hell is going on.

Once I'm in the park up the road, I regret my decision. There are lots of people about despite the bitter chill in the air, and I'm glancing over my shoulder every few minutes to check nobody is following me, or there's no sign of Ryan Beckley bearing down on me from across the children's playground. Eventually I find a bench up against a wall and sit down, confident nobody can approach me without being seen.

I sit without doing anything for a good ten minutes, just watching people going about their lives. Could the other Isabella be here in the same park, out with her family for a New Year's walk before going home to warm up with a hot chocolate? I would probably recognise her if I saw her, though I know photoshoots don't show people at their most natural. Still, I'm frustrated that I can't find a way to get in touch with her. How can I help her – warn her about this man – if I can't find her? Clearly the police aren't going to do anything about it.

Checking my phone, my spirits lift when I see I have a notification – I'm into the tennis club group. As soon as I see that, I marvel at how easy it was. Clicking through to the group, I immediately go to check the members, and after only a couple of minutes of scrolling I find her. Staring at her profile image, her name the same as mine, I wonder if I'm doing the right thing, but before I have the opportunity to talk myself out of it I click 'Send message'.

Chapter 9

Three days later, I've given up on the idea of Isabella replying to my message. Without adding her as a friend, she might not see the notification that she has a message, but it's equally possible that she's read it and ignored it. After all the time I spent composing something, the message I sent in the end was quite bland. I didn't go into any detail, just said that I really needed to get in touch with her. It was hard to decide which approach to take, because I understand that something so vague could easily be ignored as a scam, but I didn't want to launch straight into the story of Beckley and his threats.

I considered sending the message from my own profile, once I knew which Isabella Butterworth to contact, but I decided against it. If I saw a message coming from an account with the same name as my own, I would instantly assume it was some sort of virus, and I'd probably change my password as well, just to be safe. Sending it from my fake account seemed to make more sense, but that carries its own risks. Perhaps she's already friends with Jean on Facebook, or maybe she's seen the real Jean and mentioned the message to her, discovering my deception that way. There have been no repercussions so far though, no suggestion that my profile has been reported by anyone, so I keep waiting, a small flame of hope alive in my heart.

I've thrown myself into work this week, to try and take my mind off everything, but every time I take a break my mind slips back towards the other Isabella, and her connection to Ryan Beckley. Wary about leaving my flat since the police visited with their cryptic questions, I've ordered in everything I might need for a few days and tried to keep myself busy. I might have continued like that for some time if it hadn't been for an unexpected text from Kelly.

Hey Izzy, great to see you the other night. You free for lunch today?

I read the message a few times, looking for the catch, but I can't see anything untoward. Maybe she's realised they've pushed me out a little and wants to apologise, or at least rebuild some of the bridges that are damaged. Of course, I'm always free for lunch, working freelance and having almost nothing in the way of a social life, but I try not to make that too obvious in my reply. We agree a time and a place, and I'm surprised to find I'm actually looking forward to it.

As usual, I arrive first. We've picked a nice little Italian restaurant just outside the city centre, and I take a seat where I can see the door. It'll be useful to see when Kelly arrives, but she's not the person I'm concerned about. On the way here I didn't get the impression I was being followed, but I feel like I can't be too careful at the moment.

I'm handed a couple of menus, and I quickly scan the drinks options. I'm really tempted to have a glass of red wine, but I also don't want to be the only one drinking. Kelly was drinking plenty the other night, but will she drink at lunchtime if she's going back home to a baby? I err on the side of caution and order myself a soft drink, reminding myself that I should be able to eat and drink whatever I want around my friends without fear of judgement. In the last few years I feel like I've lost that, which should definitely be a warning flag for our friendship.

Kelly is late, and I start on a pack of breadsticks that's sitting in the middle of the table. The waiter casts me a few looks, but I steadfastly ignore him. The last thing I need is a stranger taking pity on me because he thinks I've been stood up. Finally, she comes through the door, looking flustered, and makes her way over to where I'm sitting.

'Sorry, I can't get out the door at the right time these days.'

I smile. 'That's okay, you have another person to be responsible for now, that must make things harder.'

She shoots me a searching look, as if she's waiting for the punchline, but then her shoulders relax when she realises I meant what I said. 'Yeah, I don't think people understand that sometimes. I can be all ready to go, but then I feel like I need to double-check his bag to make

71

sure everything is in it, or he needs changing. Then I drop him off, and my sister-in-law wants to ask me something, so I end up talking to her for fifteen minutes, by which time I'm late.' She looks down at her menu and shakes her head. 'I'm told it gets easier.'

'Maybe when they leave home.'

Her laugh doesn't have much humour behind it, and I wonder how she's doing, really. I can't imagine what it must be like, having a baby, so I can't really offer her much in the way of advice, but the dark circles under her eyes and the ragged edges of her nails tell me it's affecting her more than she's letting on.

I like this restaurant because it has good acoustics, and it's quiet right now. It's exhausting, trying to have sensitive conversations with people when I can't be sure I'll accurately hear what they tell me, but here I feel like I can manage well. I'm about to ask her if she's doing okay, if she's got plenty of help, when she looks up at me with a bright smile.

'Bottle of wine?'

I nod. 'Sure, if you want.'

'I do,' she replies with a firm nod. 'I do.'

We order the bottle and our food, then settle back in our chairs. For a few beats, neither of us says anything, and I search my mind for small talk. The moment to ask her how she's doing seems to have passed, but I make a note to ask her later. I wonder if that's why she asked me to meet her today, because she wanted to get out of the house and do something that felt more like the old her, the Kelly that wasn't a mum.

'How are you doing, Izzy?' she asks suddenly, leaning forward and looking me in the eyes.

I'm taken aback, because she's directed the very same question I was going to ask back at me. I see it as an opportunity to get her to open up, though.

'I'm fine. I'm good, thanks. How are you? How's life as a mum, really?'

She waves my question away. 'Ah, it's fine. Some days are shit, some days are amazing, most days are a mixture of both. I realised we didn't really get to talk about you much the other night, especially with Courtney's news, so I thought we could have a proper catch-up today.'

'Oh. Well, I'm okay. Nothing much is happening at the moment.' I think for a moment. 'Work is going really well, I'm glad I made the change. This way of working really suits me.'

Kelly nods as I speak. 'Good. Good! I'm really pleased for you. We were all a bit worried, with you living alone and then working on your own. We thought you might get a bit lonely.'

I shrug. 'Sometimes, but if that happens there are people I can spend time with,' I say, knowing full well that it's not as easy as that. I'm pretty happy with my routine, but I wouldn't expect Kelly to understand that, so it's easier if I embellish a few details.

'You seemed really quiet the other night, that's all.'

At this point I remember she said 'we', before. That would be her, Jess and Courtney, I assume. So they've been talking about me. My heart sinks. I was hoping this was the hand of friendship, but it's not, is it? It's some sort of interference in my life, prodding to try and find out how I could possibly be happy without a boyfriend and a house and a nine-to-five office job with drinks after work on a Friday.

'Well sometimes it's hard to get a word in edgeways with Jess and Courtney,' I say, trying hard to keep any spite from my voice. 'And as we were mostly talking weddings, it wasn't like I had much to contribute.'

I'm hoping Kelly will take this as I mean it, that not everyone is interested in planning dresses and favours and God knows what else people find to waste their money on, but instead she gives me a sympathetic look.

'Are you seeing anyone at the moment? It can take time to find the right person; just because you're not there yet doesn't mean you won't get that, too.'

I pick up my glass of wine and take a big slug, not trusting myself to answer immediately. Every way I can think of wording my true feelings seems inadequate because I know she'll misinterpret it. None of my three friends understand that I don't have much emotional space for thinking about settling down right now. My brother is in prison and I'm trying to support him, I'm only partly dealing with the gradual loss of one of my senses, and now I'm scared there's a man out there who wants to kill me. I don't say any of this, though, because I know there's too much deep emotion going on in each of those subjects to tackle over lunch, even if Kelly was the person I wanted to talk to about them. Instead, I put my glass down and give Kelly a bright smile.

'No, nobody at the moment, though I'm not short of

dates when I want them. I just don't feel like sharing my life with another person right now.'

My friends know about what Tony did because it was all over the national news as well as local, but we've never talked about it. I suppose it's awkward for them, especially as he and I lived together until then, but it's almost as if they pretend nothing has happened. His absence has affected me more than any of them realise. They don't want to see past the surface of my life, though, which really highlights why our friendship has waned.

Our food arrives, and I throw myself onto my plate as a means of escape from the conversation. My pasta dish is steaming and delicious, and I focus all of my attention on it for several minutes while Kelly pushes hers round her plate.

'We just want you to be happy, you know that, don't you, Izzy?'

Sighing, I put my fork down. 'What makes you think I'm not?'

Okay, maybe I'm not happy, but it's not for the reasons I'm sure she's about to list.

She gesticulates with her fork, as if to say, 'Well, look at you,' but she clearly can't find the right words, so I shake my head and go back to my food. It tastes great, otherwise I might have thought about getting up and leaving, but I'm not going to give her the satisfaction of thinking she's got to me.

'I mean, what have you got going on in your life that's really good at the moment? I know you say you're enjoying your job, but that's just a job. We all figured you'd go back to an office when you could.'

'Hell no,' I say with a genuine laugh. 'Inflexible hours and bitchy gossip? Working my arse off to have the bloke who sits next to me repeat all my ideas and get the credit for them? Kelly, I was crap at my job, probably because the job itself was crap. I'm good at what I do now, and I enjoy it. I get to decide when I work, and who I work for. I set my own hours, and my own fees, and it's working for me. We're not all the same. An office job just isn't for me.'

She nods sagely, as if she truly understands, but I can just imagine the conversation she'll have with Jess and Courtney later. 'She misses it, you can tell. She went on about how much she enjoys working from home, as if anyone would want to be stuck in a poky flat like hers all day every day.'

'Well, she's always been a bit weird,' one of the others would say, and they'd all laugh, and move on. I hope, anyway.

'Have you finished with the intervention now?' I ask Kelly, finishing off the rest of my wine. I'm frustrated that of all the things that could be bothering me right now, she has assumed it's my job, which is the one thing I'm truly happy with. 'Was there any other reason you wanted to have lunch, or was it solely to pick over my life choices?'

'There's no need to be defensive, Izzy. We only want you to be happy.'

'Then please believe me and accept it when I say I *am* happy.'

The two of us stare at each other across the table for a moment, until eventually she gives in with a little shrug that says she won't be convinced, but she'll drop it for now.

Ten minutes later, we've paid and we part ways. I don't hang around for extended goodbyes. What's the point? I don't really care about my old friends any more. It's time for me to make some new ones, daunting as that sounds, and cut old ties. My mind flits to the other Isabella, and I wonder if she has this problem. Is she the sort of woman for whom marriage and children are enough? Or does she have more in her life, a different purpose that keeps her going? I'm dying to know more about her, to meet her and get to know her, if only to reassure myself that she's safe from Ryan Beckley.

When I get home, I perform another online search for his name, but nothing new appears. I set up an alert, so I'll get a notification if a story matching my search criteria pops up, then go back to my emails, searching through for clues about the other Isabella and what she might be like. Now I've turned my back on my friends, I feel like I can devote more time to her. Opening Facebook, I see that she still hasn't replied to my message. I think it's time that Jean sent her a friend request.

Chapter 10

Despite the fact that it's a weekday, I pour myself another drink. I've made a plan to track down a few different Ryan Beckleys in order to try and get hold of the one I want. After all, if I can find the other Isabella, surely I can find him using the same principles?

I need food, so I order myself a pizza. After my disastrous lunch with Kelly I think it's probably a good idea to stick to the flat from now on. This is the benefit of the world today, there's nothing I need that I can't get delivered to the comfort of my own home, and quickly. Unless I need to see a doctor, I can stay here for as long as I like, really. This thought comforts me, and when my pizza arrives I settle back snugly on my sofa, relishing the solitude and the ability to do what I want, when I want.

I'm halfway through my food when I get the notification. *Isabella Butterworth has accepted your friend request.*

For a moment, I think my heart has stopped. She accepted. She actually accepted. I wipe the oil from the pizza off my hands and push the box aside, my mind only on Isabella now. Clicking on the notification takes me straight to her profile, and for a moment I just stare at the photo in front of me. It's one of Lincoln Cathedral, not of Isabella herself, but the header photo shows the family of four, taken from behind. This glimpse into her life almost takes my breath away, and I take in as much of the detail in the photo as I can.

It's not one of the ones from the photo shoot, and from this perspective I can see that Isabella herself is tall, noticeably taller than me I think, and only about an inch shorter than her husband. The two girls are standing between them. I don't know how old the photo is, of course, but the children don't look much different in age from the photos I've seen. There's something strange about the angle of their bodies, the way the four of them are walking together, holding hands. It doesn't look completely natural, as if the photographer staged something that wasn't instinctive for them, and I file this observation away to consider later.

Where the hell should I begin? Now that I'm sitting here with her profile page in front of me, I honestly don't know what to look at. I'm paralysed by indecision. Until she responds to my message there isn't a lot I can do other than find out a bit more about her. Right, I need to be methodical.

The first tab on her profile is labelled 'About' so I click there. After all, I want to know as much as I can, to figure out why Ryan Beckley threatened me, and by extension, her. There's nothing in the sections about her work, or where she went to school, which is disappointing, but I understand why people leave those parts blank. I have no interest in reliving my school days, and I know plenty of people feel the same, so maybe Isabella doesn't want to be reminded of that time in her life. As for work, maybe she doesn't have a job, or maybe she wants to keep that private. Never mind. The more I can find out about her, the more likely I am to be able to uncover that part of her life.

Her birthday is on her profile, though. She's older than me, turning forty-one in a couple of months. I open up the document where I put in the information I got from her emails, and start adding details I get from her profile, including date of birth and what I've already gathered about her family.

There's nothing else on her profile in the way of personal information, so next I click onto the 'Photos' tab. Her albums are mostly mobile uploads, so I flick through them until I find one that interests me. A picture of the older girl, grinning widely, standing next to a big helium balloon shaped like the number eight. A few of the surrounding photos seem to be from the same day, with the girl opening presents or posing with other people – I assume the children are her friends and the adults family, but nobody is tagged. The photos have no captions, either, but there are a few comments.

'Happy birthday, Olivia!'
'Happy eighth birthday, Liv!'

'So grown up, eight already!'

That tells me plenty already. Opening up a document, I type the heading 'Family information'. Looking at the date, I subtract eight, then add Olivia Butterworth and her date of birth, along with Isabella's. Another quick scroll brings me to a similar group of photographs, and soon I've added Ruby Butterworth to the list, her date of birth just under two years after her sister's. It's amazing just how much information you can get from people's photos and from the comments other people leave. Even if Isabella herself never mentions her children's names, everyone else does.

Not long before Ruby's birthday photos, I see the traditional 'back to school' shot of the two girls, standing outside the front of their house. I already know what school they go to from the PTA email, but anyone could easily get it from this one photo alone. The logo is right there on their blazers and book bags, and if you live in Lincoln you'd probably recognise it as that of one of the private schools. Whatever Isabella and her husband do for a living, they have enough money to pay for two lots of school fees. I can't imagine that Ryan Beckley's issue with Isabella is connected to her children, though, so I move on.

The husband is the one I haven't seen much of. There are no photos that I can find where he's tagged, so perhaps he doesn't use social media, but even the photos he's in are candid shots where he's in the background. There are no pictures of just the two of them, which surprises me, because all my friends who are in relationships are constantly posting selfies of them and their other halves. Eventually I give up looking through her mobile uploads and try another album instead, which has collated all of the photos other people have taken of her. Here, I have more luck. There's a photo of the two of them with another couple, and I save it to my laptop, because it's the first one I've seen with a clear view of Isabella's face, other than the posed shots I received the other week.

I take a moment to look at her, really look. There's no likeness between us; why would there be? We share a name, but we're not related. I suppose part of me thought that I'd be able to recognise her simply through the connection we share, but I could have passed this woman every day in the street and I probably wouldn't have thought anything of it. Without the lighting and airbrushing of the photoshoot, she looks normal; I don't know how else to describe her. Not unattractive, but not dazzlingly beautiful, either. A normal build, probably a size twelve. Brown hair that looks to have some subtle highlights and an expensive cut, but nothing too ostentatious. Her husband is good-looking, but he looks like the sort of man who has always taken his looks for granted and hasn't taken ageing into account. I scan the comments: Ian. His name is Ian. I add him to the list. I've had to make an assumption regarding surnames – maybe Ian has a different surname, and the girls could share it. They could even be double-barrelled, but adding anything extra to Butterworth would make it a bit of a mouthful. Still, these are details I can double-check, now I know more about the family.

Scrolling through the posts on her page, I see a few memes that friends have shared with her, as well as posts she's been tagged in. At one point, one of her friends calls her Bella. Bella – I like that. It's not a nickname I've ever used, but I think it suits her. It feels too graceful for me, plain old Izzy, but for her it's just right.

When I finally close my laptop, my pizza is stone-cold, but I don't care. I feel like I'm on top of the world now, with all of this information at my fingertips. Getting up, I cross to the window and look out at the dark street, watching a couple of cars as they pass. There's nobody outside, nobody waiting for me today, and I feel stronger, somehow. If Ryan Beckley does come back, I have information that I can barter. But as soon as I think that, I know I wouldn't do it. I wouldn't put Bella and her family at risk. The whole point of doing this, finding out what I can about her, is to try and protect her from him. Whatever this man wants, whatever he thinks she might have done, I instinctively know he must be wrong. If he had any sort of legitimate complaint against her, he'd go to the police and get justice that way. No, she's just as much a victim as I am in this scenario.

For all I know, he might have already attacked her. That might be why the police came to ask me questions. She hasn't posted anything for a few days, so she could be injured, maybe in hospital. I'm sure if she'd died there would be something on her page, so I'm secure in the knowledge he hasn't succeeded in killing her, as he threatened, but that doesn't mean he hasn't found her.

But what if he hasn't? What if she's just living her life,

completely oblivious to the fact that there's an unhinged man out there who's obsessed with finding her and hurting her? How could I live with myself if something happened to her now, after I've found her? No, I need to find a way to warn her.

I go back and sit down at my laptop, open up her profile again and click on the icon to send her another private message. How to begin? Do I keep up the pretence that I'm Jean? No, that wouldn't make any sense, because how would an elderly lady she knows from the tennis club have any of this information about Ryan Beckley? But if I tell her that I'm not actually Jean, that I'm a complete stranger who faked a profile in order to get in touch with her, she'll block me immediately. I'm not an idiot, I know how dodgy my actions look, and she doesn't know me; why should she believe that I've only done this in order to help her, to warn her? That I only have her best interests at heart, and those of her family? I could appeal to her need to protect her children, mention them by name, but that makes me look as bad as Beckley himself.

Slamming my laptop closed again, I slump back on the sofa and take a swig of the drink that has been sitting next to me, ignored. I don't see how I can warn her in a message in a way that she'll take seriously. Of course, I could go back to the police and make them listen to me this time. Tell them I've found another woman who shares my name and that I'm worried she's at risk because Beckley threatened me, but I don't think they're likely to take me seriously just because I've suggested it for a third time. Would they send someone round to speak to her? I'm sure she'd believe the threats if she was warned about them by a police officer. But if they don't send anyone, how will I ever know? I could just carry on my daily life and she might be attacked, when I could have prevented it.

An anonymous letter, then. Of course, in order to do that, I need to know where she lives. The school her children go to takes students from all over Lincoln and the surrounding areas, so that doesn't narrow it down. All I have is a photo of her front door, and the location of the tennis club she's a member of. Is that enough? I read through the information I've compiled in the document, and my heart sinks. There's no way I can figure out where she lives just from this.

I need a new plan. The important thing now is to warn Bella. All I want is to protect her.

Chapter 11

It's Friday afternoon, and I'm out for a walk. My resolve to stay in my flat forever hasn't lasted as long as I expected, partly because I need fresh air, but partly because I can't stop thinking about Bella and her family. I've put the first stage of my plan into action, but I'm waiting for someone to get back to me. It's maddening, but I don't know what else I can do right now.

I've barely been able to sleep, so I've worked through the night for the last two nights, and now I've found myself with nothing to do. So I grabbed a coat and set off, not even thinking about where I was going, just walking to try and clear my head.

Lincoln is an ancient Roman settlement, with parts of the modern city steeped in history. There are old buildings and winding streets, unexpected alleys and beautiful architecture. Then there are the parts that are more modern, with streets laid out in a grid pattern, and a confusing repetition of identical houses. I've lived here all my life and I can't imagine living anywhere else, but I still don't know the whole city.

For a couple of hours, I walk. I'm not going particularly fast, I just want to keep moving as I think. Tony called yesterday, and I felt a stab of guilt when I heard his voice. I've been so wrapped up in my thoughts about Bella, and Ryan Beckley, that I've barely thought about him. Is this what it's like? The longer you go without seeing someone, the less you think about them? I can't let that happen. He's asked me to help him, and I need to try and find the time to do it. But how? What he's asked of me, I've tried. It hasn't been easy, and so far I've drawn a complete blank. This person he wants me to find, a Dr Palmeri, clearly doesn't want to be found. It's not like tracking down Bella, which was a little complicated but not beyond the wit of most people. No, this is going to be more complex, and I might need to try and access files that I shouldn't be able to. That means doing something illegal, or at least immoral, and I'm not sure I'm prepared to go that far, even for my brother.

He was angry when we spoke. I know he was doing his best to hold it back because he wasn't truly angry at me, but it was there anyway, in his voice. I understand, I do. It's not like he can do it for himself, and there's nobody else who'll help him, not after what he did. Or what they think he did. I've always believed him, but the longer it goes on, the louder the treacherous voice in my mind becomes. The one that says maybe they're all correct, maybe he's not telling me the truth. He admitted to his part in what happened, but he insists he's not the only one to blame. Without evidence, though, I don't know what to believe.

Still, I have no way of knowing, at least until I manage to do what he's asking of me. So really, it's just as much in my best interests as it is in his. If I remind myself of this, and behave selfishly, I can get it done. Then at least I'll know the truth, and I'll be able to look him in the eye without worrying he'll guess what I'm thinking.

My walk has taken me to one of the nicest parts of Lincoln, with a mixture of old and modern houses, all huge with gardens that stretch out in front of them. I know I'm near the castle, and looking up, I can glimpse the castle walls running behind the row of houses. I keep walking, not turning in that direction. I don't feel like mingling with tourists and shoppers right now, so I stick to the residential streets, moving onwards without really thinking. To my right, I pass the fence that encompasses the Lawn, outside the old asylum, nowadays famed for the annual steampunk festival. As the road starts to slope downhill once more, I stop for a moment to look out over the green space to my left. There's a community herb garden in there somewhere; I've looked into it before, on one of the occasions when I've suddenly decided I need a new hobby. But considering I can barely keep a succulent alive on my windowsill, I quickly decided that anything resembling gardening wasn't for me. Besides, it's not like I ever cook with fresh herbs. Even ones in a jar aren't part of my cupboard staples, not when it's easier to stick something in the microwave or order a takeaway.

I continue on my way, and the railings change. A little further along, there's a familiar-looking logo, and as I approach it, my heartbeat increases in pace. It's a school. But not just any school. It's Olivia and Ruby's school. Had I known it was here, and walked here on purpose? I shake my head at the thought – no. It's just a coincidence. I'm not the sort of person to turn up outside someone else's kids' school. That's just weird.

I stop and look at the building in front of me. It looks more modern than I had expected. There's something about the nature of private schools that makes me think of old, draughty buildings with high ceilings and substandard heating, but this one looks positively cosy. I can see a class through the window, sitting at tables with paper and craft supplies in front of them. Other children are near the window, and I see the teacher busying herself gathering up paintings and slotting them into a drying rack. It's Friday afternoon, so it looks like this is time for art. I smile at my own memories of primary school, but I don't remember my classrooms ever being as well equipped as this one looks to be.

Since I gained access to Bella's information, I haven't done anything to warn her about Ryan Beckley. I've been paralysed by indecision, but that itself has led to guilt whenever I realise that time is slipping away from me. The longer I leave it, the more likely it is that he'll track her down and hurt her. What if he hurts one of the children? What if he's so bent on getting to Bella that he doesn't care if one of the girls gets in the way? My breath catches in my throat, and panic starts to rise in my gut.

The road is already lined with cars, but more are now squeezing into the few parking spots still available, and I check my watch. It's after three, so these must be parents arriving to collect their children. Oh God. Does that mean Bella is here? My emotions seesaw back and forth between excitement and panic. I could see her in the flesh, maybe even speak to her. But no, she shouldn't see me here; it might give the wrong impression. Nobody likes childless people hanging around outside schools for no good reason, however innocent their motives might be. Even though I honestly was just walking past, who would believe me?

I cross the road and move up a side street away from the school, finding a vantage point where I can still see the entrance. I wait for nearly fifteen minutes, wondering if I should just give up and leave, but in that time a crowd of people starts to gather at the gates. It's cold and grey, so they've been waiting in their cars until the last possible moment, I think. They're all women; I don't see a single man. Some things don't seem to change, no matter how much we push for equality. Then, proving me wrong, a man arrives, and is welcomed into one group of mothers like the novelty that he is. There's a younger group of women standing at the side who glance over, and I wonder if these are nannies or au pairs, rather than parents. It wouldn't surprise me, because I expect a lot of the families whose children attend this school have some sort of hired help, and some of them look too young to have children already at school.

I spend a few more minutes wondering about the

dynamics of the groups that are forming, then I see her. Slamming the door on her large red BMW, Bella runs a hand through her hair as she approaches the gate. She doesn't look particularly happy, though she smiles at the other parents she sees. A moment later, the bell goes, and children start to stream out of the school building. I almost lose Bella in the crowd, but then I spot her, one girl already by her side. They're talking, and Ruby is showing Bella something. Bella smiles, then looks over Ruby's head as Olivia approaches, then the three of them walk back to their car.

Wracked with indecision, I watch as she buckles both girls into their booster seats, and by the time I consider acting, it's too late and they've gone. It's only been a matter of minutes from when I first saw Bella, but now I'm standing here on the street, looking at the space where her car was. Almost immediately, another car fills the gap, and another parent jumps out, leaving me wondering if I imagined the whole thing. I don't want anyone to see me and wonder what I'm doing there, watching parents collect their young children, so I start walking again. Turning quickly, I leave the side street and start to make my way back up the hill. I don't stop until I reach the junction with Union Road, then turn left and make my way round to the Lawn. Here I find a bench and sit down to think.

There was an opportunity there for me, and I missed it. I could have crossed the road and spoken to Bella. Even if she'd dismissed me as a complete nutcase I would have had the time to warn her. But it all went so quickly,

I barely had time to consider my options before the three of them were gone. I know what kind of car they have, but I didn't take the registration number. Maybe I could have used that to help me find their address.

I think about the way Bella looked at her daughters, and the family unit that the three of them made together, and I'm struck by the complete juxtaposition to my own life. Yes, I have the freedom to do pretty much what I want, when I want, but when I go back to my flat later I won't have anyone to talk to, to share anything with. I might not even speak to another human being all weekend. It's something I've got used to, but deep down is it what I really want? Or do I want a life that's surrounded by other people, normal interactions and conversations? Seeing Bella like that has struck a chord with me, and has made me feel even more deeply what I'm missing in my life. A wave of melancholy passes over me, and I wonder for a moment how I'm ever going to change the situation I'm in.

Their house is probably huge, I think. They have an expensive car, no doubt more than one, and their children go to a private school. If Bella works, her hours are flexible enough that she can collect her children from school on a Friday without needing to hire a nanny or send them to an after-school club. I make enough money to get by, but if I ever want to live anywhere nicer than my flat, I'll find it hard. My bank account isn't in the red, but it's far from full. If I have a couple of months where the work dies off a bit, I'll be in trouble. I feel a little stab in my belly, and I realise it's jealousy. I want some of the things Bella has. I want to feel secure and comfortable.

Another thing I need is new friends. I should have recognised this a long time ago, but now I've seen the need to cut ties with my old friends, I can't let myself sink into a well of loneliness.

A thought strikes me. What if I make friends with Bella?

Chapter 12

I'm back in my flat after a brisk walk home, and I feel a new sort of energy surging through me, as if something fundamental in my life has changed. It hasn't, not really, other than my attitude, but perhaps that was all that was needed.

When I thought about becoming Bella's friend, at first it was simply because she was foremost in my mind, but then I quickly realised it made sense. If I make friends with her, build up a relationship, I can keep an eye on her and make sure Ryan Beckley hasn't tracked her down. I know what he looks like, so maybe I can even act as her protector, and if I see him hanging around then I can warn her. She doesn't need to know he's already threatened me; I can tell her I've seen someone suspicious following her, or whatever he might do.

Sitting down at my desk, I try to look through a couple of client documents, but my mind isn't on it. I'm going to have to pack up for the day, and maybe get a bit more done over the weekend to make up the time. Right now, all I can think about is how to form a friendship with Bella.

There are two main elements to my plan that I need to work on: firstly, I need to find a way to meet her that's natural, organic, so I need to get over my fears and go somewhere new. The tennis club might seem the most obvious place, but there's no way I can convince people that I'm looking to take up a sport. I'm uncoordinated, unfit, and I don't even enjoy watching sport, let alone taking part in it. It would be a huge challenge that I'm sure would end up leaving me feeling pretty miserable, which I don't want.

The only other place I currently know of where I could bump into Bella is the school, and that one's definitely out. I have no children, and other than Kelly I don't have any friends with children, so trying to strike up a friendship there would be a huge red flag, and rightly so. Where else could I meet Bella and manage to start a conversation? I know a couple of shops and restaurants that she's been to in the past, but I can hardly spend my days hanging around them in case she comes in. Besides, how often do you talk to strangers in shops, unless they work there and you're asking for assistance?

It's going to take a bit more digging to try and find somewhere that Bella goes regularly, whether it's something like a gym or one of those coffee mornings for local business owners. I don't know what she does, so if I can find that out then maybe it will present me with some other ideas. At least I have access to her Facebook profile now, so I can keep checking if anyone has tagged her in anything, or if she's liked any local events that I could turn up to.

The other matter is my name. I can't introduce myself using my real name; there's too great a risk that Bella will think I'm taking the piss out of her and resist my attempts to make friends with her. I know it would be easier to do it that way and hope we can laugh off the coincidence, but if she doesn't trust me I will have lost my only chance to get close to her.

I have to remember that my main aim in this is to protect her from Ryan Beckley, gain her trust so I can warn her about him. Making a friend is only a secondary aspect to it, and I mustn't let my own loneliness get in the way of that aim.

I'm scared, though. I'm scared of rejection, and of making a fool of myself in front of a woman I barely know but have begun to idolise. Creating a new name would almost give me a layer of protection, make me feel less vulnerable. I could use my middle name, I suppose. Then it's almost like I'm reinventing myself, moving away from the person I've become and creating something new. I like that idea.

I wish I could talk to Tony about all of this. He hasn't asked about the man who attacked me since I told him about it, and I haven't brought it up again either. I'm worried that if Tony finds out his name he might do something – prison has made him harder, and I worry he could find a way to track Ryan Beckley down and hurt him. While I know that would take away the threat aspect, it's not what I want.

Tony has always been protective of me. When I split up with my last boyfriend it was quite acrimonious – he cheated on me, then tried to suggest I was being over-dramatic about it. We had a big argument here in the flat, and he hadn't known that Tony was home. For a while, my brother let us have our privacy but as things got more heated Tony burst into my bedroom, grabbed my boyfriend by the scruff of his neck and threw him out. I still wonder if Tony might have gone further if I hadn't been there.

The guy wouldn't have laid a finger on me, I'm sure, it was just a row, but Tony is my big brother. He's always been there for me, and I've relied on him to solve my problems for so long that I've forgotten how to work things out for myself. He's been in prison for well over a year now, and for most of that time I've been in complete denial, pretending he'll be back soon. My life has taken a fundamental shift and it's taken me until now to notice.

So where do I go next? Can I reinvent myself, make new friends, and include Bella as one of them? Really there are loads of opportunities available to me, if I could only find the courage to take them. In the past I've found myself scrolling through photos online of outfits I wish I could wear – well, maybe I should buy some and start wearing them. The same for the places I wish I could go. I have some savings, so what's to stop me travelling? I can't move, because this flat belongs to Tony just as much as it belongs to me, and I can't sell it out from under him while he's in prison. When he gets out, then we can talk about it, but until then I'm going to stay here and at least keep this consistent for him. That doesn't mean I can't change other aspects of my life, though.

I go through to the kitchen and stare at the shelves, telling myself that's a good place to start. It's easy enough to set up a healthy food delivery, or I could maybe look into one of those subscription boxes that send you everything you need for your meals. By the time Tony gets out I could be an accomplished chef.

For now, I need some basics, so I grab my coat, hat and scarf, and go back out again. This time I don't head toward the usual corner shop, but turn in the opposite direction. There's a small local supermarket about a fifteen-minute walk away, so I'll try going there instead. It might keep me away from my usual convenience food staples.

As I walk down the road, the traffic grows heavier and I find the noise irritating, so I flick the switch to turn the volume down on my hearing aids. Moments later, a movement to the side of me makes me jump and I flatten myself against a wall, heart hammering as a jogger passes me. He's completely oblivious to the fright he gave me, and I stop for a minute to take some deep breaths and calm my racing heart. It's okay, I tell myself. I'm still spooked by sudden movements, ever since the day Ryan Beckley was waiting outside my front door.

When I get to the supermarket, I pick up a hand basket and work my way up the first aisle, scanning the shelves as I go. I haven't been here before, so I'm not entirely sure where everything is, which is frustrating. I can feel myself getting worked up, tempted to turn around and walk out of there without buying anything, but I push on.

There's a woman behind me who wants to get past, but there's a big packaging cage blocking half of the aisle and she has to wait for me. I can hear her huffing and muttering to herself, and when I stop to look at a shelf she gives up and pushes past me.

'For God's sake,' I hear her say as she passes, and I feel my face flush. That's all I can take. I turn around and walk out of the shop, taking some more deep breaths once I'm out in the cold January air.

What the hell is wrong with me? I've spent the last couple of hours imagining that I can completely reinvent myself, become someone else and start making new, exciting friends. But in reality I can't even manage a trip to an unfamiliar shop without getting stressed and tearful. Part of me knows this is understandable; I can't make huge changes in a matter of hours, it needs to be done in small steps. But there's another part of me that tells me I'm pathetic, that I should just go home, curl up on my sofa and get drunk, and just accept my life exactly the way it is.

I stand outside the shop for about ten minutes, then go back inside. I tell myself that all I need to do is go in, buy a few things, then leave, and it will be an achievement. Fifteen minutes later I've managed it, and I'm walking home with a bag of pasta and some sauce, a loaf of bread and some milk. It'll hardly be a gourmet meal this evening, but it'll be the first thing I've actually cooked for myself in months.

Once I'm back in my flat, I collapse on the sofa and wonder how long it's going to take me to build up to meeting new people. Making friends as an adult is bloody hard, especially if you don't know where to start. What if people don't like me? What if I try to get to know another group of women and they all close ranks on me, comfortable with the friendship circle they already occupy?

My phone vibrates in my pocket, pulling me out of my reverie. There's a notification from the alert I set up for any news about Ryan Beckley. My heart in my mouth, I click through to the story and read it twice before the information sinks in. Checking the photo, I'm certain that this is the right person, the man who attacked me outside my front door and threatened to kill Isabella Butterworth, whichever one of us he was referring to. I read the story for a third time, scanning every single sentence carefully in case I've missed anything, then I sit and stare at the wall for a moment, wondering what it all means. This changes everything.

Ryan Beckley is dead.

BELLA

Chapter 13

I wipe my face with the small towel that's hooked over the machine, cross the room to get a squirty bottle of disinfectant, then wipe down the whole treadmill. Some people don't seem to bother, which is disgusting and the reason I disinfect before I use a machine as well as after. The last thing I want is to be putting my hands on someone else's sweat.

Checking my 'fitness schedule' in the filing cabinet at the side of the room, I move on to weights. A few of the women I know don't bother with anything other than cardio, because they don't want to bulk up, but I follow the plan set out by my trainer religiously. Strength is important to me, and the pull of the weights on my muscles helps me to feel in control. There are so few things I feel like I have influence over these days – so little I'm able to choose for myself – that this is something I need. I'd come every day if I could.

I push myself with each rep, challenging myself to increase the weight on each machine a week earlier than my trainer was aiming for. Even at my age I like to be the star pupil, one step ahead of where I'm expected to be. It's pathetic, the glow I get from Taylor's approval, this boy who has barely left college, who was assigned to me at random when I wanted a fitness plan setting up. I think he saw I was over forty and assumed I would just want to take it easy, but that's not me. Whatever I do, I have to be the best, and my performance in the gym is no exception.

Sweating but satisfied, I go for a hot shower, allowing myself plenty of time in there as an indulgence. I'm going straight from here to Fiona's launch, so I want to look and feel my best. No chinks in the armour.

I dry my hair carefully, oblivious to the other women in the changing room. Few of them are regulars, mostly here for spa days, sashaying around in borrowed robes and slippers. When I'm happy with my hair, I pull out my make-up bag and do my best to achieve the artful-yet-effortless look that took years to perfect. I've always gone for the sort of look that men would call minimalist, having absolutely no clue just how many products went into achieving it. Even my husband can see the sheer number of items I have on my dressing table, then comments that he thinks many women try too hard, that he likes it when I hardly wear any make-up. Thanks, honey, I think. Thanks for noticing.

My mascara smudges, leaving a black streak under my eye, and I swear under my breath. Taking a tissue, I damp the corner with my tongue and try to repair the damage, but I end up removing a layer of primer and concealer along with the offending blot. Taking a deep breath, I resist the urge to throw my entire bag in the bin and storm out of there, instead taking the time to clean up and repair the area, until I'm finally happy. I look at myself in the mirror, scanning the surface of my face to see if there's any clue as to who I might be, beneath it all. There's nothing. Even I don't know who I am any more. Maybe it's best that way.

There's no parking near the shop, which I find more frustrating than the situation warrants. Eventually I find a space for my car a few streets away, manoeuvring the behemoth into a space with practised ease. I hate that car. Ian picked it for me, after seeing that his boss's wife had one. He presented it to me with a big grin on his face, so proud of himself. I didn't have the heart to tell him it was too big, too ungainly, and that it filled me with the horror of being one of those parents – the ones who drive a four-by-four that never leaves the city and is barely touched beyond the school run and the super-market. I have a keen sense of self-preservation, though, and I knew it wasn't worth the argument and the sulking if I turned down the gift, asking to swap it for something smaller and more practical. I learnt to squeeze it through the unforgiving narrow streets of parts of Lincoln, and to deftly fit it into parking spots without swearing. He'll want to trade it in in a couple of years anyway, so maybe I can get a say in the next one.

When I reach the shop, it's already half full, which is

a relief. I didn't want to be left making too much small talk, especially given the sorts of people who might be here. I'm also glad when I feel a blast of air conditioning as I step over the threshold; it's hot outside, even for June, and I don't want to make this experience more excruciating by sweating my way through it.

'Bella!' someone coos as soon as I'm inside. A large woman dressed in some sort of floaty kaftan presses a glass of champagne into my hand.

'Hi, Fiona,' I reply, forcing a big smile. 'This looks fantastic,' I add, waving an arm to indicate the shop, despite the fact that I haven't been able to look around yet. The invitation wasn't even clear what sort of shop it's supposed to be. Fiona's another mum on the PTA, though her son is a good few years older than Liv and Ruby, and all of the committee have been invited. She's the sort of woman who dabbles in various things, never taking anything seriously, and the fact that she's got as far as opening a shop surprises me. She's never struck me as the sort to get her hands dirty, meaning she probably isn't selling anything handmade, but knowing the sorts of conversations she usually holds, I have a sneaking suspicion there'll be something in here that will make it hard for me to avoid rolling my eyes.

At that moment, someone else comes through the door, so Fiona breezes off again, leaving me alone with my glass of champagne. I don't like drinking when I'm driving, especially not in the middle of the day, but I take a sip anyway. I feel like it would be far too easy for me to slip into the sort of lifestyle that saw me drinking with other bored women at lunchtime, then carrying on when I got home, so it's safest to stick to soft drinks and not risk crossing that threshold.

I don't recognise anyone else already in the room, so I decide to have a look around the shop. It appears to be some sort of up-market New Age affair. There's no shelf full of whale song and panpipes CDs, like I remember from my teenage years, but there's still a strong presence of incense and crystals. One section seems to be entirely devoted to different fragrances of incense, laid out in the way you might expect to see designer perfumes, and next to these is a shelf of intricate incense burners. When I was at college, I had a couple of incense burners – one a curved piece of wood or possibly bamboo, with a groove to catch the ash, and one just a little pottery ring. These are completely different.

Some are in the sort of shapes you'd expect, including a leather one that looks very similar to the wooden one I used to have, except that it costs sixty pounds. Others are more unusual. I'm quite taken by the aesthetics of one that holds the incense stick horizontally in the middle, allowing it to burn at both ends, though the price tag on that one makes me wince. It doesn't come close to the porcelain sphere, however, which will set its buyer back over a thousand pounds. On closer examination, the incense itself ranges hugely in price too. Clearly, Fiona is aiming her wares at a specific market.

Moving on, I turn to the next section of the shop, which is devoted to crystals. I'm just about to pick one up to look at when Fiona appears at my shoulder again, with Hazel, another of the PTA members. Hazel and I don't socialise much, but I feel like I can probably rely on her to be of the same opinion of this stuff as me. Still, I don't want to say anything negative in front of Fiona.

'Ooh, that one's very good for fertility,' Fiona says with a grin that bares her teeth in a slightly unpleasant way. 'I can do you a discount, of course, mates' rates. And I won't tell Ian if you want it kept quiet!' She gives an ugly laugh, and I force a smile, hurriedly replacing the crystal and glancing at Hazel to see how she'll respond. She's also smiling, but shoots me a sympathetic look and I feel a wave of relief. Hopefully I'm not the only one who thinks the whole thing is utter bollocks designed to part bored rich women from their money. Or maybe it's just the fertility thing. Fiona's known for her regular lamentation on only having one child, and is often quite waspish towards those with large families, particularly anyone who's rumoured to be pregnant.

Fiona talks us through the different products in the shop, dropping in words like chakras and reiki – things I don't care to know about – and pointing out some of their healing benefits. If I actually believed that burning this particular type of mineral candle would cure all my worries, perhaps I would be willing to shell out eighty-five pounds for it, but it's more likely that it would be a useless ornament that gathers dust, and when lit would burn down in a couple of hours and leave me nothing other than poorer. My face soon starts to hurt from forcing my smile.

'Let me show you our treatment room,' Fiona declares,

leading us to the back of the shop. Through another door is a small room, with a massage table in the middle and a couple of very luxurious-looking sofas. 'We'll be doing reiki, hot stones, chakra alignment, as well as the usual range of massages.'

'Do you do this yourself?' I ask her, then feel my face colour as Fiona roars with laughter.

'Oh no, Bella! Of course not. I've got a couple of people who are coming in to do that. They're sharing the rent and I get a portion of the profits.'

I should have known Fiona wouldn't be doing much of the work herself, and it sounds like she's found a couple of mugs to agree to a deal that works out a lot worse for them than for Fiona. Still, no sense in saying it and making an enemy of her. Instead, I just give her another forced smile.

Fiona presses copies of the treatment price list into our hands, then sails off to talk to someone else, leaving Hazel and me alone. We give each other wry smiles, then Hazel nods over at one of the products.

'I don't know about you, but if I'm going to pay that much for a bath in salt I want it to be part of a holiday near the Dead Sea.'

I snort and press my mouth shut to stop myself laughing too loudly, worried it'll attract Fiona's attention and she'll somehow know we're taking the piss out of her.

'I can't say it's high on my Christmas list,' I reply. 'It's good that she's got it off the ground though, even if it's not the sort of stuff I'd ever buy. You've got to admire her for putting the work in to start her own business.'

109

Hazel gives me a disbelieving look. 'Are you serious?'

I nod, determined to remain positive. 'I am. It's not easy, getting a business off the ground.'

The other woman lets out a harsh laugh. 'Well, the money all came from her husband, so it's not like she had to secure any funding. Fiona's hired a manager for the general day-to-day running of the shop, and she was the one who sourced all the products. All Fiona had to do was look at a list this other woman collated, then sign off on it all and tell her husband to pay for it. Even the treatments were the manager's idea. She's the one who should get the credit, for pulling this whole thing together and managing to keep Fiona happy without losing her mind. Of course, she's conveniently absent today, for Fiona's little party.' Hazel takes a swig from her glass of champagne then puts it down on the counter next to her. 'I've got to go, I've got a meeting at two,' she says. 'Nice to see you, anyway.'

As Hazel walks away, I try to push down the seething jealousy that's suddenly sprung up. Hazel is one of the power mums, who manages to hold down a successful career while also raising a family. That's who I'm supposed to be. That's who I would have been, if things had been different.

I stop myself from following that train of thought. My hand is squeezing my champagne glass uncomfortably tight, and I don't want to draw attention to myself by breaking the damn thing.

Hazel could never understand my feelings about Fiona's shop, because they're so complex I barely understand them myself. Even if Fiona hasn't done any of the work herself, at least it's a project, something for her to do that feels productive. Fiona had the ambition to do something for herself, she's had the vision to create it in the first place, and she has the freedom to put it into practice. These days I don't feel like I have any of those things. Whenever I've spoken to Ian about going back to work it turns into an almighty row, which I just don't have the energy for. Jesus, how did I end up like this?

Looking around, I can't see anyone else I know, and Fiona is doing the tour for another pair of women who look like they've been trapped. I wish I'd brought my friend Caroline with me, she would have enjoyed it. We could have gone for coffee afterwards and spent an hour laughing at the ridiculous things that some people will spend money on. I pull out my phone and text her, tell her about the whole experience. At least sharing it with a friend will make me feel a bit better about it.

After another ten minutes of glancing around the room and making idle small talk with a couple of other women, I think I've spent long enough here that I can leave without being rude. I slip out of the door and hurry back to my car before anyone notices I've gone.

Chapter 14

'Girls! Granny's here! Come down and say hello!'

I call up the stairs to Liv and Ruby, but I know they won't come down immediately. They dislike Ian's mum almost as much as I do, and they're not old enough to be adept at hiding it yet. Olivia in particular has been displaying a lot of attitude recently, so we might have to have a chat about being polite to people we don't like in order to avoid making a scene. It'll be hard for me to take the adult role in that situation, because if it were up to me I'd agree with her; the woman's a living nightmare and we should avoid her at all costs.

As I stand and listen for any sign of the two girls making a move, I check my watch. Ian promised me he'd be home early today in order to greet his mother and get her settled in, but of course he's not here. Marian stands in the kitchen expectantly, as if she hasn't been here before and doesn't know what to do next. Why doesn't she just make herself comfortable? At least she could put her bag down, maybe take off her shoes. I know she won't until she's invited, though, and I'm sure the fact that I have yet to specifically instruct her to do so will be brought up again later.

'They're just coming,' I say breezily as I join her. 'Why don't you make yourself at home. Tea?'

She sniffs. 'Do you have Rooibos?'

'We do,' I reply, trying my best to give her a winning smile, but I expect it looks like more of a grimace.

'Well I hope it's better than the stuff you gave me last time I was here.' She doesn't make eye contact with me as she speaks, her gaze roving around the kitchen instead. Her bag is placed carefully on the central island, and she holds the lapels of her coat, looking pained.

'Why don't I take your coat?' What grown woman walks into her son's house and won't remove her coat until she's asked? I find it hard not to roll my eyes at her, but I know this is so minor that by the end of her visit I'll have forgotten about it completely, eclipsed as this episode will be by some other, much more serious, issue. No, I shouldn't think like that, I tell myself. If I approach Marian's visits with a negative mindset they're doomed to failure; perhaps everything will be fine this time.

'Have you thought about getting the kitchen updated?' she asks when I return from hanging her coat in the cupboard under the stairs.

'No, it was done just before we moved in two years ago,' I tell her, puzzled by the comment.

'Oh.' She purses her lips, and I realise I'm holding my

113

breath, waiting for whatever is coming next. 'Maybe it's just because it needs a good clean.'

Turning away from her, I busy myself with the kettle, a forced smile helping to keep my mouth shut. Don't respond. Don't rise to it.

I know exactly what I want to say to her, and it begins with 'Fuck off, you judgemental old baggage.' But if I said anything remotely approaching that to Ian's mum, I don't think he'd ever forgive me. Though it might still be worth it for the sense of satisfaction I'd feel in the moment. Marian is still of the antiquated view that wives of men who make plenty of money should be content in the home, and should turn their hands to making that home as clean and tidy as possible. She thinks the man shouldn't have to lift a finger to contribute to that cleanliness, despite the fact that he's responsible for a portion of the mess. After all, he pays for it all, she told me once. Never mind the fact that I was the one who paid for most of what we had before we were married and then until Liv was born. Even after that, I pulled my weight. It's only in the last couple of years that I've been forced into this domestic servitude, which I loathe with a passion.

I'd love to be honest with Marian one day, to tell her how little I give a shit about her old-fashioned sensibilities, and how I don't rate my self-worth against how clean my house is. How I have better things to do with my time than clean – things like sit with a cup of tea and my feet up when I finally have the house to myself for an hour or two. That's far better for my wellbeing than bloody cleaning. Ian and I go round in circles talking about this, about my lack of purpose. He thinks I can learn to enjoy not working and being a slave – sorry, housewife – if only I put some effort into it. That's why he won't entertain the idea of getting a cleaner, because I might as well do it when I have nothing better to do. When he gets that attitude he infuriates me so much I genuinely think about leaving him, but I know it's not that easy. I'm bored, but at least I live in relative freedom and have every comfort I might want. So I have to put up with it.

Once Marian has been invited to take a seat in the lounge and I've provided her with tea, in a proper china cup with a saucer, I run up the stairs and stick my head into Olivia's room.

'Come on, Granny's here. Come downstairs.'

Both girls are sitting on the bed, newly changed out of their school uniforms, wearing matching frowns. Ruby is getting better at emulating her older sister's attitude, and I'm already dreading the years when they're both teenagers.

'Do we have to?'

'We don't want to.'

I lean on the door frame and smile at these two wild-flowers I've managed to create. Maybe there's hope for us all yet.

'I understand that. And it's hard to explain quickly, right now, but sometimes in life you need to do things you don't like. Daddy would be very hurt if you didn't come down and spend time with Granny.'

I know that appealing to them to salve Granny's feelings won't work, because they don't really care if she's offended. She's made them both cry numerous times with her sharp words, and they haven't forgotten. But they both dote on Ian, and they don't want to upset him, so they slide off Liv's bed and traipse downstairs behind me. I usher them into the lounge and they go in slowly, scuffing their feet on the thick carpet.

The lounge doesn't suggest that children live here, other than the photos on the wall of the four of us. The two of us agreed, even before we had children, that we'd keep one room in our house as an adult-only space, and we've more or less stuck to it. The girls are allowed in here, but we rarely use it as a family because they've got their playroom for that. Even if we have a family film night, Ian and I go in there to watch it with them.

I say both of us, but more often than not it's just me. He doesn't have the patience for sitting through a full children's film, so will often drift off to the bathroom and never come back, so I tend to save it for evenings when I know he's working late. The girls and I snuggle up on the sofa together with a pizza and chocolate, and watch whatever they choose. I might not admit it, but those evenings are some of my happiest.

We pass an excruciating half hour of stilted small talk until it's time for me to cook the girls some tea, and I send them off to watch some telly for fifteen minutes. I tell Marian she's welcome to join me in the kitchen while I cook, or she can have some quiet time to herself in the lounge. She doesn't follow me, but then I hear her climbing the stairs and moving about on the floor above, so I assume she's gone up to the spare room. At least she didn't need my invitation to do that.

A few minutes later, the door to the kitchen opens and she comes in, tea cup in hand.

'Would you like another drink?'

'No, thank you.'

There's silence for a couple of minutes while I get out pasta bowls and cutlery for the girls and set the table. They'll eat in the kitchen tonight, then after they're in bed the three of us adults will eat in the dining room. We barely use that room other than when Marian is here, but I know she has certain standards that Ian likes to stick to, and I can put up with it occasionally.

I drain the pasta and open a jar of sauce to stir in, hearing a sniff from the other side of the room. No, Marian, I'm not preparing everything from scratch, because I'm cooking two meals this evening. One thing you've succeeded in is making sure your son doesn't have a clue how to make anything other than a toasted sandwich, and even that I had to teach him. God knows what would happen if I ever left him alone with the girls for a night or two. I expect they'd just eat takeaway, and it'd be the most fun they'd had in ages.

'Girls! Tea!'

The two of them bustle in, and mercifully the front door opens and Ian arrives home. I leave him to take over with his mother, carrying her case upstairs and making sure she has everything she needs, then we're busy getting the girls ready for bed. Ian reads the bedtime stories while I start cooking the second evening meal of the day, peeling potatoes and slicing them carefully. Marian turns her nose up at 'foreign food', which mostly means anything from a country where the population isn't predominantly white, but also seems to include anything that has a strong flavour. So I'm preparing something as bland and British as I can while still making sure I'll enjoy what we're eating, which is not an easy feat.

The meal feels endless. While we eat, Marian makes another comment about the cleanliness of the house and how I could perhaps learn something from 'the World Wide Web', then moves on to talk about the children and how rude they were. I keep my mouth shut the whole time.

That night, when we're getting ready for bed and I feel like I can finally relax, I defend the girls to Ian.

'They weren't rude. They just weren't sure how to answer her questions. Now they're getting a bit older they don't know how to behave around her, because they don't spend a lot of time together.'

'You're the one who doesn't want to go down and see her in the school holidays,' Ian replies. I close my eyes, willing myself not to respond. That wasn't what I meant, and he knows it, but he's not willing to say anything against his mother or her attitude. When we were first married he used to joke about how difficult his mother was, and we could have a laugh about it together, but recently he's been taking her side more and more.

I sit at my dressing table and reach for the box of cotton pads I use for taking off my make-up. It's not where it usually is, but is now sitting on the other side of the mirror. Frowning, I cast my eye over the rest of my products, then carefully open the drawers. Everything has been moved, just slightly. In the top drawer I have a few boxed pieces of jewellery, and one of the lids has been left off. I know I didn't do that.

'Have you moved anything on here?' I ask Ian lightly. I see him frown at me in the mirror.

'No. Why would I?'

'My things have been moved, like someone's been going through them.'

'You probably did it yourself in a hurry. Or one of the girls came in, wanting to play dress-up.'

I know that sounds like a plausible explanation, but I don't believe it. I've always told the girls that they're welcome to try on any of my make-up or jewellery, as long as they ask first. We sometimes have little beauty sessions, or fashion parades. I reason that making things forbidden only makes them more tempting, and neither of them have ever taken anything without my permission.

I think about the footsteps I heard overhead while I was in the kitchen. 'Do you think . . .' I stop, not finishing the sentence, but Ian guesses what I was thinking.

'Oh for Christ's sake, Bella. I know you have an irrational hatred of my mum, but that's taking it a bit too far.'

'I didn't say . . .'

'No, you didn't, but I know you thought it. You're fucking losing it.'

With that, he goes into the en suite bathroom and

slams the door, turning the shower on. I get into bed and turn off my bedside lamp, feigning sleep when he finally comes back into the room. What I haven't told him is this isn't the first time things have been moved in the house, that something has turned up where it shouldn't be or vanished from its proper place. I've kept these things to myself out of a fear of being ridiculed, but also because a part of me wonders if he's right. Am I going mad?

Chapter 15

Tyler has changed my programme, so I have a few new machines to tackle this morning, and I'm looking forward to the challenge. Three days with Marian in my house have left me with the urge to try out kickboxing, but for now I'll have to settle for pushing my muscles to their extreme with the weights. Ian helped her with her case this morning and she left just before I set out on the school run. I'm glad she did; I didn't want to leave her alone in the house. Whatever Ian says, I'm not convinced she wasn't the one who went through my dressing table.

I work my way through my reps, feeling the adrenaline course through me, responding to the burn in my muscles. It feels good, and I know I need to be careful not to push myself too far. At the moment, I feel like my body is one of the few things I have any control over in my life, and working hard to make it stronger feels intensely rewarding.

As I come to the end of my workout, I notice another

woman looking at me from the other side of the room. When I've finished, and I'm wiping down the equipment I've just been using, she crosses over to me.

'Hi,' she says, and I can hear she's a bit nervous. I shoot her a quick smile, though I can't say I'm really in the mood for a chat with a stranger.

'Can I help you?'

She nods at the card in my hand. 'You've got a programme.'

I wait, assuming she'll continue. There's an awkward pause.

'Yes,' I say, hoping to prompt her to continue.

'Is it any good? I was thinking of getting one.'

'Oh. Well, it works for me. They have some decent trainers. It depends what you're hoping to achieve, really.'

She nods slowly, as if I've offered a fascinating insight into how the personal trainer system works.

'Okay, thanks. I just wondered if you'd recommend it, you know, before I sign up.'

'Sure,' I say, resisting the urge to shrug and turn away, because she's obviously expecting more. 'You know it's free, right? If you're a member here, you don't have to pay extra for one of the trainers to set up a programme for you.'

'Oh, I know. I just didn't want to commit then find I wasn't doing it, you know.'

I don't really know, but I nod anyway. 'Okay. Well, maybe try it, then you'll find out.'

'Good advice. Thanks.'

She doesn't look like she's going to leave, so I pick up

my towel and water bottle and turn to go. 'Good luck,' I offer, and she smiles.

I've brought my swimming things, because I thought I might like to have a bit of relaxation in the pool before going home. I don't have anything else to do today, other than strip the spare bed, but that can wait. Hopefully it'll be a few weeks before Marian is back. She lives a couple of hours away, but doesn't like to do brief visits. Even if we go to see her, she won't hear of us doing it in a day, so we always have to plan a weekend, or a couple of days in school holidays. It's a pain in the arse.

I wonder if I'd like her more if I saw her in small doses, if it was an hour once a week. But she'd probably still get my back up then. It wouldn't change her attitude towards me and my parenting skills, or my terrible cleaning. I ponder this while I swim a few lengths, but soon give myself a talking-to about how much space I'm letting Marian occupy in my head. This is the problem with my life now, with having so little to do; I end up focusing on the smallest things that really don't matter, things that I wouldn't even have had time to worry about a few years ago.

After a short swim I have a quick rinse in the poolside shower then let myself into the sauna. There's only one other woman in there, but I don't really pay her much attention, instead sitting back and taking some deep breaths, feeling the heat sink deep into my muscles. It's all I can do to not groan as I feel some of the tension of the last week unwinding, but the moment is disturbed by a voice.

'Hello again.'

I open my eyes and look at the other woman in the sauna, sitting on a higher level of bench than I am. It's the woman from the gym, she of the intense stare and the questions about my fitness programme. I didn't recognise her at first, maybe because my eyes are on the same level as her knees.

'Hi,' I say, with a quick smile. I close my eyes again quickly, hoping she'll get the hint, but I'm out of luck.

'That was good advice you gave me, thanks. I went and signed up for a programme. I've got a session next week, on Tuesday.'

I make a mental note not to come to the gym that day, then feel bad. This woman clearly means well, whoever she is. I'm just prickly at the moment. Have been for a while now, if I'm honest.

'Hope it goes well. Just tell them what you enjoy, and what you want to achieve. They should be able to sort something out that works for you.'

She nods, then there's a couple of minutes of silence that give me hope. We sit in the heat, gently sweating, and I just have time to think about how weird this particular human ritual is when she speaks again.

'I'm Jenny. Jenny.' She says it quickly, and the repetition makes it sound as if she's not used to introducing herself. That or she's not sure of her own name. I stifle a laugh at this unkind thought.

'Bella,' I reply. Nothing wrong with telling her my name, because I imagine we're going to run into each other here again at some point. I just hope she doesn't

124

start asking for my help with her workouts or anything like that.

The heat is getting a bit too intense for me, so I tell Jenny that I'm going to move to the jacuzzi for a while. She nods, and when I get up to leave she climbs down from her high bench and follows me out of the door. She's not following me, is she? No, she must have decided to go for a swim, or she's going to get changed and go home.

I'm wrong. A minute later, we've both showered and we're in the jacuzzi, warm water bubbling from the jets. I find a good spot and let the force of it massage my legs for a while. Thankfully, there are a couple of other people in there, which makes small talk from Jenny impossible. I sit to her right so she can't make eye contact, but I can still feel her looking at me.

The other two women are gossiping about someone's hen do, and I lose myself in their conversation for a couple of minutes before they get out. No, don't leave me! I think. Once they've gone, I make the mistake of making eye contact with Jenny and she scoots over a little closer to me.

When did I become such a bitch? She's probably just looking to make a friend, and what's wrong with that? I could probably do with a new friend myself, if I'm honest. Other than Caroline, who have I got? The other PTA mums are hardly friends, they're just people I talk to now and again. There's so much one-upmanship involved in our lives that it's exhausting keeping track of it all, even if you don't really give a shit what other people think of you. Jenny seems a bit shy, a bit mousy, but maybe once you get to know her she's perfectly nice. She might even be good fun.

I tell myself all of this, but I still wait for her to speak again rather than opening another strand of conversation myself.

'Do you come here regularly, then? I mean, I've just joined this week.'

I wonder if she knows how much this sounds like a chat-up line, then slap down my bitchy side once more.

'Usually about three times a week,' I tell her. 'I'm . . . not working at the moment, so it gives me something to do while my kids are at school.'

She nods, but doesn't volunteer anything about herself, so I decide to make some effort.

'What about you, any kids?'

'No, no kids, no commitments,' she says with a short laugh that doesn't have any humour in it. 'I work free-lance, from home, so thought I should get out a bit more during the day, take advantage while places are quiet. Hence joining the gym.'

I nod to show her I understand, and I do. Working alone isn't much better than not working at all, when it comes to human contact, and too long without seeing other people can make you go mad. No wonder she comes across as a bit awkward, it's probably been ages since she tried to get to know someone new, and it's pretty daunting approaching a stranger in the way she did. I should be giving her more credit.

She asks me a couple of questions about my family,

and I'm deliberately vague in my responses. Even if I've decided to give her the benefit of the doubt, I'm also wise enough not to tell too many personal details to a stranger the first time I've met her. I've learnt the hard way about that – a journalist with a particularly winning way once managed to get more out of me than was appropriate, and I've regretted it ever since. Ian was furious when he found out. I'm not going to make that mistake again.

When I get out to get changed, Jenny doesn't follow me, and I breathe a sigh of relief. I wasn't relishing the idea of stripping off in front of her. I'm dressed and drying my hair when she emerges, and I watch in the mirror as she goes into one of the cubicles to change. Not an exhibitionist then, at least, though I wouldn't put myself in that category, but I'm happy to change in the open part of the changing room. See, this is why I keep calling myself a bitch. I'm judging other people in the way I'm expecting them to judge me, almost as if I'm dealing a mental preemptive blow. It's a survival strategy that I've learnt recently, but I don't like myself for it.

After drying my hair I reapply my make-up, and I've just finished when Jenny comes out of the cubicle. I see her cast an eye over the products I'm using, then she smiles at me in the mirror and holds out a piece of paper.

'I've, er, written my number down. In case you want to meet up for a coffee one day or something.'

I take the paper and give her a smile. 'Sure, that sounds nice.'

There's no harm in taking it and sending her my number, I think. If I turn it down, it will only be awkward when

127

I see her again, as I no doubt will, if she intends to be here regularly. She watches me intently, so I pull out my phone, type her number in with the name 'Jenny Gym' so I remember who she is, then send her a quick text so she has mine. I do wonder if I'll regret it, but then I'm stuck between a rock and a hard place really.

'Thanks,' she says, and the smile she gives me really lights up her face. 'It was nice to meet you, Bella.'

She leaves before me, and I sit at the mirror a little longer, wondering about Jenny. I feel like I've broken down a bit of a barrier, and it's scary, but maybe this time I need to put some of my fears aside and just put some effort into making a friend.

Chapter 16

Friday means the supermarket run, a job I feel like I should loathe but I actually really enjoy. Browsing the shelves, choosing the freshest veg or the nicest-looking cuts of meat, seeing what offers they have on this week. Ian can't cook, so while I consult him on preferences for meals each week I also allow myself free rein when it comes to keeping the kitchen stocked. It's the one thing I'm glad I have plenty of time for these days.

I encourage the girls to eat lots of fresh fruit, and I try to make homemade snacks as much as possible, but I also like to treat them occasionally. Ian gets annoyed at me when I do, but then I ask him to provide some nutritionally well-balanced alternatives and he gets in a huff because he knows he's being unreasonable. My husband is one of those people who can apologise profusely for something when he knows that doing so will be of benefit to him, yet still can't accept he's in the wrong on anything domestic. As he keeps on pointing out, I'm the one who's at home all day, I'm the one who spends the most time with the girls and knows them better, so on this he can bow to me whether he likes it or not.

We weren't always so confrontational with each other. Before things went so drastically wrong, our communication and our ability to compromise were fantastic. I'd say they were one of the reasons we always worked so well as a couple. Now, with the bitterness that's taken hold and our constant sniping at each other, it's easy to see how easily things can change.

Grabbing the selection of bags I usually take shopping with me, I get in the car and prepare to set off, but something doesn't feel right. I stretch out my legs and press the pedals. Someone has moved the seat. It must have been Ian, but why the hell would he have done that? He has his own car, and won't drive mine, despite constantly telling me how amazing this enormous monstrosity is.

It takes me a minute of fiddling with the levers to get the seat back to a comfortable position, but it still doesn't feel right while I'm driving. I shuffle a couple of times when I'm sitting at traffic lights, and the unnatural sensation puts me in a grumpy mood, so by the time I get to the supermarket I'm inwardly swearing at every other driver I come across. Once I've parked, I take a few deep breaths, then try to figure out what's wrong with my seat.

It turns out the lumbar support has been tightened, so

I'm sitting more upright than usual, and I think the steering wheel might have been moved down a notch too. Why would he do that? Was he looking for something in the car, and moved the seat to have better access? That's the only explanation I can come up with.

I don't enjoy my shopping trip as much today, and find myself getting resentful towards Ian, sitting at work with his colleagues, while I'm here doing my best impression of a 1950s housewife. It doesn't seem fair. I know we discussed it all and we knew this would be the best option for the kids, for one of us to be home with them for some stability after everything that happened, but I underestimated the impact it would have on me. I'm not the same person I was even a couple of years ago, and I'm worried I'll never be that person again.

That evening, once the girls are in bed, I settle down on the sofa next to Ian. I've given up trying to get him to help me tidy up at the end of the day, but at least I get the chance to sort the kitchen while he reads bedtime stories. It's a part of the day I want to be involved in, but I have a feeling that if I ask, it'll quickly become another of my roles, and Ian won't spend any quality time with the girls during the week at all. I think he feels like his presence in the house is enough, but it's not. I want him to have conversations with them, find out about their day, what they did at school, who their friends are. It became clear last Christmas that he really doesn't know much about the girls at all – he was completely incapable of coming up with any ideas for gifts, and the couple of things he decided to buy independently were completely inappropriate, either far too young or just not something either of the girls would have been interested in.

We don't often spend time together during the week, even once the children are in bed. If we start off sitting together, eventually he'll drift off to his study to do some work, or faff about on the internet, so I end up turning the TV on. He probably thinks it's part of our routine, but I'm fed up with that, too. I miss the days when we'd talk about the news, or what we're reading, but now we're too uncomfortable in each other's presence.

As I've got him here, I need to ask him about the car before he disappears for the night.

'Have you been looking for something in my car?'

He's looking at his phone, and doesn't look up when I speak.

'Ian?'

He turns to me now, a frown on his face, a mixture of confusion and annoyance.

'No, why would I have been in your car? I never use it.'

'My seat had been moved when I got in this morning. It was further back than usual. I thought maybe you'd been looking for something.'

He shakes his head, back to looking at his phone. 'No, you must have caught it and slid it back when you last got out.'

For a moment I think this is a plausible explanation, but then I remember how much had been changed.

'No, that doesn't make sense. Someone tightened the

lumbar support and moved the steering wheel down. I can't have knocked all three.'

Ian sighs, and it's a sound that makes my fingers twitch. I hate the way he can make me feel like I'm being unreasonable without even saying a word.

'It must have been the girls messing about, then. Why would you think it was me? I never drive your car.'

'The girls won't have touched anything in the driver's seat, they know better than that.'

'Maybe you weren't watching them closely enough,' he mutters. 'It's not like you're winning any parent-of-the-year awards.'

I sit back as if he's slapped me.

'What the hell does that mean?'

'You've got them trained up now to be rude to my mum. I was so fucking embarrassed when she was here, the way they behaved towards her.'

'That's because she's a complete bitch to them, Ian. I know you can't see it, but kids are perceptive. She looks down on them because she can't stand me, and even though they're your kids too, they'll always be tainted because they're half mine.'

I don't even know why we're having this argument again. Lately, every time I confront Ian about anything, or even ask him to do something, he manages to turn the conversation back on me. It's like he's taking any opportunity he can find to have a go at me.

He stands up and puts his phone in his pocket. 'Don't try to justify the way you feel about her with that sort of bollocks. You've always hated her, for no reason, when all she's done is try to make you feel welcome. She's lonely and she wants to see us more often, but you're always putting barriers in the way.'

How has this gone from me asking him about my car to him having a go at me about his mother? We've had this argument so many times, especially since I stopped working and Marian's opinion of me dropped to a new low. I don't think I have the energy to go over it all again. Taking a deep breath, I try to calm my racing heart. He's standing over me, expectant. Is he waiting for an apology? Because he's not going to get one.

'Look, we've been over this. Your mum is welcome whenever she wants to visit,' I say, keeping my voice as calm and even as I can manage. 'We'll go and see her when we can, fitting it around the girls' school terms. We're never going to be best friends, but don't ever say I've stopped her from seeing the girls, because I haven't. The two of them are old enough to be judging people for themselves, especially Liv, and if you think they're being rude you need to ask yourself why that might be.'

His lip curls at this. 'I know exactly why it is, because they copy you. If you were nicer to her, they would be, too. Don't try and tell me this has anything to do with them, they're children. I can't believe you'd put this on them.' He shakes his head and walks to the door, then turns back to me. 'Maybe you should be thinking about what sort of example you've set in your life before you start slagging off other people.'

As the door closes behind him I pick up my coffee cup and hold it tight, fighting the urge to throw it at the space where he was just standing. I imagine it smashing, splashing the remains of my coffee onto the cream carpet and walls, soaking in until the stain is impossible to remove, a marker of my rage and frustration and impotence. Bloody Saint Ian, nothing is ever his fault, it's always mine. All I wanted to know was what he was looking for in my car, because maybe I could have helped him find it, but we can't talk about anything without it turning into a bitter row these days.

Not for the first time I think about leaving him, but as soon as the idea enters my head I know it's not possible. His hold over me is too strong, and however much I complain about my life, at least I have the girls. He can take away all of the comforts and money and convenience, but if he tries to take my children my life won't be worth living, and he knows that. No, I'm going to have to stick it out, at least for now.

I go back through to the kitchen and contemplate the drinks cupboard. Pouring myself a generous measure of one of the fancy flavoured gins we keep in, I top it up with some tonic, then go back through to the sitting room and turn on the TV. There's nothing I particularly want to watch, but I find a costume drama and try to concentrate on it, letting the first waves of alcohol wash over me. It's the only thing I can find to calm myself at the moment; I know it's not a great crutch to be turning to, but honestly what else have I got? If I thought I could convince Ian to get a dog that might work, then at least I could have an excuse for taking long walks every evening, but I've tried suggesting it before only to be shot down.

Maybe I should just get one without consulting him, but I'm scared the girls and I would come home one day to find the dog had 'escaped', and I'd have to deal with the fallout.

I'm finally starting to lose myself in the programme when my phone beeps, and I check it to see a message from Jenny.

Hi, it's Jenny from the gym. If you're not busy on Monday, do you fancy getting a coffee?

I'm meeting Caroline for lunch on Monday, and I'm really looking forward to catching up with her, so I'm inclined to put Jenny off for a few days, but then I change my mind. If I'm going to try and survive the next few months, and years, then it won't hurt to have a few more friends around me, will it? I reply and we agree a time and place.

The weekend hangs heavy on my mind. I'll take the girls to their swimming lessons tomorrow, as usual, then Ian will suggest going out somewhere in the afternoon. It won't necessarily be anywhere the girls or I want to go, but we'll go anyway. Then on Sunday he'll want to go to the gym, and read the paper, so I'll take the girls to the park or maybe the cinema. It's the same every weekend, but I'm getting exhausted with the mental energy of planning things. I prefer it when the girls have sleepovers or parties to go to, because then at least I just have to worry about collecting them at the right time, rather than coming up with something to do that will keep them entertained. One day I might just disappear for a weekend, walk out and go to a hotel, just to see what he does, but I know if I do something like that he'll make my life a misery when I come back. I know I need to put up with it for now. But that doesn't stop me from planning. One day I'll surprise Ian. He'll never see it coming.

Chapter 17

The coffee shop is quiet, with it being Monday morning, and Jenny is already sitting in a booth at the back when I arrive. It's a beautiful day that makes me hopeful for a good summer, and I had been hoping we could sit outside, but I won't ask her to move now. She grins at me and waves enthusiastically, then colours slightly. I wonder if she's short on friends, too, and doesn't want to come across as too eager. I feel a pang of pity for her, then, though it's also something I can identify with.

'Hi,' I say with a smile as I approach the booth. 'Have you ordered?'

She shakes her head. 'Not yet, I was waiting for you. The cakes look amazing. Have you tried them here before?'

I glance over my shoulder at the cabinet in front of the till, and she's right, they do look good. Cake is something I haven't really allowed myself for a while, but I'm feeling extravagant today.

'No, but I think today is the perfect day to give them a go.'

Jenny grins at this, and I settle myself on the bench opposite her.

'I hope you weren't busy today,' she says. 'I don't want to impose on you. I just thought it'd be nice to chat, get to know each other a bit. With our clothes on this time!' She gives a strangled laugh, and I can tell it's a line she's been thinking about and practising, but hasn't quite pulled it off in the way she hoped. I smile at her anyway, and she seems to sag slightly with relief.

A young woman comes to take our order, and I choose a piece of lemon drizzle while Jenny goes for chocolate and caramel, as well as a coffee each. When she's left to get our drinks, Jenny sits back and looks at me almost shyly, and I realise I never answered her question.

'I'm meeting a friend for lunch later, but that's all I had planned for the day. Once I've dropped the girls at school I find it hard to fill the time, some days, so it's nice to have something to keep me busy.'

Why did I say that? I'm embarrassed that I've been so candid with this woman I've only just met, so I fumble in my bag in order to cover how flustered I am.

'How old are your girls?' she asks.

'Olivia is eight and Ruby is six.' I spend some time telling her about the girls, how wonderful and infuriating they can be, and I see a sort of soft sadness in her eyes as I speak. Sometimes I forget how perfect my life must look to other people, and I need to remember just how lucky I am. Despite the fact that Ian and I have gone from being madly in love to hating the sight of each other, despite everything that's gone on in the last year or two and how badly things have been fucked up, I still have a wonderful life. I don't know what I would have done if it hadn't been for the girls. Perhaps it would have been simpler, but I still wouldn't change things. Sometimes I need to remind myself that other people envy what I have, those who are on the outside and don't know the full story, and I need to be mindful of that.

'What about your husband? Ian, was it? What does he do?'

I hesitate. I don't remember telling her his name, but it must have slipped into something I said, either just now or the other day when we met in the gym.

'He works for an insurance company,' I say, keeping it pretty vague. Nowadays he only talks about work when he has something to brag about, or he wants to vent about someone he works with, and the latter is only because he wants me to agree with him. Once, I told him that by the sound of it he was overreacting and he should consider apologising to his colleague, and he went completely apoplectic. I hadn't seen him that angry since the day everything came out, and I hope I'll never see him like that again.

'Insurance? Doing what?' Jenny looks interested, but I wave away her question.

'To be honest, I don't completely understand it,' I tell her with a self-deprecating laugh. This is rubbish, of course. I know exactly what he does, but I find it easiest to pull the silly-woman act and pretend I have no clue how my husband earns his money. Anyway, I don't want to talk about Ian. If I'm going to make new friends, I want to talk about them, and me, not my husband.

'And what did you say you do?' I ask Jenny, before she has a chance to probe more about Ian. She looks a bit disgruntled, but doesn't press it.

'I'm a personal assistant. You know, lots of admin work, mainly.'

I nod. 'Did you say you work from home a lot?'

'Mostly, yeah.' Jenny looks down at her half-eaten cake and picks at some crumbs. I'm expecting her to go on, to tell me a bit more about her job, but she doesn't say anything else.

'Do you enjoy it?' I try.

She appears to consider the question for a moment. 'I do, yeah. Usually. Not always.'

There's another few moments' silence, and I wonder what else I can ask her.

'Do you live alone?' I figure that's a fairly safe question, because it doesn't make any assumptions about her relationship status or sexuality.

'Yeah. I used to live with my brother, actually. But then . . .' Her voice tails off.

'Are you okay?' I ask.

Jenny looks up and gives me a bright smile. 'Yes, sorry. Doesn't matter.'

'You were saying something about your brother?'

There's a quick flash of something unfamiliar in her eyes, but then it's gone. 'Yes, I used to live with my brother but now I live alone.' I can see the challenge in

141

the tightness of her smile, so I don't ask anything else. Clearly there's a story there, but she'll only tell me if she wants to.

Our conversation drifts to the local area, and the parts of it we love and hate. Lincoln is a beautiful city, and we have a lot of cultural opportunities as well as good restaurants, but attempting to park anywhere can be a nightmare. Busy times of year, like when the Christmas markets are on, are also frustrating. We compare tales of entitled tourists and laugh together, which is nice. I've forgotten how long it has been since I've been able to just relax like this with someone, other than Caroline, and I don't get to see her as often as I'd like. Over lunch we'll have to set up our next get-together, then I won't go weeks without seeing her again. She seems to ground me, but maybe that's just what friendship is about.

Jenny reaches under the table and pulls out what I think is my handbag.

'Oh I think you've got . . .' I begin, before realising my bag is sitting next to me on the bench. I do a double take, looking between the two bags, then laugh.

'We have the same handbag,' I say, lifting mine up to compare.

'You're right,' she replies, with a small laugh, but she also looks a bit embarrassed. Hers is a lot newer than mine, judging by the lack of wear and tear, or maybe mine just gets more of a battering in everyday life. I don't even like the bag, but it was a gift from Ian and it's a practical size, so I use it most of the time. It gets chucked around a lot, and is always spilling over with things I might need for the girls, so the seams are starting to bulge a little. Jenny's, in comparison, looks like it's been well cared for. It's lost the stiff and squeaky quality of brand-new leather, but there are no scuffs or scratches on it, unlike my battered version.

'It's such a lovely bag,' she says, running her hand over it. 'It's my favourite.'

I smile; no point in telling her I'm less keen. 'Funny coincidence,' I say instead, and she forces another laugh but looks away from me, trying to catch the eye of a staff member so she can ask for the bill.

We wrangle over payment for a couple of moments, until she concedes and lets me pay.

'I'll treat you next time,' she says, and I give her a smile.

'Sure.'

'Did you say you're meeting another friend now?'

'Yes, Caroline. I've not seen her in a couple of weeks, it'll be good to catch up.' I feel like I need to defend my social life, show Jenny that I'm not the sort of woman who spends every day having coffee or lunch with friends.

'Where are you going?'

I tell her the name of the restaurant and she makes an envious noise.

'I love it there, the food is really good.' The look she gives me makes me a bit uncomfortable, almost as if she's angling for an invitation, but I don't bite. I'm happy to make a new friend, but I'm not going to invite her to spend half the day with me. Besides, I need to tell Caro about her, see what she thinks. She's always a much better judge of character than I am; she'll be able to give me advice and tell me if I'm doing the right thing by letting this woman into my life.

Jenny and I stand and walk together out of the coffee shop, then I turn to say goodbye to her.

'Are you walking there?' she asks. 'I'm going that way, we could walk together.'

I was looking forward to walking by myself, enjoying the sun on my skin, perhaps browsing a couple of shops on the way, but I can hardly lie and tell her I'm going back to my car when I'm not. I deliberately picked places I could walk to today, partly because I'm still uncomfortable driving my car knowing someone moved the seat, and partly because I want to have a drink with Caro and not worry about driving home. The girls have their afterschool sports club today, and one of the other parents will drop them home, so I don't need to worry about collecting them. I just want to enjoy myself and unwind a bit with my friend.

'Okay,' I say to Jenny, because she's really left me no option, and we set off together, walking up the hill in the direction of the castle and cathedral. We don't talk much, our small talk seemingly exhausted, and I wonder when she's going to turn off. By the time we reach the restaurant she's still with me, and I'm more than half an hour early to meet Caroline.

I glance at my watch. 'I'm a bit early, so I might do a bit of shopping first.'

'Okay,' she says, with a nod and a smile, looking over my shoulder at the clothing boutique we're standing outside.

I hesitate, hoping she'll get the hint and understand that I meant I'd do some shopping alone.

'Do you need to get back to work?' I ask.

'Well, sort of. I make my own hours, really,' she says with a shrug.

'That's good, flexible.' I pause. 'Well, it was lovely seeing you.'

I wait for her to respond, and I see the moment it sinks in, that I'm effectively telling her to go away, and another flash of pink flares on her cheeks.

'Yes, I had a nice time.' She looks down at her feet, then clutches her bag closer to her. 'Okay. Bye.'

Jenny turns and walks off quickly, back down the hill in the direction we've just come from, which confirms my suspicions that she was hoping to be invited to hang around. I feel a stab of guilt, but then I also remind myself that I've only just met her, and she's not my responsibility. Still, I watch her until she's out of sight, wondering why I feel so uneasy.

Chapter 18

Monthly book group, and once again I haven't actually read the book we picked. I can't seem to concentrate on reading at the moment; whenever I try to sit down with a book, my mind just drifts somewhere else and eventually I give up and just watch telly. Still, I've had a good look online at the plot, including reviews with spoilers, so I think I've assimilated enough information from other people's opinions to not make a fool of myself. I'm convinced half of the other women in the group don't bother to read the books either, but none of us ever admits to it.

Caroline is already there when I arrive, so I sink onto the sofa next to her gratefully.

'You haven't read it, have you?' she asks, giving me a sly sideways look, and I laugh.

'Is it that obvious?'

'I just know you,' she replies with a smirk.

'Fine, you caught me. Don't grass me up.'

'As if. I'll just ask you a couple of questions about characters who don't exist and watch you squirm as you try to make up an answer that sounds intelligent.'

I give her a playful slap on the arm at that, and she laughs. 'Come on, the wine's open.'

We meet once a month in the home of one my neighbours, Brenda, and there's always a good spread. We pay subs, which presumably go towards the cost of the wine and Waitrose finger food she provides, but I think she'd still do it even if we didn't cough up. There's something about Brenda and her love of hosting that I find both admirable and hilarious in equal measure. Ian and I were invited round for dinner not long after we bought our house, though while there have been invitations since, Ian has always found an excuse not to go. He's happy to socialise with his own friends or colleagues, but will avoid anyone I get to know. Never mind that I find his friends dull or outrageous bigoted snobs; if I tell him this he tells me I need to grow up, or I need to support him. But when he doesn't like people I know, his reasons are entirely justified and reasonable. Yet another disparity in our relationship that is so maddening, yet impossible for me to address right now.

Caro and I help ourselves to wine and nibbles, then retreat back to the sofa before someone else can nab it. We tend to always sit in the same places, but I know a couple of the women who find themselves on hard-backed chairs sometimes throw us envious glances that we've managed one of the comfiest spots in the room. If I were in my own home I'd kick off my shoes and curl my feet up underneath me, but that's not the done thing in Brenda's house.

'So, how's things?' I ask Caroline, and she gives me a shrug.

'Same old, same old. I'm still wrangling with the client who doesn't think she should pay for the time I spent setting up a whole new system for her.'

'I can't believe that,' I say, giving her a sympathetic grimace. She told me all about it over lunch the other day, as I lived vicariously through her, with her tales of awkward clients and their outlandish requests.

'I know, she thinks she can just pay for the software and then maybe a hundred quid as a one-off to be able to use the database I designed for her. Never mind that it's taken me hours over the last couple of weeks, and she keeps adding in different requirements, so then I have to go back and change something.'

'You haven't given her access to it, have you?'

Caro snorts into her Pinot Grigio. 'What sort of idiot do you think I am? No, I let her access a version of it for forty-eight hours, and now she's kicking up a stink because it's not working any more. Well, no. Not until I see my money, bitch.' Caro says this with a satisfied smirk, but I can tell this is really frustrating her. Working free-lance is hard enough without having to chase clients for payment when you've already done the work.

'Anyway, how are you? Heard any more from your new friend?' she asks me, one eyebrow raised. I told her all about Jenny the other day, and she seemed really amused by the whole situation. She reckons Jenny is probably harmless and a bit socially awkward, so I don't have anything to worry about. In fact, she told me it was about time I got myself some new friends instead of mithering her all the time – of course, she said this completely deadpan and left me reeling for a split second before I realised she was winding me up.

'She's texted a couple of times. I thought I might see her in the gym, but our paths haven't crossed again yet.'

'You could always just tell her when you're going.'

I don't really want to do that, though, I think. 'I'm not sure I want a gym buddy. I'm happy to meet her for coffee and a chat, but when I'm in the middle of a workout I don't really want to talk to anyone else. Even in the sauna it's a bit awkward, just sitting there in a swimming costume, sweating buckets, trying not to think about all the other people who've been sweating in there over the last week, or month.'

Caro pulls a face. 'You make it sound so relaxing.'

I shrug. 'It's a talent.'

'Everything else okay? Girls doing okay at school?'

I nod. 'Yeah, they're fine.'

'You seem a bit on edge, so there must be something you're not telling me.'

I pause. Just before I left the house this evening, I discovered something, and my friend has obviously picked up on my unease. Should I tell her about it? It seems so ridiculous, especially when I think about saying it out loud.

'What?'

'Nothing.'

But Caro won't drop it. 'Don't give me nothing. What's wrong?'

'I think Ian has been reading my emails.'

She raises her eyebrows. 'That's a fairly major invasion of privacy. Why do you think that? What's he said?'

I sigh. 'He hasn't said anything, that's the problem. I don't want to ask him directly, because either way we'll end up having a row, and I know he'll deny it regardless of whether he's done it or not, so it won't get me anywhere.'

'Well, why do you think he's been reading them?'

'I checked my emails earlier and there were some that had arrived this morning that had already been read, despite the fact I didn't even log on to look until after I'd picked the girls up from school. And there were some from the day before that I know I read, but were marked as unread.'

Caro sips her wine, her brow furrowed in thought. 'You're certain you didn't click on them earlier in the day, when you got a notification or something like that?'

'Positive. Three of them were just adverts, but there was one that was personal.' I don't go into details about what that email was, and Caro doesn't ask, which is one of the reasons we're good friends.

'Could there be a glitch with your email provider?'

I think about this. 'I suppose that's a possibility. That could explain why some were marked as unread when I know I read them, but I don't think the same can be said of the new ones that had apparently been read.'

She nods thoughtfully. 'Okay, so if we assume you're correct, and someone read your emails, why do you think it was Ian?'

I hesitate for a second. 'Well, opportunity I suppose. He's the only one who has access to my phone, and he probably knows my password to access them from elsewhere, anyway.'

'Right. Why would he do that, though?'

I sigh. 'God knows with Ian. He could be checking up on me, wanting to know what I'm doing. He wouldn't find anything particularly interesting, though. No steamy affair, unfortunately, or spiralling gambling debts.'

'No murky criminal past coming back to haunt you?' she asks with a laugh.

'No,' I reply, forcing my own smile. 'Just adverts for clothes and kitchen appliances.'

'Well if you get any decent discounts I might go rooting through your emails myself,' she says, and this one draws a genuine chuckle.

'You're welcome to any of my discounts,' I tell her.

'Right, I think your best course of action is to change your email password,' Caro says, looking serious now. 'That way, if it happens again, you can be pretty confident it's just a weird quirk of your email provider. You might need to update some settings or something.'

'Yeah, that's a good point. I should have thought of that.'

'You've got a conspiracy theorist's brain in there,' Caro says, tapping her own temple and giving me a searching look. 'Honestly, I'm sure it's nothing, though.'

'What if I change my password and it doesn't happen again, though? How will I know what actually happened?'

She sighs. 'You might not. Which is frustrating, but if it doesn't carry any particular real-world consequences, does it matter?'

I consider this point for a moment. 'It does matter if my husband has been reading my emails in secret.'

Caro nods. 'True, good point. In which case, you either need to ask him, or try to catch him out. From what you've said, neither is an easy option.'

'Yeah.' I sigh and look at the other women in the room. There are nine of us, and I wonder if any of the others have gradually fallen out of love with their husbands over the years. I remember the row that came out of asking if he'd moved my car seat, and I can't imagine things will be any better if I accuse him of reading my emails.

'I might just have to cut my losses,' I say, but then I don't hear Caro's response because another woman has just walked in.

'Everyone, can I have your attention please!' Brenda trills, her voice just about carrying over the sound of everyone else's conversations. 'We have a new member. This is Jennifer.'

'Jenny,' she mumbles. She'll have to learn that Brenda doesn't like to shorten anyone's name. It's taken me two years to get her to call me Bella rather than the full thing.

I lean over and prod Caroline in the ribs. 'That's her,' I hiss.

'Jenny from the gym?' she mouths back. I nod, and her eyebrows shoot up in surprise.

152

Brenda is introducing Jenny to one of our other neighbours, but I see her cast a couple of glances my way. There's a chair next to where I'm sitting on the sofa, and as soon as Brenda releases her she makes a beeline for it.

'Hi Bella! I didn't know you'd be here.' She sounds a bit breathless.

'Life is full of coincidences,' Caroline says before I have a chance to respond. 'I'm Caroline,' she adds, reaching out to shake Jenny's hand.

'Oh, hi! Bella's told me all about you,' Jenny replies, enthusiasm in her voice.

This puzzles me, because I haven't actually told Jenny anything about Caro, but I let it go for now.

'How did you hear about this group, then?'

'Oh, I saw something about it in the local newsletter and I already knew Brenda, so I asked her if I could join.'

I never read the thick amateur-looking booklet that's pushed through my door once a month, but it doesn't surprise me that Brenda might be involved in its production somehow. She does like to keep quite an elite group for her book club, though, so Jenny must have passed some sort of test in order to be invited to join.

But one thing does puzzle me, and that's how Jenny got the local newsletter in the first place. I got the impression that she lives in a completely different part of Lincoln, and I'm sure the distribution doesn't stretch that far. Still, however she got it, she's here now. Thankfully, before we get a chance to talk more, Brenda begins the evening.

When we have a break halfway through, Jenny slips

off to the toilet and Caro leans over to murmur in my ear.

'Did you tell her you came to this group?'

I shake my head. 'No, and I didn't tell her where I live, either.'

She raises her eyebrows. 'Must just be coincidence, then.'

But the way she says it makes me wonder if she believes it any more than I do.

Chapter 19

'Who is that woman and why is she in your garden?'

I turn at Marian's words, wondering what the hell she's talking about, and look in the direction she's indicating.

'I can't see anyone.'

'She's just gone behind that horrible old tree.'

The tree is my favourite part of the garden. The girls love to climb it, and we pick apples every year, only managing to get a few before the birds and worms get to them, but it's still part of an annual ritual, and I use what we get to make apple crumble. It shouldn't irritate me that Marian turns her nose up at it, but everything she does irritates me.

She's been here for two days, and I'm literally counting the hours until she leaves again. After our last row, Ian told me his mother wanted to visit again, so I tried to show willing by offering a few dates. It's only about three weeks since her last stay, and if they're going to become more regular I'm going to need some new coping mechanisms. At least I've been able to content myself with ranty texts to Caroline over the last two days while I've tried to keep my manners in check around Marian and her snide comments.

I peer out of the window again and watch the tree. Sure enough, someone emerges from behind it and looks up at the house. For a moment I close my eyes and take a deep breath, then I open them again, open the back door and step out onto the patio.

'Jenny? Is that you?'

'Oh! Bella! Yes, hi!'

I search her face for signs of embarrassment but I can't see any.

'What are you doing in my garden?'

'I . . . I was round the front, and I was about to knock on the door, but then I heard a noise down the side of the house. I thought it might have been a cat in distress, so I came to look.'

I look around the garden and listen for a moment, but I can't hear anything.

'There are a few cats round here,' I tell her, willing to give her the benefit of the doubt for now. 'I didn't hear anything, though.'

'No, maybe I was wrong. Sorry. I was just going to come round the front again.'

'Well, now you're round this side, you might as well come into the kitchen.'

I lead Jenny into the house. Marian is on her feet, with

her arms folded, looking like some sort of malevolent house spirit.

'Marian, this is my friend Jenny. Jenny, this is my mother-in-law.'

Jenny beams and holds out a hand. 'Lovely to meet you, Marian. Bella told me you were staying over the weekend.'

'Yes, well. I'm leaving this evening.' Marian looks Jenny up and down, but her expression is unreadable. 'And what were you doing in my son's garden?'

It's little things like that that gradually wear me down. Referring to everything Ian and I own as just his, as if I don't matter and might vanish to dust at a moment's notice. Jenny doesn't seem to pick up on this, though, and repeats her tale about hearing a cat. Marian doesn't look convinced, but she accepts the story with a quick glare at me, as if she wouldn't expect anything less from someone who had chosen to be friends with me.

'Tea? Coffee?' I offer. Jenny hesitates, but Marian demands another cup of Rooibos – a different brand this time – and Jenny asks for the same. The two of them settle down at the kitchen table and I get out the cake I made with the girls yesterday in a fit of domesticity. It's rather wonky, but Ruby and Liv were proud of it, which is what matters.

'Oh how lovely! Did the girls bake it?' Jenny asks, then turns to Marian. 'I think it's wonderful that Bella does things like that with her children. So many parents are too self-absorbed these days, don't you think?'

Marian looks unsure how to respond. She's clearly

judging the aesthetic appearance of the cake, but she might actually be conceding that Jenny has a point, that at least as a parent I spend time with my children instead of sitting them in front of screens for the whole day. Admittedly, I have made even more of an effort than usual this weekend, with Marian constantly looking over my shoulder, but I pride myself on spending time with my children.

'Well, I suppose,' Marian says, and I have to stop myself from staring at her in shock. Did she actually admit that I might have done something right, while I was within earshot?

'I don't approve of how much sugar they eat, though. It can't be good for them. The last thing I want for those girls is to grow up with weight problems.'

Of course, there had to be something negative to follow it. I busy myself with making coffee.

'Oh I'm sure there's nothing to worry about. Homemade cakes and things like that are far healthier than all the processed rubbish you can buy, and the girls are active enough that they'll burn off everything they eat.' Jenny says.

'Perhaps,' Marian replies, giving Jenny a suspicious look. I wonder if she thinks I've set Jenny up to come in here and say nice things about me. If only she knew I was just as surprised as she was to find the woman in my garden. I hadn't even realised she knew where I lived.

I sit down with the two of them and take a sip of my coffee, and the conversation turns to the garden. Jenny asks me a few questions about what the plants are, and

I answer to the best of my ability, but if I'm honest I don't know a lot. There's a local man who comes in once a week to help out, and I've asked him to keep it as low maintenance as possible. He's done a marvellous job, but I couldn't really tell you much about the different flowers and how well they grow.

'I wish I had a garden,' Jenny says wistfully. 'I'm going to have one, one day. Just like this.' She stares out of the window, and I can see a determined expression on her face.

At that moment, I hear the front door open.

'Mummy!'

I get up and go to greet Ruby and Liv at the door, thanking Chris, the parent who dropped them off after their sports club. They're both still wearing t-shirts and shorts, and ordinarily I'd let them stay in those clothes, but I'm aware of Marian and her judgement, squatting in the kitchen.

After a hug, I shoo them upstairs to get changed.

'Can we eat our cake?' Ruby asks.

'Once you've changed, yes. And brush your hair.'

'Why?' Liv asks, then her face falls and she glances at the kitchen door. 'Is Granny still here?'

'Yes, and she'd love to see you before she goes, so please get changed quickly then come down for your cake and a drink.' I hope that the promise of cake will outweigh their unwillingness to spend more time with their grandmother.

Back in the kitchen, Marian and Jenny aren't speaking, so I fervently hope they didn't hear the tone of Olivia's

159

voice from the hall. I don't need another lecture about Liv's attitude.

Fifteen minutes later, there's still no sign of the girls, and Marian has already made a couple of pointed comments about seeing them before she goes. I creep out of the kitchen, Jenny having made herself at home, and go up to see what the girls are doing.

'Come on you two,' I say, trying to keep my voice cheerful. They've both got changed and they look fairly respectable, but they're sitting on Liv's bed again, united in their protest.

'I'd really like you to come downstairs and say goodbye to Granny. If you don't come to see her, she's going to be annoyed, then Daddy will be annoyed when he gets home.'

'I don't care,' Liv says. 'I'm annoyed that I have to speak to her. She told me yesterday that I looked fat.'

I close my eyes for a moment, envisioning the scene I'd like to follow, storming downstairs and demanding that woman gets out of my house and never comes back. How dare she say something like that to an eight-year-old girl? I take a deep breath, then reach for Liv's hand.

'I'm so sorry, Liv. I didn't know she'd said that. First, your body is beautiful, strong, and growing perfectly. Second, do you remember how we talked about why some people say mean things?'

She nods. 'Because people have said mean things to them and they don't know any other way to talk to people.'

160

'Exactly. And that applies to adults as well as children. So when the boy at school was calling you names, it's not much different from when Granny says things like that. It's wrong, I'm not excusing their behaviour, but maybe Granny's just forgotten how to say nice things. But if we carry on doing our best to be nice to her, maybe it'll help her to think of nice things to say to us.'

I find these conversations really difficult sometimes. When Liv is a teenager, perhaps we'll have more of a candid conversation about how vicious Marian can be, and why we shouldn't have to put up with it, but also why we do. It's difficult with a child of her age, though. There's so much she sees and takes in, without completely understanding. Her view of social interaction is still very black and white. Right now, I just want to find a way to coax her downstairs for a few minutes so I don't have to feel the full force of Marian's displeasure, which I know is selfish. I wish I had the courage to stand up and say no; if my children don't want to speak to you then I won't make them.

Liv slides off her bed slowly, shortly followed by Ruby, who hasn't said a word but is taking it all in. She slips her hand into that of her big sister, and the two of them come down the stairs behind me. Once we're in the kitchen, they both do their best to ask for a drink and some cake politely, then sit at the opposite end of the table from Marian.

'Girls, this is my friend Jenny,' I say, introducing them to the woman who is still sitting at the table. She never

161

actually told me why she was coming round to the house in the first place, and it feels a bit late to ask now.

'How was your sports club?' Jenny asks them. Liv shoots me a questioning look, but Ruby launches into an explanation of the game they were playing today, so I don't have time to talk to Liv. Hopefully she can just accept Jenny in the way Ruby has, but I know she's a bit too perceptive for that.

'I really should be going,' Jenny says after chatting to the girls for a few minutes. 'It's been lovely to meet you two, and the cake was delicious, thank you.' She turns to me and beams, and she looks happier than I've ever seen her. What's going on with Jenny that I don't know about? I think I need to try and tease it out of her, maybe over a bottle of wine.

Once she's left, Liv looks at me.

'Who was that lady?'

'My friend, she's called Jenny. We go to the same gym.'

Liv takes a bite of her cake, then a swig of milk before responding. 'I've seen her before.'

'Really? Where?' I try to stop the fluttering sensation that starts in my stomach at these words, but I can't.

Liv shakes her head slowly. 'I can't remember.'

Before I have a chance to ask any more, Marian announces she's ready to leave, so I have to go upstairs to get her case. In the flurry of goodbyes and forced smiles, promises to see her soon, and so on, I don't get a chance to ask Liv what she meant, and then the moment has passed.

That night, however, I lie awake long after Ian has

turned off his light and started snoring. What did Liv mean? Was she mistaken? After all, Jenny doesn't have any particular distinguishing features; she could look like a lot of different women. Or is there something else going on, something I've missed?

Chapter 20

God, I'm late. I'm never late. If you're late, parking becomes a nightmare, and you can't fight your way through the gates with all of the parents coming out. If you don't make it within five minutes of the bell going, you end up looking like a completely neglectful parent, met by a teacher or classroom assistant who says something like, 'Oh, here she is!' in the tone that suggests you've made them wait for at least an hour.

As I dash across the playground towards the doors, I see Ruby's teacher talking to another parent, a few children still hovering inside the classroom door. I'm not the last one, then. That reassures me slightly, and Ruby doesn't appear at all concerned as she grabs her cardigan and book bag, then bundles herself out of the door with a quick wave to one of her friends.

'Mummy, Miss Yates said the school is getting guinea pigs! And each of the classes will take it in turns to look after them!' Her eyes are shining with excitement, which makes me smile.

'That sounds great! I hope your class gets a turn soon.'

'Can we have guinea pigs, Mummy? Please?'

'Hmmm, I don't think so, sweetheart. Daddy isn't really an animal person.' I have no problem making their father into the bad guy in his absence, because he's always vetoed pets of every kind.

'I'll ask him, maybe he'll say yes.'

I hope she'll have forgotten about it by the time he gets home tonight, because I know if she asks and he has to disappoint her by saying no, he'll blame me. Whenever either of the girls is upset with him, somehow it ends up being my fault. He still doesn't see his children as feeling, thinking human beings with minds of their own.

We walk round to Liv's classroom and collect her, then head back to the car, the two of them talking about the proposed guinea pigs. Apparently there's going to be a competition to name them, so the two girls put their heads together to come up with some suggestions while I walk next to them, laden with coats and bags.

'Mummy, there's your friend,' Liv says suddenly, pulling me out of a daydream in which I'm a single mum and can buy the girls a puppy without having to convince someone else.

We've just come out of the school gates and are waiting to cross the road. Liv points up one of the side streets, and I follow the direction she's looking. She's right, it's Jenny. What's she doing here?

Jenny sees us and I can see by the look on her face

that she hadn't planned on stopping to talk to us, but we're going that way back toward the car anyway.

'Hi,' I call to her as soon as we're close enough. 'Fancy seeing you here.'

I try to keep a brightness to my tone of voice, but I'm confused. She's never mentioned any children in her life, so why is she standing outside a primary school on a weekday afternoon?

'Hi Bella. Hi girls,' Jenny says with a smile that's unnervingly bright.

'What are you doing here?' I ask.

'Oh, I . . . er . . . I was just walking past.'

She definitely wasn't walking when Liv spotted her, and at eight years old she doesn't have the tact to keep quiet about this.

'You weren't walking, you were standing still, watching the playground. Were you waiting for Mummy?'

Jenny gives a little laugh that sounds forced and oddly high-pitched. 'No, not at all. I didn't know this was your school, Olivia. I was just . . . er . . . my niece, you see.'

I smile and wait for her to explain. She falters again, then speaks in a rush.

'My brother is thinking about this school for his daughter, and I was walking past, so I thought I'd just have a look.'

'Fair enough,' I reply, not quite believing her. 'They do tours if you ring and book in advance. You won't get much of an idea what the school's like from the outside.'

Jenny nods, but still looks very much like a rabbit caught in headlights.

'How old is she? Your niece?'

'Five.'

'Oh, so she's at school already? But they want to move her?'

'No, she's . . . I mean yes, she must be . . . I mean . . .' Jenny tails off.

'I can help you arrange a tour, if you like. I could speak to the headteacher about it when I drop the girls off tomorrow?'

Liv is watching this exchange with her mouth open, and I wonder if she's picked up on something strange, too. Ruby is pulling on my hand, straining to get back to the car and get home for a snack. She hasn't even told Jenny about the guinea pigs, so I'm hoping they've vanished from her mind already.

'It's fine, I'm sure they'll call when they want to have a look around,' Jenny sputters. 'As I said, I was just walking past and saw the school, so thought I'd stop and look.'

I nod, keeping my smile fixed, wondering what is going on. Jenny is clearly hiding something, but I have no idea what that could be.

That evening, Ian is in an uncharacteristically good mood, and we spend a while chatting after the girls are in bed. This mostly consists of him talking about work, but I'm happy enough to let him if it means we're sitting in the same room and actually communicating.

'How was your day, anyway?' he asks, taking me by surprise.

'Not bad. Here's a strange one, though.' I sit forward

a bit and tell him about my encounter with Jenny outside the girls' school.

'I'm sure she wasn't telling the truth about her niece. She didn't seem to know if she was at school already or not, but if she's close enough to her brother that she's getting involved in their decisions about schooling, surely she would know something like that?'

'Who is this woman again?' he asks with a frown.

'The one I met at the gym. Remember, a few weeks ago? She followed me into the jacuzzi and it was a bit awkward at first, but then we met for coffee and she seemed okay. But since then she's joined the book group, and she randomly appeared in the garden the other day. I told you, she spent an hour sitting in the kitchen chatting to your mother.'

'Oh, her.' Ian looks away and spends a moment staring out of the window. 'I think you're probably overthinking it.'

'Really? It doesn't sound strange to you?'

'Maybe she's just a bit lonely. But if it's bothering you, don't speak to her for a while.'

'That's a bit difficult,' I point out. 'She goes to the same gym, and now she's coming to the book group, too. She keeps popping up in places I don't expect her.'

'Just leave her alone, Bella. You're being dramatic.'

I sigh inwardly. It had been going so well until now. Soon enough he's got his phone out, and a few minutes later he drifts out of the room.

Going through to the kitchen, I pour myself a strong gin and tonic and find some chocolate at the back of the cupboard. Rather than going back to the living room, I settle myself on one of the dining chairs and call Caroline. If Ian isn't going to listen to me, perhaps she will.

'When you put it all together, it does sound a bit weird, doesn't it?' she says, and I feel a weight lift from my shoulders.

'That's exactly what I said. Something just seems a bit off. But I don't know what.'

'It could all be coincidence, you know.'

'Really?'

There's a pause before Caro replies. 'I know, it's unlikely, isn't it?'

'I think so. I mean, she claims she works full time, yet she's always out and about at strange times of day, even for someone who works mostly from home. I can't imagine her boss is so flexible that she can take an hour out to go and sit in someone else's kitchen.'

'Where does she live? Maybe we can find out a bit more about her.'

'I don't know,' I tell her, realising that I possess precious little information about Jenny, and far less than she has about me. 'I don't even know her last name.'

'Seriously? Right. I know your first instinct might be to avoid her, but I think you need to do the opposite. Make more of an effort to spend time with her, ask her personal questions and don't let her duck out of them. If she deliberately avoids a question, call her out on it. Ask her directly, why won't you answer this question? If she has nothing to hide, she'll either apologise or tell you to mind your own business. Or she'll freeze or make something up because she's lying. Either way you'll get an answer of some sort.'

I hadn't thought about it this way, but it sounds like good advice. After all, if I'm going to keep bumping into her it might be safest to play her at her own game.

At that point, Ian walks into the kitchen and goes to the fridge for a beer. He looks startled when he sees me sitting at the kitchen table.

'What are you doing?'

I put my hand over my phone. 'Talking to Caroline.'

He rolls his eyes, opens his beer then leaves the room. He doesn't like Caro, probably because she's the closest friend I've got. I think he feels threatened by the idea of me having someone I can confide in, someone I actually enjoy spending time with. He probably wonders just how much I've told her, about our relationship and about what happened to precipitate our move here. He lives in fear of me telling someone what he did. Well, let him wonder. It wouldn't hurt if he stews a little, thinking I'm telling Caroline about what a shit husband he's turned into.

'Sorry, just talking to Ian,' I say, realising I've left Caro hanging on a question. 'What did you say?'

'I said do you want me to come with you, next time you meet up? The three of us could have lunch together.'

I think about this for a moment, but decide against it. 'Thanks, but I don't know if that would work. She seems quite jumpy. I thought maybe she had some kind of social anxiety, which maybe she does, so if I start bringing in more people that might just scare her.'

'Okay, but let me know if you change your mind. In

170

the meantime, if you find out anything else about her, tell me and I'll see if I can do a bit of digging. She'll have some sort of digital footprint, everyone does.'

The thought of this makes me a little uneasy, but I agree anyway. What if I'm wrong, and she really is just a bit awkward? Then I'll feel awful passing on her details to Caroline and snooping into her personal life. I know just how I'd feel if it were me, and I found out someone I thought of as a friend was prying like that. Then I remember that she was standing outside the girls' school, and I feel a small shiver run through me. Caroline is right – I need to find out what's going on, and who Jenny is. She's been around my children, and she's been inside my house, so if I'm going to make sure my family is safe I need to stay one step ahead.

'Okay. I'll make a plan.'

We say our goodbyes, then before I have time to hesitate and rethink, I send Jenny a text asking her when she's free for lunch. No going back now. The girls will be finishing for the school summer holidays soon, so we'll have fewer opportunities to spend time together just the two of us, but maybe that could work in my favour. If I invite her for a few days out with me and the girls, using the excuse that I could do with a second pair of hands, then maybe we can get to know each other a little better.

Jenny replies pretty quickly and we set up a lunch date for tomorrow. I'm fizzing with adrenaline at the thought, but I need to remember there might not be anything strange going on at all. But if there isn't, at least I might come out of it with another strong friendship.

IZZY

Chapter 21

The walk to Brenda's house is particularly enjoyable this evening, with the warmth of late summer in the air, but the days shortening as autumn approaches. Bella's kids are back at school after the summer holidays, and I'm hoping to get her to myself a bit more now.

I'm usually the first to arrive for the book group. It's my one evening out with other people, and aside from the times I meet Bella for coffee or lunch it's my main point of social contact in the real world. A lot of the women are older than me, including Bella, but we still get on pretty well.

When I ring the doorbell, I feel a familiar fluttering of nerves in my stomach. Despite the fact that I feel like I belong here now, I'm still scared that someone will realise I'm not who I say I am. So far, however, it's been easy. When I introduce myself, nobody looks suspicious or seems to be sizing me up. It's almost as if, along with my new identity, I've found a new level of confidence.

The more time I spend with Bella, however, the more I wonder if she really is the person I was looking for. When Ryan Beckley threatened me, he was absolutely furious about something, but I can't see how there can be anything remotely unpleasant about Bella that inspired such strong emotions in him. She's bored and lonely, restless at home without a purpose in her life, but not sinister in any way. Not that it really matters now Beckley is dead.

When the police came to interview me, they didn't give me any details, but I found out myself when the story finally broke online. Since then, they've been back a couple of times to check my alibi, as if I could have had anything to do with his death, but in the end it was ruled a suicide. He jumped off the railway bridge in the city centre, the footbridge that takes you over the level crossing. There wasn't a train coming, but the fall killed him anyway. It's strange, because despite the fact that he terrified me that night, now I know how his life ended I feel sorry for him. I don't know what demons were haunting him, but they must have been far worse than anything I could have imagined.

After becoming friends with Bella I considered trying to drop his name into conversation at some point, just to see how she reacted, but then I couldn't think of a decent story if it turned out she did know him. The longer I leave it, the more pointless the whole thing seems. Since his death was ruled a suicide the police haven't been back to bother me, and as far as I know they never questioned Bella about it, though of course it all happened before I met her. Still, even though he's dead I want to know why he attacked me, and why he threatened someone with my name. Maybe I can still protect Bella somehow. Maybe she still needs me.

Sometimes I wonder why I went through with this, getting to know her, when I know she's not in any danger from Ryan Beckley any more. But I'd already come so far, found out so much about her, that I felt I had to see it through to satisfy my burning curiosity about her. And now I've met her, I actually want to be her friend. Since the row with my old friends I haven't seen any of them, haven't bothered trying to get in touch with them, because why would I? I've got Bella now, and she's a better friend than I ever could have hoped for. We had a bit of a rocky start – I could tell she was reluctant to let me into her life – but then something seemed to click and we've got on really well ever since. I feel like this sort of friendship is something I've been missing out on my whole life, and I'm so glad I found her.

Brenda beams at me as she opens the door.

'Always keen!'

I laugh. 'You know I just like to get my favourite seat,' I tell her with a wink, and she stands back to let me inside. I'm clutching the book we selected for this month; it's well worn, because I've taken my time over it. To be honest, the books we read are never the sort of thing I'd choose myself, but I'm not sure how they'd all react to me suggesting an epic fantasy novel or a

Star Trek tie-in. It's been nice to expand my horizons, but it does take me most of the month to get through some of these books, simply because I don't find them that interesting, or I can't read too much in one go without feeling like my brain is going to run out of my ears. I know half of the others don't always read the book, including Bella, but I don't want to embarrass myself. Besides, now Bella has realised I always read them, she relies on me to tell her the plot and the key characters ahead of time.

I help Brenda to set up the room and lay out the wine glasses and nibbles she's bought. Despite the fact that they all come in packets from Waitrose, she still removes them all and arranges each type of food neatly on plates. There's even a plate reserved for gluten-free items, and it's a different colour from the others. Brenda takes her hostessing seriously, and I'm flattered she allows me to help. It's a novelty to me to be trusted with something, rather than offering to help only for someone to sigh and behave as if I'll be more trouble than I'm worth. I've always been quite clumsy, but I've really improved.

I've been wearing my hearing aids regularly again, and I've even been to audiology and had the settings tweaked. Pushing through the discomfort has meant that I finally notice the benefit of them and don't feel as self-conscious about my hearing loss. It's as if this new identity is who I've always wanted to be, but couldn't as Izzy. A couple of times, lying awake late at night, I've considered changing my name by deed poll. That way, I never have to face up to the lies I've told, and I can carry on being Bella's friend without her ever finding out. Because I don't know what I'd do if I lost her now.

By the time we're finished, a couple of the others have arrived, and they help themselves immediately. I always wait until at least half of the group are there, because I feel awkward sitting there with a drink in my hand right from the start, as if someone will think that's the only reason I'm here. Of course, Bella was the reason I started coming to this group, but I wouldn't want anyone to know that, either. It was a stroke of luck that someone tagged Bella on Facebook in a comment about their book club, because I knew straight away it was something I could use. Of course, I had to find out where it was, and I knew I couldn't start asking about it without looking suspicious, but a bit of online digging took me to Brenda, who is very open online about her schedule. After that, I did some volunteering in the same charity shop as her, and within two weeks I'd been invited to the group. The effort of going about it that way meant Bella trusted me more because Brenda was our mutual friend. She didn't need to know we'd only just met.

There are a couple of things I've done, though, mistakes I've made. I need to be more careful, but I've learnt my lesson each time. Besides, now we're close friends I don't need to do quite as much sneaking around as I did at first, which is a relief. I'm more worried about Ian noticing me. I have no idea what he'd do if he caught me doing something underhand, or loitering somewhere I shouldn't really be. Bella would be suspicious, but I think I could talk her round. Ian, however . . . he scares me. I think Bella would be better off without him.

When Bella arrives I move over so she can sit next to me, but she hesitates before she sits down.

'I need a drink first,' she says, turning her back on me and heading over to the table with the wine. She then goes to get some food, and stops to have a chat with a couple of the other women before eventually returning to sit next to me.

'Have you read it this time?' I ask her, nodding at the book beside me.

She snorts. 'God no. I've had too much on my mind.'

'What's up?'

She shoots a look at me, as if only just realising I'm there. 'Nothing. Forget I said anything.'

I resist the urge to reach over and squeeze her shoulder; I've learnt she's not a very tactile person, and my attempts at hugs and other physical contact have often been rebuffed. Still, I want to find out what's going on and show her I'm here if she needs me.

'Seriously, Bella. What's wrong? Is it the girls? Ian?'

She shakes her head curtly and looks back at the rest of the room. 'I said it's nothing.'

I sit back in my seat, suitably chastised. What's going on? Bella's never like this with me. Is it something I did? Quickly, I go through the last few days in my mind, since I last saw her. No, there's nothing I've done that she could have seen or found out about. I've been busy with my own work. Since meeting Bella I've been squashing my working hours into just a couple of days in order to make sure I have more free time. Before we were friends I needed that time to work on my plan, and sometimes to follow her. Now I keep space in my diary for lunch with her whenever she asks, although that's not as often as I'd like, as well as having some time to get through these bloody books.

Throughout the meeting I try to draw Bella out of herself a little, but it doesn't work. She contributes very little about the book, and I notice she drinks more than she usually does. By the break, I'm starting to wonder if I should intervene, but I don't want to be that sort of friend. The two of us drift over to the table with the nibbles on, and join someone else's conversation, which Bella barely makes an effort to listen to, but she also won't be drawn when I try to ask her anything quietly. My heart is racing by the time we sit down again, and once more she blanks me while we continue to chat as a group.

I'm fighting down the panic by the time we finish. Does she know? Has she found out about me, about who I really am? Bella gets up to leave almost as soon as we finish, and I have to grab my things in a hurry and practically chase her out of the door in order to keep up.

'Bella, wait! Please!'

She slows down slightly but doesn't stop.

'What's wrong? Tell me what's wrong.'

I know I sound like I'm begging, but I can't help it. I can't lose this friendship, not when we've come so far.

She turns to face me, and I can see she looks completely exhausted, worn down by life.

'I've had enough. Enough of the lies, enough of the secrets. If it wasn't for the girls I think I would just run away, start all over again.'

I nod, breathing evenly to try and calm my racing heart. 'What lies, Bella?'

'Fucking Ian,' she mutters. 'It's all his fault. Everything is his fault.'

I feel as if a weight has been lifted off my shoulders. She's mad at her husband, not at me. I just got the cold shoulder today because she's feeling done in by everything that's going on in her life.

'Marian's here again this weekend,' she tells me with a brittle smile. 'You should come round, help defend me.'

I nod, remembering the one time I met Bella's mother-in-law. It had been a particularly awkward experience, and not one I was willing to repeat, but I'll do anything she needs right now.

'I can do that. Just tell me when.'

She nods, and turns away, and I wonder if that's a tear I see roll down her cheek.

Chapter 22

I decide to take the following week off work. I don't have any projects that won't wait, and there are too many things I want to do for myself now, things that will take time and focus. If I really want to help and protect my friend, I need to help her get away from her husband.

Since I met Bella, I haven't really bothered to focus on Ian very much. I've had a look for him on social media, but aside from a professional profile page on LinkedIn, I haven't been able to find anything. That doesn't mean he's not on them, though. It just means I'm going to have to hunt a little more. I'll find a way to get into his phone, just as I got into Bella's emails, then I can have a snoop around. It wouldn't surprise me if he's on Tinder, at least, if not on some other dating or hook-up sites under a false name. Would Bella know about it? I think about this for a moment and come to the conclusion that she probably wouldn't care.

Most of what I know about Bella and Ian's marriage has been gleaned from observation and from odd comments Bella has dropped. When she drinks a lot she sometimes lets more slip, but even then she's very guarded. I wonder sometimes just what has gone on between them, for them to be so bitter towards one another yet stay together. It's not like they couldn't easily separate – neither of them would have to worry about money, looking at everything they have. Bella has told me herself that she has plenty of her own to support herself and the girls should she ever need to. I think that was the time she was telling me the best piece of advice she'd ever received was to never give up full control of her own money to anyone else, and to always have her own bank account. At the time I laughed, because I've never been in the position to share finances with anyone, but I stopped when I realised she was deadly serious. That's when I first wondered if there was more to the barbed comments.

I make a few notes on what I can do to find out more about Ian, but at the moment there's not much action I can take. Frustrated, I glance at my phone and see there's a notification from the local news site. I still haven't turned off the alerts for Ryan Beckley's name and there must be some mention of him in this article.

Quickly scanning it, I see there's nothing new. The council have added new, higher barriers to the footbridge where Ryan was killed, in the hope that it will prevent further tragedies. It's a while since I've looked for any information about Beckley, but my heart sinks slightly; I had thought for a moment I might suddenly have a lead.

Even after Beckley died I kept looking for links between him and either Bella or me, just out of curiosity. After a couple of months I thought maybe I'd been going about it in the wrong way. Instead of trying to rack my brains about my life, or find out more about Bella's, I needed to look further into Beckley. Who was he? Did he have any family who might be able to tell me more about him? Searching for him online was easier once I had references to his death, but it still took a lot of sifting to find anything useful. It was only when I found one newspaper article that mentioned his sister that I felt like I'd actually got anywhere. Even then, she wasn't named, so finding her proved tricky.

Eventually, my interest in Beckley and his sister waned because my friendship with Bella became more important. It's September now, and he died in January, so I haven't thought about him for several months. But with this article piquing my interest, I wonder if it's worth trying to track his sister down, just to try and find a few answers at last.

I've searched Facebook plenty of times before, always hoping to find some glimmer of information that I've missed previously, but there's never been anything that I've been able to use. I knew there was a chance his family had shut his profile down, but I'm still disappointed every time I check. What I really need is one of those pages set up in tribute to him, because there I'd be able to get all sorts of information – family, people he worked with, maybe even where he lived – but there doesn't seem to be anything.

After an hour or so of digging, I've come up with nothing, and I slam my laptop closed in disgust. I thought this was supposed to be the digital age, where everyone shoved all of their personal information online without a thought for their own security? I'm fed up, so I grab my phone and keys, shove my feet into a pair of shoes and go out for a walk.

Now that I know he won't be coming back for me, I feel a lot more comfortable leaving the flat and walking alone, though I wonder if this is also a side effect of me slipping into my alter ego. Is this other woman more confident in her own safety and security? Does she think she could happily fight off an attacker should the need arise? I ponder these questions as I walk, my feet automatically carrying me towards the city centre.

I don't know if my subconscious brought me here intentionally, but I find myself standing opposite the level crossing where Ryan Beckley died. Looking up at the footbridge, I shudder at the thought. There's now a high glass barrier lining the walkway, which would be almost impossible to get over. As I watch, a woman with two small children stands and looks down over the top, the toddlers pressing their faces against the glass, probably hoping they'll get a good view of a train coming past.

The level-crossing barriers are down, so I wait for a while until a train goes past and we're eventually allowed to cross. I linger as I cross the tracks; I know it's morbid, but now I'm here I wonder if I can get any sort of feel for the man. Of course, that's absolute rubbish, but once I've crossed I find a bench to sit on and think. If he killed himself, maybe he had a history of mental illness and I can track down his doctor or therapist? No, far too difficult to get any sort of information out of either of those avenues. Even after his death, they're not going to give anything away unless it's to the police. I sit and drum my heels on the pavement, waiting for inspiration to strike.

Gazing up at the footbridge, my eye is caught by a flash of colour. What is it? I can't see from this distance, so I leave my spot on the bench and walk up the steps, crossing to the centre of the bridge. It's a bunch of flowers, and it looks fresh. Checking that nobody is watching me, I step closer and pick it up. There's a card attached.

Miss you every day.

That's all it says, and I sigh in frustration. Someone could have left them here in memory of Ryan Beckley, but equally there might have been other tragedies on this bridge. They could even have been dropped by someone crossing the bridge in a hurry. Putting them back down, I lean on the glass for a moment. The card has the name of a florist on it, so I take a quick picture then Google them. They're about a mile away, so at least I could pop in and see if they know anything about the person who bought them.

'She leaves a new bunch every week,' a voice behind me says, startling me. I turn round to find a woman sitting in the corner of the footbridge, near the top of the steps on the side opposite the one I came up. She appears to be homeless, sitting on a shabby-looking coat, with a bag and a sleeping bag rolled up next to her.

'Who does?'

'Some woman. Has done for months, ever since that bloke went over.'

I pull up a picture of Ryan Beckley on my phone. Crouching down so I can hear her more easily, I show her the photo. 'This bloke?'

The woman casts a sideways glance at the picture, then nods. 'That's him. Police say it was suicide.' She sniffs, but doesn't offer anything else.

'Do you know who the woman is? The one who leaves the flowers.'

'Nah. Just some woman. Typical sort, looks away when she passes me, pretends she can't see me.'

I nod and put my phone away. 'Does she come at the same time every week?'

'More or less. Every Tuesday, in the afternoon.'

'Thank you.' I wonder if I could come back on Tuesday and see this woman, find out who she is and how she knew Ryan Beckley. 'Is there anything you need?' I ask the homeless woman. 'Food, toiletries, anything like that?'

She colours slightly, then nods. 'Nobody usually asks, they just give me ham sandwiches.' I bend down as she mutters something, then I nod and head off to the Boots on the high street for a stash of sanitary towels and tissues, then stop at McDonalds for a veggie meal. When I deliver the goods, the woman smiles and thanks me, and I make a mental note to come back and check on her. I can combine it with seeing if I can spot the woman who leaves the flowers.

My next stop is the florist where the bouquet came from. A little bell jingles as I push the door open, and there's a pleasant-looking woman I judge to be in her sixties standing behind the counter.

'Hello love, can I help you?'

I take out my phone and show her the photo of the flowers from the footbridge. 'I just wanted to check, did someone buy these from you?' I tell her what the card said, and she nods slowly.

'Is there a problem?' She gives me a wary look, and I realise I should have come up with a story first.

'No, I just saw them and thought they were lovely. My mum's not been well recently, so I thought I'd pop in and get her some.'

The frown vanishes from the woman's face and she beams at me. 'Of course! Do you want the same arrangement?'

'Yes please,' I say, watching as she bustles around, picking stems and arranging blooms in her hand before laying them on some coloured tissue paper.

'I thought you were going to say something had happened to that woman, you know,' she says while she's working. 'Comes in every week, picks something different, but always writes the same message on the card before she goes. I worry about her. One week she didn't come in, and I wondered if I should say something. You know, report her missing or something. But then I thought, what business is it of mine? Maybe she just decided to stop buying flowers.'

'Did she ever say who they were for?'

The woman gives me a sad smile. 'Her brother, she said.'

'How sad.'

She nods in agreement. 'But she was back the next week. She must have just been on holiday or something. I'm glad I didn't poke my nose in, imagine the embarrassment if I'd called the police and she was sunning herself in Lanzarote!' She laughs and shakes her head as if despairing at her own silliness, but I find it warms my heart to know there are still business owners who care that much about their customers.

I leave with my bunch of flowers, pleased that my impromptu walk has got me further than I expected. Now I know Ryan Beckley's sister leaves him flowers every Tuesday, the next step is to wait, and let her come to me.

Chapter 23

Time seems to drag so slowly until Tuesday. I occupy myself with rereading all of the articles I can find about Beckley's death, in case there's some minute detail that I missed, yet is somehow vitally important. But there's nothing and I just become more frustrated.

I message Bella a couple of times, but don't hear anything back, even when I ask her if she fancies meeting up for lunch. This lack of communication isn't like her, and I'm worried. Have I done something to upset her? If she'd found out about any of the things I've done, surely she would have said something? But she keeps so much close to her chest. There are a lot of things to do with her past that she never talks about, and shuts me down if I try to ask, so if she was mad at me, she might just ghost me. Maybe she suspects what I've been up to, and she's waiting to find out more? A little shiver runs through me at the thought. I need to speak to her, check everything is okay.

I've already sent two texts that have gone unanswered, so I don't want to send another and come across as completely needy. I'll have to think up a way to bump into her. Or, being the new and confident person I am now, I could simply go round to her house, knock on the door and ask her. That idea makes me shrink into myself with horror, just thinking of all the ways it could go wrong, but I might need to consider doing something like that. Contrived meetings aren't my style any more, not since I met Bella and became my new self.

While I'm thinking over different ideas, my phone rings, and I perk up in the hope that it's her. I glance at the screen and my heart sinks. It's Tony.

'Hi,' I say, trying to inject some cheerfulness into my voice.

'Hey. How are you?'

'Not bad,' I tell him. We have a few minutes of small talk, and I can hear some noise in the background. I wonder how public his conversations with me are. Is someone listening in? Quite possibly. I haven't told him anything about Bella – of course, I can't tell him about my new identity, this new double life I seem to be leading, but I might ordinarily have told him about making a new friend. I know he never liked my old friends. It would probably cheer him up to know I've got someone new to spend time with now, even if she's different from me in so many ways. Right now, though, I don't want to run the risk of his phone calls being recorded. Nobody can know about my friendship with Bella, just in case.

'How are you getting on?' he asks, and I know what

he's talking about. He's been asking me for months to help him find this doctor, but try as I might I can't track him down. It's as if all trace of him has been scrubbed from the internet.

'Are you sure you got the spelling right? Palmeri?'

'Yes,' he says, exasperation clear in his voice as he spells it out again, exactly as I have it written down.

'Without a first name it's really hard,' I tell him, trying to keep my voice calm. 'Obviously, after everything that happened, someone has gone to a lot of effort to hide his identity.' The irony of this comment isn't lost on me, as that's something I've been doing myself recently.

'I know that, Iz, but I thought you'd be able to dig something up,' he says. I can just picture him, pleading in his eyes. I really want to do this for him, but I don't know what he thinks I can achieve even if I find this Dr Palmeri. Does he really think all I need to do is ask some questions, and suddenly Tony will be believed? Is he convinced that Palmeri will agree with him, and everything will go back to the way it was? Whatever happens, he's still guilty of gross negligence manslaughter, even if Palmeri changes his own testimony.

I shake my head in despair, then feel relieved that Tony can't see me. My brother needs to feel like I still believe in him, or he'll lose all hope completely. And I do, it just gets harder the longer this goes on.

'I'm trying, I promise. It's just really difficult without doing something illegal.' I hear him draw a breath as if he's about to speak but I cut him off. 'I'm sure that's not something you want me to do, I know,' I say firmly,

193

hoping to remind him that someone else might well be listening to our conversation.

'You haven't been to see me in weeks,' he says quietly.

'I know, I'm sorry. I'll come soon, I promise.'

There's a thump on the end of the line, and the strains of an argument.

'Iz, I need to go, I'm sorry. Come see me soon, please. Love you.'

'Love you too,' I say, but the dial tone is sounding in my ear before I finish speaking.

I have no idea what time in the afternoon the woman comes to lay the flowers, so I make my way into town for midday. Before I climb the steps to the footbridge, I buy another bag of basic toiletries and some vegetarian food to give to the homeless woman. I didn't ask her name last time, which I feel bad about, and when I get to the top of the bridge there's no sign of her. She probably moves around; I can't imagine the council are happy about her camping out on top of the footbridge, making the place look unsightly, so she's probably been told to move on. Still, I keep hold of the bag in case I see her, or anyone else who can make use of the things I've bought.

Leaning against the glass wall of the bridge, I look down over the railway line, then quickly straighten up and set my gaze further afield. From here it looks like a long way down, and that drop isn't really something I want to think about. Besides, I don't want someone thinking I'm contemplating following in Ryan Beckley's footsteps and causing a scene. When the woman arrives

194

to lay the flowers I want to try and speak to her, not put her off.

After a while, my legs start to ache from standing in one spot. I should have thought this through a little better. I haven't missed her, because there's no fresh bunch of flowers there, but she could come at any time between now and about five, really. That's a lot of standing around and waiting. I'm going to need a different plan.

Walking down the steps again, I glance around for somewhere to sit that will give me a good vantage point. The height of the footbridge means I won't find somewhere that gives me a perfect view, but I'm on the right side of the level crossing for the florist. I have to work on the assumption that she will go to buy her bunch of flowers then walk straight here and onto the footbridge to lay the new tribute.

There's a bench that looks perfect, but it's currently occupied by a couple of older ladies. I walk up and down the street a couple of times, watching carefully for any sign of a woman carrying a bunch of flowers, and when the women finally get up and leave, I take their place. Putting the bag on the bench next to me I feel a pang of guilt for being selfish, but I really don't want anyone sitting next to me and distracting me right now.

While I wait, I glance occasionally at my phone, but there's nothing from Bella. I carry out a couple of half-hearted searches for Dr Palmeri, but there's nothing new, as I suspected. At least I can make good on my promise to visit Tony. I've neglected him recently, and I can't do that. We're all each other has left now, and I can't let him think I've given up on him, even if I do privately think the whole thing is hopeless. I sort out the visit for later in the week, then put my phone away, just in time to see a familiar face walk past.

I feel a jolt when I see she's carrying a bunch of flowers, wrapped in the same paper as the ones I bought from the florist the other day. What the hell? I watch as she climbs the steps to the footbridge, then disappears from view for a moment. Should I follow her? No, I decide it's best not to. When I thought Beckley's sister was going to be a stranger to me, I had planned to stop her and talk to her, maybe play the compassionate bystander and ask her who the flowers were for, and so on. But my plans changed the moment I saw her face.

There are so many questions racing through my mind, but I don't have time to try and answer any of them now. From where I'm sitting, I see her head and shoulders appear along the top of the footbridge, then disappear again as she bends down to lay the bunch of flowers in the same spot. Then she stands again, and leans on the side for a few minutes, just as I did a couple of hours earlier. I stand, hoping that she'll come back down this side of the bridge, but I'm out of luck. As I see her cross to the other side, I leap into action.

Thankfully, the level crossing is up, so I don't need to cross the footbridge to catch up with her, and a few moments later I'm following her along the high street. She isn't moving particularly quickly, and at one point she stops to dig into her bag for her phone. After checking it, she moves on, but it's given me a chance to get my breath back.

Seeing her here, I feel a small sense of satisfaction, because I've finally made some progress, and I feel justified that I've pursued this friendship with Bella. I don't know what Beckley's sister wants, or what her aim is, but I'm determined to find out. I feel almost re-energised, and I realise I'm actually enjoying this, stalking someone through the streets of Lincoln.

We continue up the high street, to the base of Steep Hill. It's aptly named, and I hope she isn't venturing all the way up, but she soon stops and goes into a restaurant. What should I do now? I stay where I am for a moment, then take a few steps back towards the shop on the opposite side of the street, so I can watch the front door of the restaurant in case she comes out again.

As I see it, I have a few different options. I've found out who she is, so I could leave now, go home and work out how to use that information going forward. I could stay and wait, just to see where she goes afterwards; or I could go into the restaurant and consider confronting her. The last option is definitely the one I'm least inclined towards, so I push it to the back of my mind. I suppose the real question is what else I think I can learn from waiting here? After a few moments of consideration, I decide there isn't much, but something keeps me hovering. I'm rewarded because I soon see someone else I recognise walking towards me up the high street. I turn to look in the shop window, hoping he doesn't see me, but he's too wrapped up in himself to pay any attention to the people around him. He enters the restaurant, and as the door closes I let out a long breath.

Of course, it could be a coincidence, but I'm sure it can't be. Crossing the road, I make a pretence of looking at the menu that's fixed in a glass case outside the door. I take a step to my left and peer through the window, and from there I can see quite a few tables, including the one I'm looking for, which confirms what I'd thought.

So why is Ryan Beckley's sister meeting Ian Butterworth?

Chapter 24

I'm on my way home when I get a text, and my heart leaps when I see it's from Bella.

Sorry I've been shit, want to come round tonight for drinks? Girls are at a sleepover, Ian is working late.

The mention of Ian makes me uneasy, but I have plenty of time to decide what I'm going to tell Bella.

Sure, sounds good. Let me know what time you want me.

I'm picking the girls up from school then taking them through to Scampton, do you want to say after 5?

I agree, then an idea starts to form in my mind. I know Bella will be leaving the house around three to go and collect the girls, so that means it'll be empty for a good couple of hours. Maybe I can use that time to go snooping, but this time I'll be looking for information about Ian.

Changing direction, I head through the city in the direction of Bella's house. They live close to a park, and

I've found there's a decent vantage point where you can see the front of their house without being too obvious, as you're mostly concealed by a couple of trees. Heading to that position, I see Bella's car is still in the drive, so I sit down at the base of one of the trees and scroll through my phone to look at the pictures I've captured.

Unfortunately, there's nothing incriminating in any of them. I tried to take one through the window of the restaurant, but all I've ended up with is a blur of my own reflection and the outlines of two people in the background. Even though I stayed outside long enough to watch the two of them leave, they didn't make it obvious that they'd been in there together. To my mind, that made them look even more suspicious, but the photos just look like I've taken pictures of two people leaving a restaurant separately. There wasn't even a backward glance from either of them, never mind an awkward goodbye. They just left.

I've been wondering about it ever since, about why the two of them were meeting. An affair is the obvious one, and I know Bella and Ian aren't happy. The way she talks about him, I know that deep down she loves him, or used to, but there's a distance between them that she won't talk about. Could he have started looking elsewhere? If so, would he really have the audacity to have an affair with one of her friends? I wonder how long it's been going on, and if the woman feels any shame at how two-faced she is, cosying up to Bella while she's sleeping with her husband.

I'm still confused about the link to Beckley and his

threats, though. Could that just be a coincidence? I won't know until I find out a bit more about what's going on. Maybe while having an affair with Ian, Beckley's sister is trying to finish what her brother started. I feel like this justifies my decision to become Bella's friend, though, because it looks like there's still at least one person in her life who means her harm in some way.

Glancing up, I see Bella getting into her car, and a moment later she drives away. I sit and wait for a while, then reach into my bag for the set of kcys I've had made for myself. It was quite easy really – once I'd managed to get myself invited into her house, I had a quick rummage through some kitchen drawers when Bella was out of the room, and that's where I found the spare set of keys. Well, there were three sets, all different, so I had one of each cut. It took a bit of trial and error to work out which ones were for the house, but I got there in the end. The others must be for friends' houses, or for Marian's. I replaced the sets of keys before either Bella or Ian noticed they were missing, as far as I know.

Now, I go up to the house then slip down the side and let myself in by the back door. I try to walk with confidence, as if I'm meant to be there, but I still don't want to be seen unlocking the front door and walking in so brazenly. In this area I imagine there are plenty of people with CCTV outside their houses, and I don't just mean those doorbells with cameras, so I go in the back door just in case.

Once I'm in the kitchen, I pause for a moment to listen. The girls should be at school, Bella has just left, and there's no sign of Ian's car, so I assume I'm safe, but it's always best to check. I feel like I know this house pretty well now, the number of times I've been in and out, mostly when it's been empty. Of course, the first time I came in I was invited in. I've never had to break in, I wouldn't go that far.

Satisfied that the house is empty, I take care to wipe my shoes on the mat. I don't want to leave any footprints on the pristine carpets. I consider taking them off, but if I have to leave in a hurry I don't want to find myself leaving them behind and having to make a run for it in my socks.

I resist the urge to have a wander through the rooms, something I did the first few times I let myself in, enjoying the experience of occupying someone else's space in secret. This time I have a purpose, so I go through the living room and open the door that lies on the other side – this is Ian's study, the space that I know he now mostly uses when he wants to keep out of the way of Bella and the girls, or at least that's what I've picked up from Bella's comments. If he ever works from home, he shuts himself in there all day, with strict instructions that he can't be disturbed, and he uses it as an escape from spending time with his family. It surprised me when Bella said that because I got the impression that he loves his girls and enjoys being with them. Maybe it's her he's trying to get away from? Well, if he's having an affair then that might explain it.

The first time I let myself into the house, I had a quick look in here, but then went to look in other rooms. I know Bella doesn't really use this room, and Ian doesn't like her coming in here, so what was the point? It was Bella I wanted to know about, not Ian, but now my mission is a little different.

It's a relatively small room, certainly compared to the rest of the house. The desk is hideous, which probably means it was expensive, but there's no computer sitting on it. He must have a laptop that he carries to and from work with him. No personal computer, then? My first thought is that he's a man with something to hide, if everything is done on his work laptop and kept away from where his wife and children might find it. It's a blow, not having that to try and look through, but it would surely be password protected anyway.

Bella was pretty easy to snoop on because she doesn't really care where she leaves her phone. The passcode for it is her own birthday, which I didn't even have to guess because she types it in quite openly when other people are around. From there it was simply a case of waiting for her to go to the toilet or to sort out one of the girls, and over a few weeks I built up my own access to her email and her social media accounts, accessing them from home now whenever I want to. I did make a mistake once with her emails, forgetting to go back and mark them as unread after I'd been nosying, but thankfully she just assumed it was Ian. One benefit of their difficult relationship is that her mind automatically jumps to him when something suspicious or inconvenient happens.

My next step is to have a look through the desk drawers. None of them are locked, which makes me think

I won't find anything interesting in them. There's a notepad with a few numbers scribbled in it, and a couple of phrases crossed out, but there's nothing that means anything to me. No suspicious receipts or incriminating letters, not that I expected to find anything like that. Still, I was hoping there might be something that, combined with what I saw today, might help me to find out what's going on.

The only other thing of any interest in here is the tall filing cabinet, but of course that's locked and I can't see any sign of a key. I run my hands across the top of it and search down the side, then along the bookshelves. Even though I've just been through the desk drawers, I check them again, just in case I missed a small key, but I come up blank. There's a comfy chair in the corner so I stick my hands down the sides of the cushions. I don't find a key, but there is a piece of paper, which I pull out and open up, smoothing some of the crinkles so I can read it.

It's a plain piece of notepaper, with a date and time on it, nothing else. Something about the date seems to ring a bell, but I can't remember what about it might be familiar. I put the piece of paper in my pocket, hoping that I'll be able to remember what it is later on. For now, though, I've drawn a blank. I've been through the rest of the house enough times to know there's very little in any other room that will tell me anything about Ian, so I leave by the back door in frustration.

'I feel like I should be doing something wild with an evening to myself,' Bella says with a laugh as she tops up my wine glass. 'Shall we go clubbing and pick up a couple of twenty-year-olds?'

I laugh, fervently hoping she's joking. I can't think of anything I'd like to do less, but I think I'm so enamoured of Bella now that I'd do anything she suggested, if it was what she wanted to do.

'Isn't this wild enough for you?'

She snorts into her wine. 'It's a bit more lively than the book group, but not much. At least I can have a good gossip with you.'

'What's up, then?'

Bella sighs and puts her wine glass down, then rubs her face. 'Oh, it's just life at the moment. I feel like I'm living an endless cycle of school runs and cooking meals for people who don't appreciate it. Ian and I do nothing but snipe at each other . . .'

She tails off, and I nod sympathetically, but my mind is racing. What's going on between her and Ian? Why was she so upset the other day?

It takes all of my willpower not to bombard her with questions, and just to sit patiently, allowing her to talk when she wants to.

To my dismay, she waves a hand dismissively. 'Ignore me. I'm just hormonal and feeling sorry for myself.'

I'd really hoped that she was about to open up to me a little more, but the shutters have come down again. Knowing I can't push it, I launch into a tale about a terrible date I went on last year, though I tell her it was more recent. My hope is that, by sharing a tale of my disastrous love life, she'll be inclined to share more about the difficulties in her relationship with Ian. It doesn't help to draw any more details out of Bella, and she changes the subject soon after, but I feel like she's closer to letting me in.

As I'm walking home later, something occurs to me and I root through my pockets until I find the piece of paper from down the side of the chair in Ian's study. I smooth it out again and check the date. When I realise why it seemed familiar, I shiver. The date and time correspond with when Ryan Beckley died. There's no reference to him that I can find in their house, but this can't be a coincidence, not after seeing Ian with Beckley's sister. Maybe Beckley's threats weren't directed at Bella at all, and he was only looking for her in order to find the man sleeping with his sister. So why did Ian write down the date and time that Beckley was on that bridge? I don't know how long that piece of paper had been there before I found it. To me, it looks like the quick scribble of someone who's arranging something and needs to remember the time. Did Ian arrange to meet Beckley that night? My mind jumps to another question. If he did, did Beckley really commit suicide, or was it actually murder?

Chapter 25

A couple of days later, I have a plan in place to help me find out more about Ryan Beckley and his sister, but there's something I need to do first. I've spent two days walking around Lincoln looking for the homeless woman I saw the other day on the footbridge, but I haven't been able to find her. How do you locate someone who lives on the streets, especially when you don't know their name? It's not something I've ever tried to do before, so I have no idea where to start.

There are homeless shelters, which I've looked up, but short of turning up to one and standing outside to see if I recognise the woman going in, I don't think I'd be in with much luck. I've tried hanging around the footbridge, but there's been no sign of her there. Maybe she moves around the city, but in that case I have no chance of finding her quickly. Lincoln isn't that big, but it's still full of different places where a homeless person could sleep or spend their days, and there's no way I can check all of them.

I'm out and wandering again, when I see a man begging near the railway line. This was the next option on my list – find another homeless person in the same area and see if they know her. I go up to the man, put some money in front of him and stop to stroke his dog. As I did with the woman, I ask if there's anything he needs, but he tells me that money suits him just fine. I'm not going to argue with him, so put a few more coins down before asking my next question.

'I met a woman up on the footbridge a few days ago,' I tell him, trying to keep my voice casual. 'I bought her a few things, and some food, but I haven't seen her since. I wanted to make sure she was okay, see if there was anything else she needed.'

He eyes me suspiciously for a minute. 'Why? What do you get out of it?'

I shrug. 'Nothing. She helped me with something, told me something I needed to know, so I wanted to help her in return.'

After a moment, he nods, as if he finds my explanation acceptable. 'You mean Lucy. You won't be speaking to her again, love.'

'Why not?'

'Died a few nights ago.'

I'm stunned; all I can do is stare at him. 'What happened?' I ask eventually.

'Someone stabbed her. Probably someone after her stuff, some pathetic shit like that.' He shakes his head sadly, and I sit back on my heels for a moment, overwhelmed. I'd been walking round with some soap and snacks for her, and she might have already been dead.

I thank the man and put a third handful of change down for him, give the dog another scratch between its ears then stand up, wondering what I should do next. This wasn't part of the plan. I had thought I would find her sooner or later, but now I can't talk to her or ask her anything else.

For a moment I just stand there in the middle of the street, before shaking myself and wandering away. I need to gather my thoughts, so I stop at the nearest café and order myself a coffee, sitting down in a corner where I don't have to interact with anyone else.

This is awful. Poor woman. Lucy, the man said her name was. I sip my coffee and think about our brief encounter, and I imagine her sitting up on that bridge, alone at night, but not safe. God knows what it must be like to sleep on the streets, never knowing if you're safe or where your next meal is coming from. But why the hell would someone stab her? Is it really something as simple as wanting whatever meagre possessions she might have had? Or could there be something more sinister behind it?

Something occurs to me; I need to go back. Finishing off my coffee, I go to a cash machine and withdraw some more money, before heading back to find the man who told me about Lucy's death. If he wants money I'm happy to oblige if it means he might talk to me, because this all seems like too much of a coincidence.

209

When I get back, he looks me up and down. 'Yeah? What now?'

I pass him a tenner. 'What do you think happened to Lucy?' I look him right in the eye, and he takes the money carefully, tucking it into an inside pocket, then glances back at my wallet.

'I don't know anything about it.'

'Look, I'm not the sort of person who carries round fifty-quid notes or anything,' I say, passing him another tenner. 'I know you might well be wasting my time, and the money is going to run out very quickly if we keep playing this game.'

'One more'll do it.'

I roll my eyes, but give him the third note anyway.

'Reckon she was done in because she knew something . . . something bad,' he says, once the money has been squirrelled away out of sight.

'What was it? Why would someone want to kill her?'

'She reported a murder, and the police ignored her. Kept telling her she was talking shit, they didn't want her messing up their nice shiny police station. So I think the murderer came back for her.'

His eyes are glinting. I'm frozen to the spot. Could it be true? It sounds completely outlandish, but knowing what I know, it fits. If Lucy was up there the night Ryan Beckley went over the bridge, maybe she saw something. Maybe she saw someone push him over. Was that the person she saw killed? And could their murderer have been Ian? I still can't think of any other reason why he would have written down the date and time of Beckley's death.

210

'Did she tell you anything else, anything about what she saw?'

The man eyes my wallet but I shake my head. 'I don't have any more.' It's a lie, but I don't want him thinking I'll just stand here handing out money, not until he gives me anything concrete.

He shakes his head. 'Nah. Just asked me what she should do if she thought she'd seen someone killed. I told her to do nothing, just keep her head down, but a couple of the others told her to tell the police. Gullible bastards. I don't trust 'em.'

'Thank you, you've been really helpful.'

He gives me another nod before I turn and walk away. Not knowing what to do next, I turn my feet in the direction of my flat, and it's only when I'm safely back in my own space that I really start to process what I've been told.

Of course, there's a possibility that whatever happened to Lucy was nothing to do with Ryan Beckley. She might have seen a fight outside a pub, or a domestic on the street one day. And maybe she was killed by a complete stranger who gets their kicks from attacking women, or maybe it really was just someone who wanted to take her stuff. But I can't shake the feeling that this is all linked.

I can't remember any suggestion that Beckley's death might have been anything other than suicide, but I search online anyway, before I do anything else. Every reference I have to his death says he fell, and that his death was not treated as suspicious. It happened nearly nine months ago now, so I assume the case is closed. I double-check the date of his death, to make sure I'm not mistaken about the note I found in Ian's study, then take a deep breath before picking up the phone and calling the police station located closest to where Beckley died.

When a woman answers the phone, I explain that I'm a journalist and I'm looking for information about a case from a while ago. She directs me to their press officer, and I sit on hold for a while before being transferred to a bored-sounding man.

'What publication are you from?' he asks once I've explained what I want to know.

'I work freelance,' I reply, prepared for this question. I've given him the name of my alter ego, rather than my real name, and I'm using the second phone I bought for the purposes of assuming my new identity. I don't want anyone trying to track me down.

'And you're looking for information about the Ryan Beckley case?'

'Yes, I'd specifically like to know if his death was ever considered suspicious. For instance, if anyone reported having seen anything untoward that night, on the footbridge.'

There's a pause, and I can hear him typing.

'I'm afraid that's not the sort of information I'm authorised to give out to someone over the phone,' he replies, not sounding at all apologetic. 'Even if a case is closed, we can't give you details about the investigation.'

'What if I said I have a source who told me you had a witness claim Ryan Beckley was murdered, yet you never followed up on it?'

There's a pause. 'If you have information pertaining to a crime, I would ask you to come in to the station and give a statement.'

'Someone already did that, a homeless woman, and you ignored her. And now she's dead.'

I know I'm pushing it here, but I want to get some sort of reaction out of him.

'I can't give you information relating to an ongoing case, either,' he says.

'So you admit that I'm right? Ryan Beckley isn't an ongoing case, but the stabbing of the homeless woman who reported his murder is, yes?'

Another pause, presumably as he curses himself for his choice of words.

'I can't give you information about an ongoing case,' he repeats, the pitch of his voice slightly higher now. 'Was there anything else you wanted?'

'No, I think I've got all I need for now,' I tell him, and I'm not surprised when he hangs up straight away.

So I'm pretty sure I was right. Lucy saw someone push Ryan Beckley off the railway bridge, and when she reported it, she wasn't believed. Then someone murdered her. But why did they wait so long before killing her?

A horrible thought crosses my mind. Is it a coincidence that she died so soon after speaking to me? What did she tell me about that night? She said she saw him go over. If anyone else had spoken to her about that night, maybe she would have told them the same thing, but perhaps they didn't think to ask her until I started sticking my nose in. Did my interference get Lucy killed?

I'm still working on the theory that Ian could have met Beckley that night and pushed him off the bridge. Could he also have killed Lucy, the only witness to his crime? It's a stretch, but I need to think about how Ian could have known that I'd been talking to Lucy. There wasn't anyone near enough to overhear our conversation. Maybe a couple of people walked past, but they didn't hang around long enough to have understood the context of what we were talking about. Ian works in the city centre though, so he could have walked past, seen me looking at the flowers, then talking to Lucy. Could he then have gone to talk to her himself, to ask her the same questions I did? That sounds possible, certainly. If he knew what the flowers represented and why they were there, then seeing me poking about with them might have made him nervous.

But I can't just assume it's Ian, I tell myself. He's my friend's husband. He could be having an affair, but can my imagination really stretch to him being a murderer? Anyway, whoever the killer is, either they didn't see Lucy that night, or they didn't think a homeless person could be any threat to them. I wish they'd realised that even though Lucy reported what she'd seen, she was completely ignored. Then perhaps they would have left her in peace.

I swear out loud. Why didn't I ask her more about that night when I had the chance? If I could have gained her trust, perhaps she would have told me what she saw, then I'd be a bit closer to understanding what the hell's been going on. As it is, everything is just getting more and more confused. One suicide has now become two murders. This is far more serious than I ever could have imagined.

I follow this train of thought and my blood runs cold. If the person who killed Lucy and Beckley got to Lucy because they saw her conversation with me, does that mean I'm next on their list?

Chapter 26

I lie awake for most of the night, twitching every time I hear a sound. My neighbours downstairs don't usually bother me, but now every thump or creak puts me on edge. Outside, the wind knocks a tree branch against my front window, and I have to resist the urge to reach outside and hack the thing off with a pair of kitchen scissors.

When morning arrives, I make myself a coffee then huddle on my sofa, bleary-eyed, wrapped in a blanket, for comfort more than warmth. All I can see in my mind is one face – Ian Butterworth's. Not only might he have been the one who saw me talking to Lucy, but he was in the city centre on the day I followed Beckley's sister from the footbridge over the railway, too. What are the chances he saw me following her, when he was walking that way to meet her himself? It wouldn't have been hard for him to hang back and see where I was going. The fact that I stopped outside the restaurant after she went in, then crossed to the other side of the street to watch the door, will have made it obvious that I was keeping an eye on her. It had never occurred to me that someone might be watching me, too. If it had, I would have behaved differently.

So, what do I do now? I know the obvious thing would be to cut ties with Bella and her family in order to keep myself safe, but I don't want to do that. I don't think I can. Her friendship means too much to me now, and if her husband really is a murderer then I feel even more strongly that I need to try and keep her safe. Just when I thought one threat had been removed, it turns out there might have been an even greater one there all along.

I could warn Bella. If I put together everything I know, maybe she'll see how it all connects. She might even be able to give me more information to fill in some of the gaps that are still confusing me. And if she believes me, then maybe the two of us can go through Ian's filing cabinet and find something more concrete, something we can use to take to the police. After all, the only thing I have pointing towards Ian is a piece of paper with a date and time on. It doesn't prove anything by itself.

My heart is racing and I can feel my breathing getting faster as the full implication of this sets in. I sit down quickly and drop my head between my knees, doing my best to regulate my breathing before a panic attack sets in fully. I need to be able to think, to function, in order to decide what I'm going to do next.

I can't give up on Bella, not now. If Ian sees me as a

threat, then me backing off won't make a difference, he'll still come after me. But what if I actually face up to him, tell him what I know? Will that make him more wary? I could tell him that I've written everything down and sent it to my brother, then at least he can't do anything to me without becoming the prime suspect.

As my heart rate gradually returns to normal, I slump back onto the sofa and try to think of what I should do. How can I protect myself, and Bella? How can I get the proof I need to make sure Ian pays for his crimes?

The most important thing is to keep him from doing anything to me, or Bella. If he saw me talking to Lucy, then he probably suspects I know something about Ryan Beckley, so I need to convince him otherwise. If I focus on the affair, and my desire to protect Bella, can I make him think that's the only thing I'm interested in, rather than Beckley's death? He doesn't know how I came to be on that bridge; I might have found out about the affair first, then found out his mistress had a brother who killed himself, rather than the other way around. If he thinks I believe Beckley committed suicide, maybe he won't see me as much of a threat, and that way I might be able to get some more information out of him that I can show to Bella. I think it through for a while, but can't come up with anything better. Time is short, so if I want to put my plan into action I need to get moving.

Ian's office is in an old building near the cathedral, and once again I find myself sitting on a bench and watching the door. I consider going in and trying to see him, but

I decide against it. While I'm sure he wouldn't do anything to me in front of his colleagues, I don't want him getting me alone in a small office. Also, me turning up there will tip him off to the fact that I want to talk to him, giving him chance to come up with a story that might put me off the scent. No, safer to wait outside and try to catch him off guard, out in the open where anyone can see us, and somewhere that's not automatically his territory.

I have no idea if he's likely to leave for lunch, so I've accepted I could be sitting here for a full day, possibly even late into the evening. According to Bella, he works late at least two nights a week, but does that mean he's actually in the office at those times? Or is he down the pub with his colleagues, or meeting another woman? Nothing would surprise me, especially not now.

The bench I've chosen isn't particularly comfortable, but it gives me a good enough view of the front door to the building, so I suck it up and make do with shifting position whenever I can, to keep the blood flowing to my extremities. It's cold for late September, and I feel like winter is approaching even though autumn has only just begun. I scroll through my phone mindlessly, not able to fix on anything in particular, then jump when someone comes and sits down beside me. Shit. It's Ian.

'Morning,' he says brightly, though there's something decidedly snake-like about the smile he gives me. 'Can I help you?'

I'm speechless for a moment, so he continues. 'I really like my office. It gives me a great view out across here, towards, the cathedral. So imagine my surprise when I look out to see one of my wife's friends sitting on this bench, watching my building? I thought it must be coincidence, but the fact that you're still here over an hour later suggests not. So I'm going to ask you again, can I help you?'

His tone is far less friendly now. I swallow, and pull out a couple of the photos I took of him and Beckley's sister leaving the restaurant the other day. I got them printed out, but of course they're backed up digitally, too. Handing them to him, I don't say anything, but watch his face as he looks at the images.

'What's this?' he asks, scowling at me. 'You've been following me? That's fucking creepy. Does Bella know you're stalking her husband?'

'Does she know you're sleeping with one of her friends?' I say, jabbing my finger at the photo of the woman.

He laughs, and it's not a pleasant sound. 'Seriously? Is this all you've got? You think that taking two separate photos of me and this woman coming out of a restaurant proves anything? How can you even show these were taken on the same day?'

'They're digital, the metadata shows when they were taken,' I snap, riled by his scorn. 'Are you going to try and tell me it's a coincidence that the two of you were there at the same time? I saw you sitting at a table together, so don't try and tell me you didn't even know she was there.'

'So, do you have a photo of that?' he asks, still full of snide amusement. 'No, I thought not,' he continues when I don't reply. 'Don't come to me and make accusations if you can't prove what you're saying. And don't even think about trying to tell Bella about it, because you already know I can completely deny it.' He laughs again and shakes his head. 'You are completely fucking stupid, you know that?'

I'm taken aback by his comment. 'All I'm doing is trying to look out for my friend.'

'Your friend? Really? How much do you actually know about her? What did she do for a living before you met her, before the current version of her life that she presents to everyone she knows?'

'What does any of that matter? I'm friends with her now, and all I can see is you manipulating her and lying to her.'

Ian laughs openly at this, and I clench my fists to stop the urge to smack him.

'Seriously? You think that I'm the manipulative one? I suppose that just proves how good she is. Whatever you might believe about my wife, I promise you don't know her. All of the things she doesn't tell you are far more indicative of her character than the things she does.' He looks me right in the eye as he says these words, and I'm knocked off kilter. What is he talking about?

There's a pause as I let his words sink in. He's right that Bella is a very private person, and there are things she doesn't like to talk about, but I've always respected that part of her personality and not pushed it. Ian obviously knows her better. Could there be something in what he's saying?

I notice he's screwed up the photos, which pulls me back to the conversation I'd intended to have with him.

'This isn't about Bella,' I tell him. 'This is about you, and what you've been doing. I care about her and I don't want her to get hurt.'

His desire to destroy the photos shows me my plan's working; he's fixated on what I know about his affair, not on what happened to Beckley.

'Don't you worry, Bella is perfectly capable of taking care of herself,' he says with a sigh. 'Look, I know you think that your little trips to coffee shops or the gym, or your book club, or whatever it is you do together, mean that the two of you are best friends, that you share everything, like thirteen-year-olds at a sleepover. But that's not how it works, not with Bella. She only has people around her who are useful to her, so you need to figure out what purpose you serve in her life. Then you might begin to understand her a bit more.'

I have no idea what he's talking about. If only he knew, I was the one who pushed my way into her life rather than the other way round. I wish I could tell him that to wipe the smug smile off his face, but I can't give it away, not now. If I have my way, Bella will never find out who I really am or why I came into her life, but if she does, I want it to be on my terms, with a rational explanation.

I've had enough of this conversation with Ian; he's obviously deflecting to hide his affair, and I don't want to listen to any more of it. Getting up from the bench, I make to leave, but he grabs my hand.

'Let go of me,' I snap, and to my surprise he does as I ask.

'Watch yourself,' he says to me. 'You don't want to get mixed up in things you don't understand.'

He stands and stalks back over to his building, not looking back, leaving me looking after him, wondering if that was a warning or a threat. Even though his words sent a shiver down my spine, I'm relieved. I think I convinced him I'm only interested in the affair, so I might be safe, at least for now.

As I turn to leave, I think I see someone over the road, watching me, but when I look again she's gone. I must have imagined it; I've spent so much time in the last couple of days thinking about Beckley's sister that it's no surprise I've started seeing her everywhere. Still, I can't help thinking that she is more mixed up in this than I previously thought.

Chapter 27

The prison visiting room somehow feels even more bleak than it usually does. Ever since Tony was sentenced I've been counting down the weeks until he'll be eligible for release, but it still seems too far away to start thinking about. I was so lonely without him, but now at least I've got my friendship with Bella.

Tony's always needed a purpose in life – that's why he became a paramedic, because helping people on a day-to-day basis gave him such a sense of satisfaction. He knew he was doing something worthwhile, that he was needed and a valuable member of society. How is he coping now, without that purpose? Well, I know he has one resolve, related to tracking down Dr Palmeri, but I'd rather he gave up on that and just found something to keep him occupied for the time he has left in here.

We'd hoped he would only get two years, but it went up to four because of his statement and how vastly it differed from Palmeri's. Tony accepted responsibility for the child's death, for the things he should have checked but didn't. It was Palmeri who screwed him over, whose account of the incident differed so vastly from what had happened. The recording of their conversation somehow got lost in the depths of the emergency system, and now my brother is stuck in here while the other person who should have been prosecuted is out there living their life quite happily. I completely understand why this haunts Tony, and why he's so obsessed with making sure Palmeri pays the price too, but I don't see what it will achieve at this stage. Tony won't be able to work as a paramedic again, after what happened, so it won't get him his job back. I suppose there's the hope that Palmeri changing his testimony could mean Tony's released earlier, but he's served two and a half years already now, so I'm still hoping that I can persuade him to just focus on himself and move on.

He reaches across the table and squeezes my hand.

'Thanks for coming to see me, Iz. I've really missed you.'

'I know, and I'm sorry. It must be hard being here without a friendly face.' I feel another stab of guilt. While I've been out making new friends and getting mixed up in dangerous things, my brother has been sitting here, day after day, probably going out of his mind with boredom. I know he has his routine, and they have access to plenty of books and things like that, but for someone who was always so active and full of life I can see how this place has broken him.

Gross negligence manslaughter. That was what they settled on in the end. It could have been a lot worse, we were told, but at least everyone agreed that Tony had an exemplary work record and this tragedy was caused only by a momentary lapse, due to stress and exhaustion at the end of a long and traumatic shift. It was the sort of mistake anyone could have made, and his legal team made a point of that when he was in court for sentencing, but of course that didn't bring any comfort to the poor girl's family. I try not to remember them, sitting there in the gallery, so close to me that I could hear every sob. Well, the mother was there. I never saw the father. I assume he couldn't bring himself to go – to look at the man he thought responsible for his daughter's death.

'How's it going?' Tony asks, looking at me intently. 'You look really well. Like, happier than before. That's good. Have you met someone?'

I laugh and shake my head, embarrassed. 'Not in the way you mean. I've made a couple of new friends, that's all. People who are better for me than the last lot.'

Okay, there's only really Bella, but I've got the other women at the book group too, and since I've been using my alter ego I've even reached out and been doing some in-person freelance PA work for a few people, too. So it's not a complete lie.

He nods approvingly. 'That's really good, I'm pleased for you. The girls you've been hanging around with since college are no good for you, especially recently. I'm glad you've found someone else to be friends with.'

Buoyed up by his response, I tell him a bit about Bella.

226

'I feel like she takes me seriously, you know? My old friends just saw me as dull Izzy, the one who was never as lively or exciting as they were, who went home early from nights out and didn't appreciate their jokes.' I shake my head at the memory of that last night out. 'I should have realised ages ago that we'd grown apart, but I think I was just blind to it. I didn't want to put the effort into making new friends, but now I've gone out there and done it, I wish I'd done it years ago.'

'That's great, Iz. I'm really pleased for you.' Tony gives me a genuine smile, and I wish I could tell him everything, right from the start. I know if he hadn't been in prison I would have called him straight away when Ryan Beckley showed up at my door, then maybe we would have handled the whole thing together and it would have gone very differently. As it is, I don't feel like I can explain it to him now. How could I make him understand why I've made friends under a false name? And that I feel like I'm turning into that person now, to the extent that I can feel myself becoming a different woman? I know it's all in my head, psychosomatic or something like that, but whatever it is, it's working, and even he can see the positive change in me.

When he gets out, I assume he's going to come back and live with me, at least to begin with. I'm not sure how I'll keep my new identity a secret from him, unless he never meets my friends, but I feel like it's so far away at the moment I don't really need to think about it. I'm not going to leave my brother stranded, no matter what happens. But how can we go back to being as close as

227

we were, when most of the people I'm now spending time with know me by another name? Will Tony understand any of that, how it came about? Or will he think I'm completely mad, and ruin everything for me under the guise of trying to protect me? One thing is certain, by the time he's released I need to have reached some sort of conclusion by myself, then I don't have to keep living a lie.

'How are you getting on with Palmeri?' he asks me eagerly, leaning forward. There's a glint of desperation in his eye that makes my heart sink. I wish he would give this up, but I don't think I'll ever be able to convince him to let it lie. My only hope is that Palmeri turns up before Tony gets out, then he doesn't waste his life on the outside on this fruitless search just as he has on the inside. I wish Tony could see that Palmeri would hardly change his statement if it meant implicating himself.

'I'm no further on, I'm sorry. I can't find anyone with that name who might be the man you're looking for. Obviously, after what happened, he's done something drastic to keep himself hidden and covered his tracks really well.'

'But there are people out there, private detectives, who can help with this sort of thing,' he insists.

'Tony, do you know how much that would cost? I'm doing okay at the moment, but I don't earn enough to keep a private investigator on retainer. I've done as much as I can, and short of hacking into hospital databases I don't know what else I can do.'

Tony licks his lips then glances over his shoulder at

another inmate a few tables away. 'Maybe I can find someone who can do that, so you don't have to get your hands dirty.'

'No!' I look round to check nobody is listening, then lower my voice. 'No, Tony. You can't get involved in anything else criminal, especially while you're still here. Do you want to get caught and have your sentence extended? I want you home as soon as they'll allow it, and I know you think if they get an accurate statement from Palmeri things might be different, but do you really think that's going to happen now? It's been nearly three years.'

I can see a mixture of emotions fighting for dominance on his face, then he sits back in the chair looking disgusted. 'I really thought you'd be able to come through for me on this, Iz. I just . . . I need to find him.' He rubs a hand across his face. 'Fuck. How the hell did this happen?'

'That doesn't matter. Look, let's go through the whole thing again, together. Tell me again exactly what happened that day, the whole truth, including the names of anyone you remember being involved, what you did, what the doctor said, and how this whole sorry mess came about. There might be something you've missed, something I can use. A first name would help.'

He sighs and rubs his face for a second time, and for a moment I think he's going to refuse, but eventually he nods.

'Fine. But I told you everything at the time, you know that. As soon as it happened.'

I nod, remembering the day Tony came home distraught,

229

how he sobbed in my arms at the death of one of his patients, a child he felt he should have saved. He'd worked almost a double shift, and was running on so little sleep. I was sure he was exaggerating, that there'd been nothing he could do. But then it all happened so quickly – the inquiry, his suspension, his statement taking responsibility, then sentencing. But he'd never counted on the doctor lying and leaving everything at Tony's door.

'I know, but maybe we'll think of something this time, a way to track down Palmeri. He obviously knows he's in the wrong, if he's gone to ground. I certainly can't find him working at any hospital in the UK.'

'I'll do what I can. They never gave me any details about what he'd said happened, though. As soon as the inquiry decided that I was completely at fault, they didn't let me anywhere near Palmeri. I don't know his first name or even what he looks like.

'I've always told you the truth, Iz. I never said it wasn't my fault. A child died, and I've accepted responsibility for that. The only thing I won't accept is that it was entirely my fault. Someone else needs to pay the price for that girl's death, just as much as I do, and justice isn't done until that's happened.'

The intensity of his stare scares me slightly, but I give him a nod to show I accept what he's just told me. He drops his head and starts speaking, keeping his voice low, and gradually he tells me the whole story of what happened that day. He never had a trial because he admitted culpability, so I haven't heard him go through it like this before. When it happened, I got information

230

in pieces, but now he tells me the whole process from the beginning.

A couple of times his voice breaks, and I want to reach out and hug him, but I know he has to get through the story uninterrupted. By the time he's finished I'm regretting having put him through this, because there's nothing I can use, no little detail he left out before, or anything useful at all. I've begun to lose hope we'll ever find Palmeri, and my concern is that even after Tony gets out, this obsession will never end.

Chapter 28

It's ten in the morning, and I've been up half the night practising some of the things I found online. I reckon I can do it now, though, so there's no time like the present. Just like last time, I wait until Bella has gone out, then cross over from the park and let myself in by the back door, making my way straight to Ian's study.

I don't waste any time, pulling out the cheap pair of nail clippers I've brought with me. The video made it look incredibly easy, but I'm doubtful. Surely it can't be that simple? I pull out the nail file attachment and wiggle it into the lock gently, then a little firmer when I come up against some resistance. To my surprise, I manage to get it the whole way into the lock, then try to turn it, and it responds smoothly. There's a click, and I try the top drawer to be sure. It's open.

If there's anything worth finding in this cabinet then I bet Ian has no idea how easy it is to break into it with something as simple as a metal nail file. Marvelling at it, I slide the top drawer all the way open to begin my search.

A lot of the papers are things to do with the house, and various bills, which I gloss over. That's not of any interest to me right now. I don't even know what I'm looking for, but I don't think details of their mortgage payments are going to help me find out what happened to Ryan Beckley and Lucy. Every so often I stop and listen to make sure nobody is outside. Bella will be a while at the gym – I know her routine pretty well by now, so I've got at least an hour and a half in the house before she gets home, possibly more. That should be enough time to search the cabinet.

The second drawer down doesn't offer anything of any interest either, and it's only when I get to the back of the third drawer that I finally find something. There's a cardboard folder tucked down right at the back, so it's half underneath the folders that are hanging in the drawer, and as I pull it out I feel a tingle of excitement. What is this, and why was it hidden away at the back? I open it up and scan the first sheet, then sit down on the chair in shock.

Taking my time, I read through the whole file. There are only a few sheets of paper, but I read them all twice before sitting back and trying to take it all in. I don't know exactly what I was hoping to find, but this wasn't it. I'm confused and disorientated, and for a moment I forget where I am and what I'm doing there. When I finally shake myself I realise I can't leave without these papers. I don't want to waste time taking photos of them, so decide to stuff the whole folder into my bag. I can scan them when I get home, keep the copies, then return the originals at a later date. Hopefully whoever hid them back here won't check on them regularly, so nobody will miss them, at least for a few days. And that might be all the time I need to get this finished.

I feel jittery the whole way home, looking over my shoulder to make sure nobody is watching or following me. I haven't felt like this since Beckley attacked me that night. For the first time, I feel like I need to call Tony and explain some things to him, tell him what's going on and ask for his advice. He might be able to answer some of the questions I have, and help me work through the rest. I don't think I can just call on the off-chance they'll let me speak to him, though, so I'm going to have to wait until he calls me.

Back in my flat, I lock and bolt the door, then get to work copying the documents. I save them in a couple of different places, as well as printing out hard copies, just in case. Is it enough to take to the police yet? I don't know. Chewing my lip, I sit down and think for a while, then I decide it's time. I need to talk to Ryan Beckley's sister. It will mean showing my hand, but if that's what I need to do in order to find out what the hell is going on, it'll be worth it.

I need to talk to you about your brother.

My message is concise, but hopefully it will attract her interest. I consider calling her and having it out over the phone, but then think better of it. I want to talk to her in person, then I can record what she says and see her facial expression at the same time.

Why? comes the reply. *What do you want to know?*

It's interesting that she doesn't ask who this is. I got her number from Bella's phone, but it seems she's already got mine, which makes me shiver. Has she been watching me, the way that I've been watching her? Maybe I didn't imagine seeing her the other day.

We need to talk in person, I type back.

What about?

She's obviously stalling, so I wonder how much I can tell her. I think for a few minutes, then carefully craft a message. It gives away a little of what I know, but not everything. I don't want to scare her off, but I need to show her that I know more than she's told anyone.

It seems to work, because her reply comes back very quickly.

Meet me tonight and I'll tell you everything.

I hesitate. Part of me had expected her to refuse, but now she's agreed I don't know if I want to go through with this. Am I strong enough to stand up to her and get what I want? My phone beeps again and I snatch it off the table to check the message.

You need to come and meet me. You're right, we can't talk about this over the phone. Your choice.

Another message follows shortly after, with an address, and a time: eleven tonight. Why has she picked so late? I check the location on the map and can see it's a residential street, which sets another alarm bell ringing. Is this her home? Is she trying to unsettle me by meeting me somewhere she'll hold the balance of power? When I suggested this, I thought we'd meet during the day in a park, or a coffee shop or something. Not in a quiet street in the middle of the night.

It was a stupid idea, I tell myself. I'm not going to go. I'll just tell her I'm not prepared to meet her unless it's on my terms, and we'll see what she says.

I don't delete the messages, but instead take some screenshots and print them out, adding them to the pile. Right now, I feel like I should be making sure I save everything, document exactly what I know and what's been said.

For a couple of hours, I try to get some work done, but my heart isn't in it. I still haven't replied to confirm if I'm going to meet her or not. Why am I hesitating? I know the answer, and it's linked to the documents I found in Ian's filing cabinet. I look over them again, picking out the important bits of information, and wonder how I could have missed it before.

I can't let it rest, and soon I'm getting my coat and shoes and I'm out the door. I'm not stupid enough to do what she's asked, going there alone, at night, but at least I can check out the location. It's in a different part of the city, and it takes me an hour to walk there. When I arrive, I stare up at a house that looks like any other. There's nothing sinister about it, but I can't help feeling like I'm missing something. Maybe my own behaviour has made me overly suspicious of other people's, but now I'm here I might as well check out the house.

Before I can stop myself, I ring the doorbell. While I wait to see if anyone will answer, I look at the house itself. It's a really standard, small, red-brick terraced house.

236

The front door is made of white PVC, with a semi-circular window at the top, too high for me to see anything through. It has two windows at the front, one on each floor, and I try to peer through the one next to me. It's dark inside, and I can't see anything without pressing my face to the glass. There's no sound from inside, so I risk it, shading my eyes with my hand to get a better view, but all I can see is a sofa and a TV, along with a couple of magazines on a coffee table. It doesn't tell me anything.

If this is Beckley's sister's house, why does she want me to come so late at night? I still think it could be a trap. I'd like to be able to watch the house for a while, see who comes and goes, but there's absolutely nowhere to hide on this street. I might have a spare webcam at home, but I don't have the necessary equipment to set it up so I can access it remotely, and there's nowhere obvious I could leave it. Checking my watch, I don't think there's time for me to go and buy anything either.

Kicking myself, I turn in the direction of home. Once I'm away from that street I feel a bit more comfortable, but there's still a nagging sensation at the back of my mind. Could I be doing more? Surely there's an option available that will allow me to find out more about Ryan Beckley without putting myself in a potentially risky situation?

If Tony were here, I'd just ask him to go with me, but I don't have anyone else I feel I could ask. Of course there's Bella, but right now I don't want to involve her, either. If this woman means me harm, I'm pretty sure she won't hesitate to hurt her, too, even if she is her friend.

No, if I want to find out the truth, I need to do it alone.

Getting back to my flat, I make a decision. There has to be somewhere nearby I can wait and see if I can keep an eye on the house, make sure she's alone and not setting a trap for me. Then, if it's all innocent and it's simply that she's busy until late at night, I can go and speak to her.

For the next couple of hours, I prowl around the flat restlessly. My intention is to get to her road around nine, then I have loads of time to scout out the area and figure out where I can wait to catch someone arriving.

I choose the darkest collection of clothing I've got, including a black beanie hat, then I'm ready to go. Stepping out of my building, I take a deep breath of the evening air to steady my nerves, then set off. Whatever happens this evening, I'm determined to find out the truth once and for all.

BELLA

Chapter 29

We've just put the girls to bed when there's a knock at the door. Both Ian and I look at each other, but it's clear from our expressions that neither of us is expecting a visitor. He shrugs and goes to the front door, but I follow close behind him, wanting to see who it is.

'Mr Ian Butterworth?'

'Yes?'

I can see two people in suits standing on the doorstep, a man and a woman, and each of them holds out a wallet of some sort for Ian to look at. Police. And plainclothes police, which means something more serious than a burglary or some kids causing a nuisance. Sweat begins to prickle at the base of my skull.

'Is your wife at home?'

'Yes, I'm here,' I reply, stepping forward. 'What's happened?'

'May we come in?'

Ian leads them through to the living room and I follow, where they introduce themselves. I'm too flustered to remember their names or ranks, but I expect Ian is taking it all in. He shoots me a searching look, wondering if I know why they're here, but I just give him a shrug. I know he's angry, because he hates being caught off guard by having strangers in his house, and an official visit from the police is far worse than that. This isn't something I could have prepared him for, though, because I have no idea why they're here.

'We have a few questions for you, if you don't mind,' says the man. He pulls something out of his inside pocket and pushes it across the coffee table towards me. 'Do you recognise this woman?'

I pick up the photo and glance at it, then back at the detectives, passing the photo to Ian.

'Yes, that's my friend Jenny.'

The man nods, while the woman writes something down.

'Can you tell us when you last saw her?'

'Er, one night last week, I think. She came round one evening for a drink.'

The man looks over to Ian, who shakes his head. 'I wasn't here.'

'You were working late,' I tell him. 'She'd gone by the time you got home.'

'And how do you know her?'

'I met her at the gym,' I tell them. 'We exchanged numbers and got to know each other that way.'

'Doesn't she go to your book group, too?' Ian interjects, and I nod.

'Look, what is this about?' he asks, directing his question to the male detective. 'Why are you here? Has Jenny done something?'

The woman clears her throat. 'I'm afraid we have some bad news. This woman was found dead a couple of nights ago. Her death is being treated as suspicious.'

I sit and stare at them for a moment, and the room spins slightly. Before I know what's happening, I feel bile rushing up my throat and I have to dash from the room into the downstairs toilet, where I vomit three times. Once everything is out, I stand clutching the sink, rinsing my mouth out and spitting water until the bitter taste has gone, but it still leaves a residue clinging to my teeth. I go to the kitchen and get a glass of water before returning to the living room.

'I'm sorry,' I say, aware that my hand is now shaking. 'I just . . . it's a shock.'

The woman gives me a sympathetic smile, and nods. 'We understand. We found your name and address on a notepad in her home, hence why we're here.'

Ian rubs his chin and lets out a long breath. His face looks grey and I can see his hand is trembling slightly. 'And you think she was murdered?'

'Could there be a mistake?' I interject, before either of them has a chance to respond.

'There's no mistake, I'm afraid,' the man says.

'Well, thank you for coming to tell us,' Ian says, rising

to his feet in a gesture that clearly shows he expects the detectives to leave, but they both stay seated.

'I'm afraid we have a couple more questions, Mr Butterworth.'

Ian's lips twist slightly, but I can see he's trying to keep a civil face on. 'Really? What could we possibly tell you?'

'Well, we'd like to ask you if you know of anyone who might wish her any harm?'

I shake my head. 'No, not at all. I mean, she didn't really talk to me much about other people she knew, if you see what I mean. She told me a bit about her work, and we talked about things we'd been doing, but I never met any of her other friends, or her family. I got the impression she didn't really have many people in her life.'

The two detectives glance at each other, then back at me. 'Were you aware that the name she gave you, Jenny Holdsworth, wasn't her real name?'

I frown. 'What does that mean? Why would she have told me a fake name?'

'That's something we hoped you might be able to tell us.'

The man leans forward then, and tells us Jenny's real name, then sits back. He never takes his eyes off us, obviously waiting for a reaction and hoping to catch one of us out in a lie.

'What the hell? What's this supposed to mean?'

'Again, we were hoping you could tell us that.'

I sit back and think about the way Jenny came into my life, introducing herself at the gym then practically forcing her number on me. The shy and awkward way she came across made her seem completely harmless, but it's obvious now that she intended to befriend me, and specifically me, not just anyone she came across at the gym who looked friendly. I swallow, then take a big gulp from the glass of water that's sitting in front of me.

'She told me her name was Jenny Holdsworth, and I had no reason not to believe her,' I say slowly. 'Now I think about it, she was very keen to become friends with me, but I just thought she was lonely and perhaps a bit socially awkward. I didn't think there could be anything sinister behind it. Maybe there isn't. Maybe it's just a coincidence.'

Ian snorts and I glance over at him. 'She was bloody obsessed with you,' he says, then looks at the detectives. 'She found all sorts of excuses to come over. She even tried to become friendly with my mother, but she's a smart woman and was having none of it.'

I open my mouth to say something, but then think better of it. Anyone who Marian dislikes would automatically be on my popular list, but there's no need to bring the detectives in to one of our many arguments about my husband's mother. I'm pissed off with Ian though; when I saw Jenny hanging around the girls' school that time I tried to tell him there was something strange going on, and he told me I was imagining it. He said I should leave Jenny alone, that she was harmless, but now he's rewriting the narrative to suit himself.

'And you had no suspicion that she might not be who she said she was? You didn't see anything, a credit card with a different name on, anything like that, for example?'

245

I shake my head. 'No. I mean, we went out for lunch sometimes, but I never looked at her card when she was paying. Why would I?'

I look across at Ian but he doesn't look at me, as if all of this is my fault. How could I have known she lied to me?

'How did she die?' I ask. Despite what I've learnt about her, I had grown to like her. After Caroline suggested I go on the charm offensive and spend more time with her, I did just that. Admittedly, I didn't find out much more about her, which had been the aim of the exercise, but I found myself enjoying her company. Now, though, I'm worried about what's going to come out into the open. It's obvious why she avoided some of my questions about her personal life, because she didn't want me to find out who she really was, but I still don't understand what she hoped to gain by befriending me.

The detectives shuffle awkwardly, and I can tell they don't want to answer my question.

'I'm afraid we can't give you specifics.'

'Could it have been a random attack, a mugging?' Ian says. I can tell from his tone that he's had enough and he wants them to leave.

'Of course, that's certainly one possibility,' the man says, his voice calm and placating. 'However, given the connection to your wife, we felt it was important to come and speak to you, to see if you could help us any further with our enquiries.'

I have no desire to be someone who is 'helping the police with their enquiries' and I know Ian will be feeling

246

the same. The detectives seem reluctant to leave, but neither Ian nor I offer anything else, so they stand and walk towards the front door.

'If you think of anything else, please give us a call,' the woman says, handing me a card. I don't look at it, but put it in my pocket. I don't think I'll be using it.

Once Ian has shut the door behind them, he leans on it for a moment, then glares at me.

'What the fuck?' He keeps his voice low, not wanting to wake the girls, I assume, then turns and stalks into the living room. I know he's expecting me to follow him, but for a moment I hesitate. I have no interest in talking to him about this. I just want to go upstairs and curl up on the bed, pull the duvet over my head and pretend this hasn't happened, but I know I'm not going to get that opportunity. Sighing, I follow him.

'Why the hell did this woman make friends with you? And why do the police think her death has something to do with you?' He's standing there, primed for a fight, the moment I join him.

'How was I supposed to know who she was, Ian? You're acting like I planned this, like I've been keeping some huge secret from you. Trust me, I'm as shocked as you are to find out she wasn't using her real name.' I want to point out his hypocrisy, that he was quite happy to have Jenny in our lives if it meant I had someone to spend time with other than him, but I decide it's not worth riling him further.

He glares at me, then crosses to the window, picking up an ornament and passing it between his hands for a moment. I tense, wondering if he's going to throw it. There's only one time in our marriage when he's really lost his temper, and I get a sudden flashback to that time.

Almost as if he's read my mind, he puts the ornament down again, his movements exaggerated, then turns back to me.

'Has she spent time with the girls?'

I pause. 'Yes. You know she has, over the summer.'

'Did you ever think to find out more about someone who you were allowing to get to know our children?' His voice is quiet but dripping with menace. He can hardly talk – one of his former colleagues was convicted of sexual assault of a minor a couple of years ago, on a girl he met in a club who was only fifteen, but before then we'd spent plenty of time with him at family barbecues and the like. I've never thought to accuse him of improperly vetting the people we meet, but I know that argument won't make it through to him right now.

'She was never alone with them,' I snap. 'It's not like I've been asking her to babysit on a weekly basis. She's just been to the park with us a few times, and out for lunch. Christ's sake, someone murdered the woman, and this is what you're worrying about?'

'And why did someone murder her? What the hell was she mixed up in?'

'You're the one who asked if it could have been a random mugging!' I wrap my arms around myself to stop myself from lashing out, because I know if I do that he'll find a way to use it against me.

He steps closer to me, getting his face right into mine, but I stand my ground.

'If I find out my children have ever been put at risk, I will make sure you never see them again.'

Before I have a chance to reply, he stalks out of the room and slams the door.

Chapter 30

It's windy, but I don't care. I need the fresh air to try and clear my head, as if everything awful that has happened to me can just be blown away. I keep obsessively checking the news in case there's anything about Jenny's murder, but I haven't seen anything yet. There's a story about her, but she hasn't been named in the press yet, and there aren't any details about how she died. I don't know why, and that in itself worries me, especially given who she really was. Will they report that angle, her real name but also what she was doing, pretending to be someone else? Will they get hold of the story of how she deliberately came into my life under a false name, wormed her way into my friendship and used it to her advantage? The thought makes my breath come a bit faster, and I have to shake it away as soon as I think of it.

Caroline doesn't know, or at least I don't think she

does. I told her I needed to meet up this afternoon, urgently, and thankfully she didn't question it. We're meeting in our usual place; I need normality, need to feel like things haven't gone spinning out of control around me. For once I actually wish I had a friend who knew the whole truth about me, everything that's gone on in mine and Ian's past, but I can't take the risk of exposing myself now in case we lose everything we've fought to claw back over the last couple of years. Maybe Caro would understand, and would stand by me, but maybe she wouldn't. I need her right now, more than she could ever understand.

When I arrive at the restaurant, she's already there. She stands up to greet me and I pull her into a tight hug.

'What's up?' she asks immediately, as we pull apart. She doesn't let go of my arms straight away, but holds onto me and gives me a searching look, as if she's worried I'm going to turn round and run out of the door again. I can't say it hasn't crossed my mind. I don't think I want to talk to anyone about this right now, because where do I begin? And where do I end?

Before I can say anything, Caro turns to a passing waiter and orders a bottle of wine. I don't know if it's a good idea to have a drink, especially at lunchtime, because it will only increase my chances of saying something I shouldn't, but I'm weak and I want to give in to the intoxication. It might make me feel better, I tell myself, though really I know nothing will do that right now.

'Come on, tell me what's happened.' Caroline pours the wine and we push the menus to one side. I don't feel like eating, though I know we'll end up ordering some-thing because Caro won't let me drink on a completely empty stomach. She's strangely attentive like that, a trait I found difficult to understand when I first met her. Part of me actually feels sorry for her, ending up being friends with me, because she had no idea what she was getting herself into.

'Jenny's dead.' Saying it bluntly is the only way I know how to get the words out. 'She was murdered.'

Caro just sits there for a moment, her mouth hanging open.

'Shit,' she says eventually. 'Bloody hell. When? How did it happen? Do the police know who it was?'

I shake my head. 'They came round to see me last night, to tell me, and to ask me a few questions about when I'd last seen her, stuff like that.'

'Oh God. That's awful.' Caro shakes her head, and I can see fear in her eyes. I know she never took to Jenny, and maybe I should have trusted her judgement. 'Was it a mugging or something? Or a psycho boyfriend?'

'I don't think so. They said they're not ruling anything out at this stage, but I got the feeling they were only saying that to avoid giving too much away. But if they have any suspects at this stage, they didn't tell us last night.'

'Us? Ian was there then?'

'Yeah, why?'

She has a guarded expression as she answers. 'No reason. I just wanted to make sure you weren't alone when they were talking to you.'

I don't believe her, but I let it pass. It doesn't matter right now.

'God, I can't believe it,' she says, sitting back in her seat and shaking her head. 'It's not the sort of thing you expect to happen to someone you know, is it?'

'No,' I say quietly, taking a sip of my wine and staring out of the window. We sit in silence for a moment, then Caro pulls the menus closer.

'We need to eat.'

'I don't feel like it.'

'Tough. You've had a shock, and you're drinking. If you don't order something, I'll do it for you.'

I go through the motions of choosing something, though as soon as I've given my order I can't remember what it was. Not that it matters.

'When did you last see her?' Caro asks me once the waiter has left and we have some semblance of privacy again.

'Just a few days ago. She came round for a drink, and I just spent the whole time moaning at her.' I run my hands over my face, not really caring about the state of my make-up. I barely remembered to put any on this morning, and the only reason I bothered was because I couldn't cope with a snide comment from Ian about my appearance. He doesn't seem to give a shit about what happened, about how my life has been turned upside down, and I was hit with the shock of how much our relationship has changed. Not that long ago, something like this would have pulled us even closer together, and he would have supported me through the confusion and the grief. Now, it's like he can't even bear to look at me. Will we ever get back to the way things used to be? I hope so, that the Ian I married is still in there, but that's a thought for another day.

'There's something else,' I tell her, looking at my wine glass and not at her. 'Jenny was lying to me. To us. About who she was.'

'What do you mean?'

I tell her what the police told me, that Jenny Holdsworth wasn't her real name.

Caroline is quiet for a few moments and chews her lip thoughtfully. 'So what did she want? Why did she lie to you? I know you said it was to us, but she was never interested in me. You were the one she made friends with, she couldn't have cared less about me.'

I take a deep breath, then shrug. 'I have no idea.'

'I shouldn't have encouraged you to spend more time with her, I'm sorry.' Caro hangs her head, and I want to reach out and hug her, tell her that none of this is her fault, that her intervention wouldn't have changed things either way, but I don't. I can't say too much.

'She was determined,' is all I say.

Caro nods. 'She was. I should have realised when she turned up at the book group that she'd planned it. I mean, I can't remember there ever being anything about the group in that newsletter, certainly not that would have had Brenda's contact details in it. She's pretty protective over who she invites to join.'

'I don't know, maybe she followed me one day and managed to get herself invited that way.' I sigh and pour myself some more wine. Our food arrives then, and Caroline asks for a second bottle of wine. Of course I should say no, but I don't.

'Ian is absolutely furious about it,' I say, trying to keep my tone casual as I poke at my food. 'He thinks I shouldn't have let her in the house or anywhere near the kids. But the first time she came to the house she wandered into the garden, so I couldn't exactly leave her out there, could I? And Marian was there. If she'd seen me being rude to Jenny she only would have used it as more ammunition. I can't think straight around that bloody woman as it is.'

'I mean, I know we talked about her being a bit weird, a bit pushy, but how were you to know?' Caroline says, ever the voice of reason. 'When you make a new friend, you trust the details they give you. If we didn't, we'd never get to know anyone new, would we?'

'I suppose not.' I sigh and take another gulp of wine. 'And Ian will take any opportunity to lay into me about pretty much anything these days, so if it hadn't been that, it would have been something else. He's on edge enough about us having the police in our house again.'

I freeze, realising what I've just said, and look down at my food. Caroline is looking at me, I can feel her gaze on me, but I keep my attention on my food, suddenly showing an interest and wolfing down several mouthfuls. Please don't say anything. Please don't pick up on what I said. One stupid word. 'Again'. Please don't ask.

'Maybe he's just worried about you,' she says, and I feel like I can breathe again. If she noticed the significance

255

of what I said, she hasn't mentioned it, which knowing Caroline means she won't bring it up.

I let out a harsh laugh. 'Whatever Ian is worried about, it's not me.'

She frowns and reaches forward to squeeze my hand. 'Bella, if it's that bad, why don't you just leave him? I know you're thinking of the girls, but it won't be good for them to grow up around two parents in the same house who can't stand each other. At least if you're apart you can relax a bit. I feel like you're constantly on edge.'

Pulling my hand away from hers, I pick up my wine again in order to give myself time to think of an answer. I know it seems simple to an outsider, but it's not. I've told her that before, but she's clearly not convinced.

'What does he have over you? Why do you feel you can't leave him?'

I feel the tears well up and squeeze my eyes closed in an effort to stop them spilling over. No, I can't cry, not now. If I get upset, God knows what I'll end up saying, and lovely though Caro is, I don't think she'll understand.

'I can't. Just . . . don't ask me that. Please.' Whatever has happened between Ian and me, I still love him. I know exactly how the distance between us came to exist, and what caused the huge chasm that's there now, but I still have to hope that we can fix things. The longer it goes on, though, the less likely it feels.

We sit in silence for a few minutes, each of us pushing food around on our plates without eating anything. I'm worried I've offended her; I can't push her away, not now. Apart from the fact that she's the only friend I have, I need her. Caroline is the one who will be able to save me, I know that, but I can't do anything yet. I need to wait, and then when the time is right I can do what I need to do, leave Ian if we can't fix things, and start over yet again.

I don't tell her any of this. I just sigh and top up her wine as a peace offering.

'I'm sorry. It's complicated. I promise I'll tell you everything at some point, but not right now. There are things I need to do first, things I need to arrange and put in motion.'

She nods but doesn't say anything else. I stare out of the window for a moment and try not to think back to when I was younger, when I had dreams about what my life would be like. Despite the material advantages I have, I'd trade them all in to be able to go back in time and fix some of the worst decisions I've made.

'Do you think the police will want to talk to you again, about Jenny?'

'I hope not,' I tell her with a grimace. 'I don't know what else I can tell them.'

'I'm sure it was just something random,' she says reassuringly. 'Nothing to do with you at all.'

I nod, but in my heart I know she's wrong.

Chapter 31

My phone rings as I'm dropping the girls off at school. I don't recognise the number, so I ignore it, walk them into the playground and don't think about it again until they're both safely inside the school building. Their good-byes seemed a little more intense today, and I wonder if they're okay. I've been so distracted by this business of Jenny's death that I might have missed something, and I feel a stab of parental guilt. Making a resolution to spend some quality time with the two of them after school, I walk back to the car, deep in thought.

The second time my phone rings, I look at it with exasperation. I answer with a curt, 'Hello?'

That usually weeds out the spam callers pretty quickly.

'Mrs Butterworth? This is DS Watson, we met the other day.'

She pauses, obviously expecting a response.

'Yes,' I say eventually. 'How can I help you?' I feel a

sensation of panic starting in the pit of my stomach, and I clench my jaw. Now isn't the time to start losing it, I tell myself.

'We were wondering if you were free to come into the station to speak to us, preferably today? There are some more points we'd like to discuss with you regarding Jenny and what happened to her.'

I take a slow deep breath, then gradually let it out as I think about what to say. 'Can't you just tell me over the phone?'

'No, I think this would be better to discuss in person.'

'Do I need a lawyer?'

'You're not under arrest, Mrs Butterworth, we just want to talk to you about a couple of things.'

The way she says my name makes me flinch, and I wish she'd stop using it. I make a mental note to tell her to call me Isabella in future, which might have the added bonus of making her think I'm cooperating as much as possible.

'Fine,' I say with a sigh. 'I can come in now, get it out of the way.'

'Perfect, we'll see you soon.' She tells me the location of the police station, then hangs up.

Shit. What the hell is it now? Isn't it bad enough that the woman's dead; now I'm being dragged into the investigation? I should never have made the effort to get to know Jenny, that's where all the trouble started. I should have gone with my gut instead of letting Caroline influence me.

I drive through Lincoln, for once unconcerned about

sitting at traffic lights every few minutes. Anything to delay my arrival at the station. I'm dreading whatever it is they might say. What if they do actually plan to arrest me when I'm there? No, they wouldn't have lied about that, would they? Or they would have told me to contact my solicitor. I kid myself that I have any idea of how these things work, when really my only knowledge of what the police can and can't do comes from watching *Silent Witness* and *Vera*.

When I arrive, I park up the road rather than using the car park. The last thing I want is anyone to see me going into a police station, even if I do have the explanation that one of my friends was killed. It's not something I really want to hear being gossiped about at the school gates. We've told the girls the basics, that Mummy's friend Jenny died, but nothing more than that. I don't want to traumatise my children, and so I'd rather keep it away from their environment altogether if I can, though I recognise that might not be within my control.

I ask for DS Watson by name when I go in, hoping that by my demeanour alone I make a good impression; I don't know anyone here, but I still don't want anyone looking at me and assuming I'm a criminal. For all of my adult life, I've relied on giving people a strong first impression in order to influence how the rest of our interaction plays out, but I'm concerned I might have lost the knack in recent years.

'She'll be through in a moment,' the man on the desk tells me, then nods at the seats bolted to the floor around the lobby. Choosing one furthest away from the door, I perch tentatively, but soon another door is opened and I'm ushered through to an interview room. This room has a sofa and a coffee table, with a couple of padded chairs for the detectives. So I'm not being treated as a suspect; they wouldn't have put me in the comfy room if they thought I had anything to do with Jenny's death.

'Thank you for coming in, Mrs Butterworth,' the detective says. This time she's been joined by another young woman in plain clothes, who is introduced as DC Patel.

'Please, call me Isabella,' I say hurriedly.

'Okay, Isabella,' Watson says with a nod of acknowledgement. 'There are a few things we'd like to talk to you about, things that have come up in the course of our enquiries into the death of the woman you knew as Jenny Holdsworth.'

I'm jarred by that phrase, 'the woman you knew as'. I still don't understand how I can have been so easily taken in by her. How did I not notice that she had cards in another name? Why didn't I think to look her up online when she started showing up in the same places as me? Hindsight is a wonderful thing.

I nod my understanding, and she continues. 'We've carried out an extensive search of her home in order to look for evidence that might help us to find her killer. In the course of this search, we found some things that we wanted to discuss with you.'

'I've never been to her house,' I tell them. 'I don't have a clue where she lived. Every time I asked her about it she changed the subject.' This was one of the things I discussed with Caroline, something I tried to push Jenny on several times over the summer. In fact, I was getting ready to take her to task about it the next time we met.

The detectives are looking at each other, and I remind myself not to volunteer too much information. That's something I learnt when everything went wrong for me and Ian: only answer questions, and then only give them the immediate information related to what they asked. Don't elaborate if they haven't asked for it, and don't enter into a dialogue until they ask you a specific question.

'Can you give us a few more details about your relationship with Jenny?' Watson asks. 'For example, do you remember when you first met, and where?'

I think back to the day she approached me at the gym, and describe it as best I can.

'I can't remember exactly when it was,' I tell them, giving them an approximate date. 'If I check my diary I can probably work it out.'

'If you can let us know, that would be useful. And she was the one who initiated the conversation?'

'Yes. I don't tend to talk to anyone while I'm at the gym. She's the only person I've ever chatted to there, I think.'

Patel takes some notes and Watson pulls out a file. 'And you hadn't met her before this date?'

'No. I mean, I might have passed her in a shop or something, but I'd certainly never spoken to her before, and she didn't seem familiar when she approached me that day.'

'Can you be sure about that?'

'What? Yes, I'm sure!' I'm getting frustrated now, and

I've had enough of this. 'Why are you asking me these questions?'

Watson pulls a photo out of the file and slides it over the coffee table toward me as if she's handling something dangerous yet fragile.

'When we entered Jenny's home, we found a number of references to you and your family.'

'References? What do you mean, references?' I look down at the photo, which appears to be of a notebook and a folder. 'What is this?'

'Jenny seems to have been keeping track of you for quite some time. Some of the things she's written down occurred several weeks before the two of you spoke in the gym on that first occasion.'

'Keeping track of me?' Her words make sense, but I still don't understand what she's saying. Watson pulls out another two photos and hands them over.

These are both photos of photos, presumably because the originals have been taken into evidence. One of them shows me leaving our house one day, obviously in a hurry judging by the state of my hair. The other leaves me cold: a photo of the outside of my daughters' school. The playground is full of children, but there are no adults hanging around the gates, so this must be their morning break, or possibly lunchtime.

'She took these photos?' I ask, and I can hear my voice shaking.

'We assume so. We've found a camera, so our forensics teams are checking that and her computer to confirm she took them. But we think it's a safe assumption at this point.'

'She was watching my children?' It comes out almost as a whisper. From what they'd told me, I thought they would just pass her off as a weirdo who had latched onto me, but this is far more sinister than I had expected. If I had known about this . . . but then, if I'd known, I would never have let things get as far as they did.

'Do you have any idea why she might have been stalking you?' Watson asks.

Stalking. Of course, that's exactly what this was. I'm innocent in this, the victim of an obsessive. Not just me, my whole family. And that's what I need to make sure the police understand.

'No, this is just awful,' I say, allowing them to hear my voice quaver as I speak. It won't hurt to sound weaker than I am. 'She was watching my children? How could I not have known about this?' I point at the photo of me leaving the house. 'She's been outside my home, and I don't even remember telling her where I lived. The first time she came round, she just turned up and wandered into my garden. I assumed I must have told her my address and forgotten about it, but I didn't, did I? She followed me or something.'

I take a few deep breaths, and out of the corner of my eye I see Patel taking some notes.

'Are there many of these?' I ask, indicating the photos.

'A few,' Watson says, avoiding eye contact.

'How long has this been going on?'

'We haven't been able to date any of the photos yet, but the digital files should be able to tell us more. We do think it was probably several months before you met in

264

person, however. Could she ever have had access to your emails?'

'My emails?' The shock on my face is genuine, I don't need to exaggerate this emotion. 'How the hell would she be able to get my emails?'

'We've found some emails printed out, some that appear to be from your account. We'll be looking into this further, but we might need to ask for your phone or computer in order to find out how she accessed them.'

I feel myself break out in a sweat at this suggestion. I know I need to cooperate as much as possible, but I can't have the police going through my phone.

'Let me know what you need,' is all I say. I'll work out a way to avoid it when it comes to it.

There's nothing more that they want to talk to me about, so I get up to leave. Patel escorts me out of the room, but then leaves me to find my own way out of the building. My legs are feeling weak, so when the DC goes back into the room I lean against the wall for a minute, concentrating on my breathing. The door isn't shut properly, and I quite clearly hear DS Watson's next words.

'We need to get Ian Butterworth in next, and find out if these photos mean he was having an affair.'

Chapter 32

When I get home, my first instinct is to go to the kitchen and pull out a bottle of vodka, but I resist. I need to keep a clear head. The clock shows that it's only eleven, so I have hours of the day yet to fill, and I don't want to waste them. By the time Ian comes home tonight I need to be calm, so that I can have a measured conversation with him.

Of course, it won't actually happen like that, because as soon as I confront him with anything he will either completely deny it and accuse me of being crazy, or a liar, or he'll admit to it and blame me anyway. Either will make me furious, and no amount of practising my response will prevent that. I just hope he works late tonight so the girls are in bed by the time we get into a fight, because I don't think I'll be able to prevent myself having a go at him the moment he walks in the door.

The hour I spent with the police served to show me

that I had absolutely no idea who Jenny really was, but also that there's something deeper going on that they haven't shared with me. If Ian has been having an affair, was it with her? Maybe she intended to get rid of me and take my place in this family. I shiver at the very thought of it, looking at the dining table where she sat, chatting so easily to my hellish mother-in-law. Probably imagining this was her house, her kitchen, and her family. God, how can I have been so stupid to let her into my life? And the worst thing is, I know the police are going to keep asking questions, and soon everything is going to come out, whether I like it or not. It's all going to be raked up again, and I don't know if I can take it.

However, one thing has occurred to me. If there was something going on between Ian and Jenny, and the police have proof of it, then maybe this means we really won't ever have the same relationship again. The thought itself is so enormous that I have to sit down for a few minutes. Even with everything we've been through, we've stuck together, which gave me hope that things could go back to the way they were eventually. We've both needed time to process things, to get used to the way our lives were affected and how things changed. But if he's started looking elsewhere, I don't know if I can ever see past that.

Hold on, I tell myself. You're running away with this idea now, and you don't even know what happened. From what I overheard, the police don't know for certain if he even was having an affair, and DS Watson didn't actually say who it was with. If Jenny has been taking photos of my family, maybe she caught Ian doing something he shouldn't have been. Maybe her stalking behaviour led her to find out something that the police are now looking into.

I look again at the vodka bottle. It would be nice to just get drunk and forget about the whole thing, forget about all the times I've made a monumental fuck-up, each of which has led me to this exact moment, but practicalities still stay my hand. After all, who would pick up the girls and sort them out after school if I get myself blind drunk?

I think about calling Caroline and talking to her about all of this, the stalking and the photos, but I hesitate. She'll ask questions, and there's still plenty I haven't told her. She's already curious, and I wouldn't put it past her to be reading everything she can find online about Jenny's murder. If any smart journalist links Jenny to me, and then starts looking for anything about me, maybe it will come out anyway. In which case, would it be better if I'd told Caro myself, beforehand? A sort of preemptive strike. But it could backfire if the story soon dies out without any mention of me.

These thoughts go round in my head for ages, until I'm so frustrated I want to scream. How am I supposed to know what to do for the best? Can't someone just give me a glimpse into the future and tell me which option keeps me safe?

Safety. That makes me think of some of the things I need to get my hands on, just in case the police come round here and want to look at any of our electronics or papers. I go straight to Ian's study and try the drawers of his filing cabinet. It's unlocked, which is strange. I briefly wonder where Ian has put the key; I know he keeps it hidden from the girls, and has conveniently not told me where it is. He must have forgotten to lock it last time he was in there, which is useful for me now because I don't have to hunt for the key. I slide open the drawer I want, then start shuffling through papers. I wonder if I should take anything that proves what I own in our marriage, just in case, but then most of those are only duplicates. Anyway, they'd be of no interest to either the police or any nosy journalists. No, right now I just need to locate the few documents that are the most important to me.

For fifteen minutes I go through the cabinet, searching every single drawer, and when I can't find what I'm looking for I go through it a second time. Where the hell are they? By the third time, I'm panicking. They should be here. I know he was keeping them in here; I saw him tuck them away right at the back. Would he take them and keep them somewhere else, as his own little insurance policy? I wouldn't put it past him, and this realisation is the strongest one yet to make me wonder what our marriage has become.

The time drags until I need to leave to pick up the girls from school. In those hours, I don't do anything practical whatsoever, I just sit on the sofa flicking between mindless daytime TV programmes, wondering what to do. I don't know where the files I want have gone, but I also don't know where to start looking. If Ian has taken them, they won't still be in the house. He's not that stupid.

I can't exactly march into his office and demand to search his desk, but I also can't ask him about it, because then he'll want to know why I'm looking for it. Could the girls have been playing in there and somehow got into the filing cabinet? I think it's unlikely, but I'll ask them anyway. They're pretty honest, so I think I'll be able to tell if they're lying to me.

I sit in the car outside the school, drumming my fingers on the steering wheel. I'm not going into the playground, not just yet, because I can't cope with the conversation. I feel like some of the other parents will be able to see straight through me to the chaos underneath, and they'll know something is wrong. It's vitally important that I present a normal face to the world right now, to prevent everything from crumbling beneath me, not least my own sanity.

With the car window open, I can hear the bell go for the end of the day, and I don't get out of the car until then. I smile and greet other people on my way in to collect the girls, enough to not cause any suspicion, but I don't stop to chat. Liv chatters away all the way back to the car, but I barely hear a word she says, I'm so lost in my own thoughts.

'Mummy, are you listening to me? Can I go?'

'I'm sorry, sweetheart. I was thinking about the traffic. Ask me again.'

She gives a big dramatic sigh, as only a girl of her age can. 'Sienna asked me if I can sleep over at her house tomorrow night.'

'Can I go too?' Ruby pipes up.

'Sienna is my friend, not yours,' Liv replies, and in the rear-view mirror I can see my younger daughter's lip begin to wobble.

'Ruby, we'll do something fun together if Liv is at her friend's house,' I tell her quickly to avoid a meltdown. 'Yes Liv, of course you can go. I'll give Sienna's mummy a call later, to check it's okay.' I've learnt by now that sometimes the invitations that come by word of mouth through the children are completely unknown to the parents. Still, I'm sure we can arrange something so the girls aren't disappointed. Ian doesn't like the girls having sleepovers because he doesn't like having other people in his house – what he means is he doesn't like not being able to control who's in his house, which includes both the children who are friends with his daughters, and the parents who drop them off and collect them.

When we get in, I tell the girls to get changed, then once they're back in the kitchen I get them a drink and a snack. Sitting down at the table with them, I try to relax and stay casual.

'Girls, have either of you been playing in Daddy's study?'

Liv glances at Ruby, then back at me. 'We're not allowed to go in there.'

Clever girl, I think. Stating a fact, but not actually answering the question. Future lawyer, perhaps.

'I know, but sometimes we do things we're not allowed to do, just for a bit of fun. If you have been playing in there it's okay, you won't be in trouble. I just want you to tell me the truth.'

'We didn't break anything,' Ruby says, and Liv glares at her.

'No, nothing has been broken,' I agree with her. 'And nothing was untidy, either.'

I can see Liv relax a little, knowing the secret is out but I haven't gone ballistic.

'What I really want to know is did you touch the big filing cabinet? Did you open any of the drawers and take anything out?'

Both girls shake their heads, and they're looking at me rather than each other, which is reassuring. When they're complicit in a lie, they always glance at each other first, just to check how the other is responding.

'You weren't looking for some paper to draw on, and thought there might be some in there?'

'No,' Ruby says, and I can see her bottom lip begin to quiver again.

'No, Mummy. We said we hadn't,' Liv replies, indignation creeping into her voice.

'Something has gone missing, you see,' I press on. 'Something very important, that was inside that filing cabinet.' I'm trying to keep my voice calm, but I know the volume is rising.

'Mummy, we said we didn't,' Liv says again, and I can see tears in her eyes too now. 'We're sorry we played in Daddy's study, but it was hide and seek and there's a big gap under Daddy's desk that's good for hiding. That's all we did.'

'Are you sure? You know I don't like it when you lie to me.' I say it before I even think about it. Liv jumps up from the table, her cheeks flaming red and the tears starting to spill down her cheeks. Ruby is crying now too, and I reach for both of them instinctively. Ruby is stiff but responds to my cuddle, whereas Liv pulls away.

'I'm sorry, girls, you're right. I know you're telling the truth. I'm just feeling stressed and worried because something has gone missing.'

'It's Daddy's study, why don't you ask him?' Liv snaps at me, then gets up and storms out of the kitchen. I hear the thumps above us as her small feet run up to her bedroom, but I don't go after her. We both need some time to calm down. At least this has clarified things: the only person who could have moved those papers is my husband, so now I need to find out what he's done with them. But how do I do that without tipping him off?

Chapter 33

After another cuddle with Ruby, I give her another biscuit before heading upstairs to try and sort things out with her sister. I don't want the girls upset when Ian comes home because that always puts him in a bad mood. In the future, I hope that the pressure of their emotions having to regulate those of their father isn't something they both need to address in therapy, but I'm not optimistic.

'Liv?' I knock on her bedroom door and wait. Part of me really wants to just walk in, but I know she needs her privacy, and it's only going to get more important that I respect that as she gets older. 'Liv, can I come in?'

There's no response, so I wait for a moment, then sit down on the floor outside the door.

'I'm sorry I didn't believe you. Adults get things wrong all the time, you know. I try my best, but I still make mistakes.' I resist the urge to point out that she and Ruby broke the rules about going in Ian's study because I know that won't help right now.

'We didn't touch anything,' came Liv's voice, muffled by the door.

'I know, and thank you for telling me the truth.'

The door opens slightly, and I see Liv standing in the small gap she has created. 'I don't like it when you don't believe us. You tell us to tell the truth, so we do, then you get mad.'

I nod. 'I've been very worried about this paper that's gone missing, so I had to make sure you hadn't taken it by mistake. But now I know it wasn't you, I'll ask Daddy if he's seen it when he gets home.'

A look of concern crosses her face. 'Are you going to tell Daddy we were playing in there?'

My heart aches when I see her expression, and hear the fear in her voice. When did she become so worried about upsetting him? I thought that we'd managed to hide our difficulties from the children, that they were too young for it to affect them, but I was obviously wrong. This is something I have to take responsibility for just as much as Ian.

For the first time, I wonder if I should just accept the fact that Ian will never feel the same way about me again, will never be the man he used to be. I'm not the same person I was, either, and perhaps it's too much for me to expect that things will eventually be like they were. I'm in full flight mode now, and I wonder if I'll ever be happy unless I find a way to completely start over. But separating from him would be so hard because I know he wouldn't want to be parted from the girls, and I worry that he'd find a way to stop me leaving.

Despite that, I think it's doable, if I plan. It needs to happen quickly, though, because of this business with Jenny. Even the thought of it takes my breath away – getting out of this house, finding a little flat or maybe a cottage somewhere rural, living there with the girls. They don't need an expensive private school, and I don't need the monstrosity of a car Ian insists I drive. I can get a job, any job really, as well as using my savings to support us. At least I have plenty of money in my own account, and that's something he won't be able to get his hands on. He's never threatened that he'd try because he knows he wouldn't get anywhere; he's always focused on the one thing he knew would make me stay: the kids. But now I'm willing to take the risk.

I need to lay some groundwork, though, and that begins with telling people that I'm unhappy. I don't know exactly what the police were referring to, but if they suspect he's having an affair that's a good place to start. If I tell Caroline about it, I know she'll be on my side and she'll listen to me.

Liv is still standing in her doorway, looking down at me with frightened eyes.

'No, sweetheart. I won't tell Daddy.'

She opens the door fully and throws herself into my arms, and I hold her for as long as she'll allow me. Perhaps I can arrange a meeting with her teacher to discuss how she's getting on, check up on her emotional wellbeing at school. Is it possible that she's seen something, noticed something that I haven't? I can't ask her, though, because I don't want to add to her anxiety. She's old enough to know about divorce and I don't want to put any thoughts into her head before it becomes a reality. Whatever I do, I have to try and do it as honestly as I can, to avoid too many repercussions.

By the time Ian gets home, the girls have had their tea and the three of us are curled up on the sofa in their playroom watching a Disney film. It's nearly time for them to go to bed, but I haven't made a move yet because I've been imagining our future life, just the three of us. Rules and routines will be different – still important for structure, but definitely more relaxed, and more focused on what the girls need rather than what we as parents want. Sometimes I try something different, responding to them, and Ian gets so annoyed I give up and go back to what we were always doing. To their credit, the girls rarely complain, though I sometimes worry that we're making them too compliant, which won't serve them well in future. Well, it won't be forever, and while I'm not stupid enough to think they won't miss him, or that it'll be easy, I know what I have in mind will be the best for all of us.

Ian sticks his head into the room and I smile at him, but he just looks at his watch.

'Girls, bedtime,' he says, walking over and turning off the TV without giving them a chance to even watch the end of the scene. I bite my tongue and don't respond to their disappointment, shooing them upstairs instead.

'I'll be up for stories soon,' he tells them, then turns to me. 'Bit late, isn't it?'

'I lost track of time.' Might as well let him win this one.

He rolls his eyes at me but doesn't say anything, so I start tidying up some of the things the girls have left out. I usually help them to do it, but I don't mind doing it myself sometimes. It helps me to think.

Once the girls are in their pyjamas, I say goodnight then leave Ian to do the storytelling, while I sort out a meal for the two of us. I don't want a row on an empty stomach. I prepare a salad while the potatoes and fish are cooking, so it's nearly ready by the time he comes back downstairs.

'Oh, didn't I say? I'm off out again, drinks for Simon's leaving do.'

'No, you didn't say. Have you eaten?'

'I'll eat there.'

'So what the hell am I supposed to do with this?' I ask, indicating the food I've just cooked that will now go to waste.

'Just throw it in the fucking bin, Bella. It's not like we can't afford the odd wasted meal.'

That's not the point, which he well knows, but I don't respond, instead changing the subject to what I really want to talk to him about. I'm not letting him go out without having my say.

'Were you having an affair with Jenny?'

He stops in the doorway then turns to look at me. 'What the hell?'

I repeat the question, looking him dead in the eye, determined to stand my ground as I see a whole range of emotions flash across his face.

'Where the fuck did that come from?'

'The police asked me to go and see them today,' I begin, and he gives a harsh laugh.

'Oh great, so we're being dragged into something else again, are we? What have you been doing, Bella? If you end up in jail I'm not bringing the girls to visit you, you can rot there for all I care.'

'Let me finish,' I snap, and I'm briefly rewarded by the look of surprise on his face that I've stood up to him for once. 'She was stalking me, Ian. Stalking us, our family. She had photos of the girls in the playground at school.'

The concerned frown on his face shows me he didn't know about this, at least. He's always been a terrible liar, brought on by the size of his ego. He assumes people will automatically believe him because of who he is, so has never needed to learn how to hide his true feelings.

'What has that got to do with me? You're the one who's sitting on your arse all day, and you're the one who was friends with her. Can't I even trust you to keep our children safe?'

I recognise this as a hallmark of his behaviour in the last two years, turning it all back on me, but I'm not letting him distract me.

'You know what else she had? Photos of me, and you. The police are going to ask to talk to you, because they think you're having an affair. So I'm going to ask you again, were you having an affair with her? Or is it with someone else, and Jenny found out about it?'

His face turns an impressive shade of red as he struggles

279

to find the words to respond to me, and I wonder if I've finally caught him out. Will he confess?

'No I fucking wasn't,' he eventually hisses at me, his eyes flashing dangerously. 'Whatever you think might have been going on, you're wrong.'

'Oh, of course, I must be mistaken. It's always me that's wrong, isn't it, Ian? You can never take responsibility for anything, can you?'

I know I'm goading him now, but this is exactly what I want. I want him to get angry, because then he might let his guard drop and say exactly what he thinks. What I have to remember is that a lot of Ian's anger is actually directed towards himself, to his own actions that changed our lives, but he'll never admit that. He bottles it up, and one day I think it'll explode. It hits me then – the police wanting to talk to him. Could Ian be a suspect in Jenny's murder?

'Yes it's you who's wrong,' he growls. 'I'm not having an affair, and I never have. Whatever's happened, I still take our marriage seriously, you know.' His eyes are wide, and I can't tell if he's frantic because he's so angry or because he's scared. 'I don't know what the police think is going on, or why they've got that impression, but they won't have anything to prove it because it didn't happen.'

'If I find out you're lying, and you really were having an affair with another woman, I will make you pay,' I tell him, keeping my voice quiet but enunciating clearly so he knows I mean it. Every single word. 'After what she's put us through. Did you know her real name all along, who she really was?'

280

He laughs at this, but it sounds strangled. 'Of course I bloody didn't. Don't you think I would have told you if I knew one of your friends was a psycho?'

'Not if you were sleeping with her.'

He glares at me, breathing heavily, his fists clenching and unclenching at his sides. I hold my breath, wondering what he's going to say next, but he just sags and shakes his head.

'Believe whatever the fuck you want. This conversation is over, Bella.'

He turns round and walks out of the kitchen, then a moment later I hear the front door slam and the screech of wheels as he pulls out of the drive far too quickly. As I slowly scrape the food I've cooked into the bin, my hands are shaking, so I put everything down, pour myself a drink and sit at the table, waiting for the adrenaline to subside. Then I call Caroline.

Chapter 34

Ian didn't come home last night. I can't sleep, waking up at every creak and rustle in the house. When I eventually give in and get out of bed, I check the spare room in case he crept back in and slept there. Nothing, and his car isn't on the drive, though given he was probably drinking heavily it wouldn't be unusual for him to get a taxi home then retrieve his car the following day.

I wake the girls up and get them ready for school, enjoying the fact that we don't have to skirt around him. Oddly enough, neither of them ask where he is. He spends so much time at work, or at least claiming he's at work, that it's probably the first thing they assume when he's not here.

Periodically, I check my phone, but I haven't had any messages or calls. I would have thought he'd do me the courtesy of letting me know he wouldn't be home, despite having had the worst row of our lives before he left.

Maybe something has happened to him . . . No, I can't start thinking like that. An image appears in my mind unbidden, of his car sitting in a ditch at the side of the road somewhere, his body having been thrown through the windscreen because he attempted to drive home after far too much to drink.

Caroline did her best to comfort me last night, and I opened up to her about how I've been feeling, about how our relationship has changed over the last few years. I even implied that he and Jenny might have been having an affair, and I touched on the fact that if we separated he might try to make life difficult for me. Of course, I still didn't tell her the whole story, because the whole point of asking her to come round last night was to get her on my side, so I have someone who can support me and help me get through the next few weeks or months.

I feel guilty for still keeping things from her, especially when she's so supportive. I will tell her the truth, in time, but when we have the opportunity for me to present my side of the story, so she can understand it from my point of view. Until then, I just have to hope that it doesn't come out somehow.

Once the girls are at school, I spend the rest of the morning making plans. At first I'm not sure how to keep a record of everything I want to do. I'm pretty sure Ian has access to at least some of the apps on my phone, including my email, so I can't risk making notes on there. If I do it on a piece of paper, what if I forget and leave it lying around somewhere? It's a quandary, and to begin with I refuse to do either, simply going through a few things in my head and trying my best to remember what I might need.

The first thing I do is go back to the filing cabinet and find the documents I'll need to take with me: birth certificates, mine and the girls', passports, and a couple of other pieces of identification and some qualifications. There isn't much that's essential, but I make sure the things I need are filed away together, so I can just grab them when I need them. I'm not going to start putting things together yet, not until I have a definite plan in mind.

I didn't tell Caroline that Ian might be a suspect in Jenny's murder, but I talked around it in a way that meant she got there herself. She was shocked, but the fact that I didn't have to feed it to her meant that she believed it, and guaranteed she'd do pretty much anything I asked. It also meant I didn't have to explain why I finally decided I should leave him and take the girls with me.

Caro promised to help me get some information on my rights regarding the children. I don't want to find myself in a situation where I'm being accused of kidnapping or anything like that. That's why we agreed I had to stay in the UK, rather than try to go abroad. I mentioned the idea of getting fake passports but Caro shot it down. Nothing illegal, she insisted, because then I would be putting myself at risk of losing the girls.

After I've finished with the documents, I go upstairs to the girls' bedrooms and have a look around. Clothes should be fairly easy, because I can pack some basics for them then we can buy new. It's their toys and keepsakes that are going to be the hardest part. They both have a lot, they've wanted for nothing, to the point of being spoiled, and I know it's going to be impossible to take everything. Ruby has clear favourites still, both in the teddies she sleeps with and the toys she plays with most often, but Liv is more difficult. I'm going to have to spend some time playing with her and watching her carefully over the next few days, then I have a better idea of what she'd miss most.

I have to assume there'll be no opportunity for us to come back for anything. In an ideal world, we'd be able to leave, then gradually bring everything with us to our new home, wherever that might be, but I can't see Ian letting that happen. And I can't ask the girls to help me pack their things because that would take far too long and would be too emotional. I will have to pack for them, pick them up from school one day, then get on the road. We would have at least three hours before Ian got home, even on a good day, and if I leave a note saying I'm taking the girls out for tea and a playdate, he might not even miss us for another hour or two after that. Long enough for us to get pretty far away, anyway.

At the moment I have no destination in mind, but of course I'll need to have something booked, even if it's just a holiday cottage. I told Caro my concern about Ian accessing my emails, and she immediately volunteered to book something for us, even paying for it on her own credit card so he couldn't track us that way, either. I just need to make up my mind, tell her to book something, and go. I don't even care where it is, so I told her how far away I want to be, and asked her to look for something for me. That way, there aren't even any searches that can be traced back to me.

Going into our bedroom, I sit down at my dressing table and look at the selection of expensive toiletries, knowing I don't really need to take any. I've become used to a certain lifestyle, but I know I can go back to using the discount supermarket soap and shampoo, with a cheap all-purpose moisturiser, rather than the hideously expensive stuff I can usually only find at airports. Opening my jewellery box, I sift through the various chains and pendants, diamond earrings and ornate bracelets. Most of it has no sentimental value, though its monetary value could be of some use, so I'll probably take a few things. Other than the necklace and brooch I inherited from my grandmother, almost everything in here was chosen and purchased by my husband.

As I go through the box, I wonder if I should call his office to check he's okay, but immediately veto the idea. I never call him at work, so I don't want to draw attention, because that will only make him angry. Despite our fight last night, I need to live with him as best I can until I leave. I don't know when that will be – a few days? A couple of weeks? It depends on so many things, but mostly my courage. I need to be brave enough to fight the fear that something will go wrong and someone will take my children.

There's a knock on the door. I'm not expecting anyone, so I check my appearance in the mirror before going downstairs. I look a bit tired, but make-up has covered up most of my sleepless night.

Opening the front door, my heart sinks. DS Watson and DC Patel are standing there, their car parked on the road at the end of our drive. There's no sign of the male detective who came here the first time, so presumably he's found something more important to do than bother me.

'Hi,' I say, trying not to sound too friendly. 'Can I help you?'

'Do you mind if we come in, Isabella?'

I need to cooperate, I remind myself, so I open the door to invite them in, then lead them through to the living room. They both turn down my offer of tea or coffee, so I sit opposite them and wait.

'Is your husband at home?' Watson asks. 'We'd really like to have the opportunity to speak to him again.'

About his affair with Jenny, I assume, though I don't say this.

'No, he's at work,' I say, not hesitating.

'We went to his office, but they told us he called in sick today.'

'Oh.' He'll be furious, that's my first thought. He's not there to spin some sort of tale, so the office rumour mill will be working overtime wondering why the police are asking for him, especially on the first day he's called in sick in his entire time working there.

I clear my throat, thinking honesty is the best policy.

'We, er, had a disagreement yesterday. He went out with some work colleagues in the evening, and didn't come home.'

The detectives look at each other. 'So he's missing?' Watson clarifies.

'I didn't think of him as missing, I assumed he was cooling off. Ian has never missed a day of work, so I naturally thought he would stay with a colleague, if they were drinking heavily last night, then go straight to work this morning.'

'He hasn't been in touch to tell you where he is?'

'No.'

'Did you call him to ask?'

I hesitate. 'No. I . . . didn't want to make him angry.'

Watson looks up at me from her notebook and I feel like she's looking right through me. Just with that sentence alone, I think she's beginning to understand what I'm trying to say.

'Okay. Well, we'll see if we can track him down. If you could give us his mobile number and car registration, that would be really useful.'

I do, and Patel writes them down.

'Why did you want to see him?' I ask.

'We have some questions for him regarding some of the photos we found at Jenny's home.' Watson doesn't elaborate, but I want to know what these photos show, what sort of sordid details they contain.

'Please, just tell me the truth,' I implore them, tired of the constant prevaricating.

Watson pauses, clearly choosing her words carefully. 'I'm sorry to have to ask you this, Isabella, but to your knowledge has your husband ever been unfaithful to you?'

I let out a long breath and sit back in the chair, feeling all of the fight go out of me. So I was right, he was sleeping with Jenny.

'That's what our disagreement was about last night,' I tell them wearily. 'I heard what you said about him having an affair, so I asked him about it. He denied it, of course, but he was so angry, it felt like he was furious that he'd been caught out, rather than because he'd been unjustly accused. Is this why she was stalking me, because she was having an affair with my husband? Because she wanted to make friends with me then somehow use that to get between us?'

Pulling out a folder, Watson selects another photograph and holds it out toward me. 'I think we're possibly talking at cross-purposes here. These aren't photos of your husband and Jenny together, they're ones we found on Jenny's camera, and we assume she took them. Do you know who this woman is?'

I stare down at the photo, uncomprehending. The idea of Ian having an affair with Jenny is bad enough, but I don't understand what I'm seeing here. This photo isn't of Ian and Jenny. It's one of Ian and Caroline.

Chapter 35

'I don't understand,' I say quietly, looking at the photo. They're sitting together, deep in conversation. Whatever it is, it looks serious, and I expect they're not aware of the fact that they're being photographed.

'So you know her?' Watson asks for clarification.

'Caroline. Caroline Devlin. She's a friend of mine.'

I wish I hadn't said that. I can imagine what they're both thinking, what they'll say to each other in the car on their way back to the station. Poor woman. Her husband is sleeping with one of her friends. What they don't know is that this woman is the only friend I have now. I've never managed to get on with any of the other school mums, the PTA enthusiasts whose main concerns are the contents of school lunches and whose child raised the most money for the sponsored walk. And now it seems the one person I really trusted has betrayed me.

Caroline, though? I can't believe it. I look at her body

language in the photo, and that of my husband, and I don't see anything intimate in it. Of course, I still want to know why they were meeting and what they were talking about, but this photo doesn't necessarily show they're having an affair, does it? Am I in denial?

'Is this the only photo?' I ask.

'There are several from the same day, all taken around the same time. But we haven't found any other photos of them together on a separate occasion, if that's what you mean.'

'Good. So they might not be having an affair. They might have bumped into each other in the street and stopped for a conversation.'

Watson nods slowly. 'That's possible, yes. Are your husband and Caroline close?'

I let out a sharp laugh. 'Definitely not. She tends to avoid coming round when he's here, but I think that's because he never makes anyone feel welcome in our home. He never has anything nice to say about her, and he's a terrible liar, so I just don't think it can be possible.'

'Jenny kept a notebook, and in it she wrote her suspicions that Ian and Caroline were having an affair. It sounds like she followed them at least once, and she was sure there was something going on. Of course, she may have been imagining it. As you say, the photos don't show anything other than two people talking, but we have to consider every angle in a case such as this.'

The expression on DC Patel's face is pitying, but I shake my head. 'I'm not saying he's not capable of having an affair. I had actually thought he might have been sleeping with Jenny,' I admit, 'and that's where her stalking behaviour stemmed from. But I don't think that's what this is,' I say, indicating the photo of him with Caroline. 'I trust her more than that, anyway.' I put as much conviction into my voice as I can, but I'm not sure it's convincing.

'Okay,' Watson says. 'Well, the thing that interests us more is the fact that Jenny is the one who took the photo, which suggests she was following Ian as well as you.'

I run a hand across my face. 'This is all so confusing. I don't know what the hell is going on.'

'I understand,' Watson replies, and I have to suppress the urge to laugh. She really doesn't.

'We'd really like to speak to your husband,' she continues. 'If he arrives home, we'd like you to call us. Hopefully we can locate him soon.'

In among this, I'd forgotten that nobody seems to have any idea where my husband is. If he called in sick to work, clearly he must have been alive and well this morning, but that doesn't help me to find him. Though right now, I think I'd be happiest if he never came home at all, because then I'd never have to face up to the truth of what he's been up to.

After promising once again to get in touch if I hear from Ian or if anything else important occurs to me, I see the two detectives out. Once they've left, I go to the kitchen and sink down into a dining chair, resting my head on the table. What now? What the hell am I supposed to do from here?

Caroline is the person I trust, the person I've shared

my plans with. Could she have betrayed me? The idea of it is so unbelievable, I'm sure there must be a rational explanation. Picking up my phone, I consider calling her and asking her about it, but then I hesitate. Maybe I should do a bit more digging first, just in case. I know the police expect me to confront Ian about it, but I don't see the point. He won't tell me the truth, and even if he did I wouldn't believe him. I'm so used to him lying to me.

The idea that she might have been holding back from me stings for a moment, especially after I opened up to her about Ian and our relationship issues. But maybe there really is a simple explanation about why there's a photo of her talking to him, when she's never told me about meeting him by herself. She's not into social media, so I can't exactly start snooping to see if she's been to anywhere she might have been meeting up with Ian. Anyway, she'd be smart enough to keep that hidden.

My phone rings, making me jump, and as if she's read my mind, it's Caroline. I hesitate before answering it, but I need to see what she wants. Maybe the police have been in touch with her, too.

'Hi.' I try to make my voice sound as normal as possible, but by overthinking it I'm probably making it sound strange.

'Hi, how are you doing?'

I sigh. 'Ian didn't come home last night. He's called in sick today. I have no idea where he is.'

'Bastard probably drank too much and now he's licking his wounds,' she says, and I hear almost a grim satisfaction in her voice. No, I'm still convinced that Caroline dislikes my husband. 'He'll turn up eventually, grovelling, with a bunch of flowers he got at a garage.'

'No, not Ian. He'll just walk in and carry on as if nothing happened.'

'Well, fuck him,' she says decisively. 'He doesn't deserve you, and you've got a plan now. I just wanted to let you know I've already started looking. I think it should be pretty easy to find something that will work, at least for two or three weeks. Hopefully that should be long enough to find somewhere more long term.'

'Thank you,' I tell her, and I mean it. She's done exactly what we talked about, and I feel bad for not trusting her. Of course, there's still the issue of the photo, but we can discuss that next time I see her. She'll have a rational explanation, I know.

'You just need to let me know when you're ready.'

'I will.'

She hesitates. 'Don't leave it too long, Bella. If you give yourself too long to think about it, you'll end up talking yourself out of it. You'll find reasons and excuses to push it back, and it'll always be "next week" or "soon". You need to do it, and do it fast, before the doubt sets in.'

I can't help the strangled laugh that escapes my lips. 'I'm already there, Caro. The doubts were there the moment I told you about it all last night. I need someone to show me the future, to tell me I'm doing the right thing.' I think about the police turning up at my door yet again this morning, and wonder if she's right, if the best thing would be to just do it now. Ian isn't even here, and God only knows when he'll bother to come back. I could go upstairs and pack some bags now, fill up the car and be ready to collect the girls at the end of the school day, then just drive. Caro would find us somewhere to go, even if it's just a cheap hotel for a couple of nights before we can get a holiday cottage booked.

Suddenly, I remember my search of the filing cabinet, and the crucial piece of documentation that's missing. I can't go until I've found it. I need it for so many reasons. Could it have been destroyed? Ian wouldn't have done that, and I know I haven't. So it must be somewhere. If it's not in the house, he must have taken it to his office. He's not there today – would his colleagues let me in to look for it? No, I'm sure they wouldn't, because he'll have far too much confidential client information kept there. And I can't ask one of them to look without telling them exactly what it is, because I expect they'd call him to tell him what I was up to. If I did it, I'd have to be ready to run straight away, but even the fact that I'm looking for it would tip him off that something was amiss. When I'm ready to go, I'll only have one opportunity, so I can't screw it up.

Could I go without it? I feel like it will protect me, but really I know Ian can still do plenty without it. He doesn't need that piece of paper. My sinuses hurt, and I press my hand to my head to try and massage some of the pain away.

'I wish it was easy,' I mutter, and Caro makes sympathetic noises.

'I know, but I will help you, I promise. You know Ian won't get anything out of me, and I'll see what sort of protection we can get you. Even if the police need to speak to you, we can stop them from letting him know where you are. If he had nothing to do with Jenny's death then you don't need to worry, but until the police have finished their investigation you're better off making sure you and the girls are safe.'

'Hmmm,' I say noncommittally, knowing he wouldn't stop until he'd tracked us down.

'Look, why don't we have lunch tomorrow,' she suggests, her tone clear that she's trying to cheer me up. 'We can talk strategy, and you can tell me everything you're scared of, so we can close up any loopholes.'

I agree, reluctantly, and we set a place and time. Once she's hung up, I continue to sit at the table for a few minutes. The house seems eerily quiet. My conversation with Caroline has convinced me that whatever her reasons for talking to Ian on the occasion that Jenny took that photo, they must have been innocent . . . right?

Chapter 36

The following day, I'm jittery when Caroline and I meet for lunch. I get to the restaurant before her, and resist the urge to start on a bottle of wine. I want to keep a clear head for this.

I can't stop thinking about that photo of her and Ian. Even if there's nothing going on between them, they still met up or bumped into each other at some point and neither of them mentioned it. I want to believe there's a logical, rational explanation. But how do I even address it, especially when we're here to talk about how she's trying to help me? Even if she's hiding something from me, the best part of me still believes she's genuinely on my side.

Ian eventually turned up after the girls were in bed last night. I put them to bed and made a meal, leaving a portion covered in the kitchen in case he did come home. I spent a while thinking about what would seem most normal – if I made some food and left it for him, or if I didn't. Until this police investigation is over, and until I know the girls and I are safe, I need to watch my step around him. Just in case.

I was in the living room when I heard him come in, but he went straight upstairs and into the shower. I didn't move, but carried on watching the television, listening in order to track his progress through the house. He came downstairs and went into the kitchen, and I could tell by the sounds of crockery and cupboards that he looked at the food I'd left for him, threw it in the bin, then made something else. Not before he'd poured himself a drink. He ate in the kitchen, probably standing up because I didn't hear the sound of a chair being scraped across the tiled floor, and only then did he come through to the lounge.

He looked at me, then walked past and went into his study, drink in hand, closing the door behind him. I sagged into the sofa cushions. So it was going to be like this. We'd have a couple of days of silence before things went back to the way they'd always been. No discussion, no apology, no explanation of where he was the previous night. I wanted to ask him if the police had tracked him down, but I didn't want to draw his attention to the fact that they were looking for him. If he felt threatened, what would he do? I feel like I'm seeing my husband in a completely new light now, and it maddens me that I don't know what's true and what's just in my head.

I did, however, dig out the card that DS Watson gave me. Going into the kitchen, I called and left a voicemail to tell her that Ian had come home, in case they hadn't managed to get hold of him. He was still in his study, so I just had to hope he hadn't heard me on the phone.

When Caroline slides into the booth opposite me now, I can see that she's desperate to tell me something. She doesn't stop to order a drink, but leans forward and fixes me with a look.

'There's something you need to know.'

I freeze. Is she going to tell me why she was meeting Ian?

'There are rumours going around online about Jenny's death, about how she was killed.'

'What?' This isn't what I was expecting, and she's thrown me. 'What do you mean?'

'The police are linking it with another murder.'

The churning in my stomach increases and I start to feel sick. Another murder?

'Which murder? They haven't said anything to me when they've interviewed me.'

'I don't know if they're making it public yet.'

'So how do you know about it?' I ask, suspicion starting to grow.

She shrugs. 'I told you, it's just a rumour. I'm in a couple of local groups and someone said something about it.'

'What are they saying?'

'Well, a homeless woman was killed a few weeks ago, stabbed, the same as Jenny.'

'They think the death of a homeless woman is linked to Jenny's? That sounds a bit far-fetched to me.'

Caro shrugs again, but I can see by the disappointed

look on her face that she was hoping for a different reaction from me.

'Sorry, you might be right,' I say, trying to appease her. 'And if they are linked, surely that means it's nothing to do with me and my family. So the police can leave me alone.'

'Have they been bothering you?' she asks, and I realise I've piqued her curiosity. This could be an opportunity for me to say something.

'They found some photos that Jenny had.'

'Photos? What of?'

'Plenty of me, and some of the girls.'

Her jaw drops. 'Oh God, Bella. Seriously? That's creepy. I'm sorry.'

I nod. 'There's more. There were also some photos of Ian.'

'So that's why you thought they might have been having an affair,' she says, realisation dawning.

There's a pause as I consider my next words. 'And there were a few of you with Ian.'

I watch the expression on her face change from shocked to embarrassed, then she averts her eyes.

'Oh Bella. I'm really sorry.'

I wait, not asking her to explain. I know if I stay silent, she'll continue, and a moment later I'm rewarded.

'I should have told you, but I wanted to give Ian the chance, first.'

'Tell me what?' I ask, aware my voice is icy.

'I met Ian one day because there was something I wanted to talk to him about.'

She hesitates, but when I glare at her she frowns.

'Oh God, hang on. You don't think I'm the one having the affair with him, do you? I wouldn't do that to you!'

I fold my arms to cover my discomfort. She saw right through me, and now I feel bad for suspecting my friend of going behind my back like that. Still, she hasn't answered the question yet.

'What were you asking him about?'

She waves a hand. 'It was something for a client. Basically, they hired Ian's firm and someone messed up, someone in IT. They suspect it was Ian. I met up with him informally in order to give him the opportunity to rectify the mistakes before it was escalated.'

'What?' This is so far from what I expected to hear, I can't quite get my head around it. 'Why the hell would you do something like that without telling me about it?'

Caroline leans back and runs a hand through her hair. 'Because I didn't want to upset you. I wanted him to have the chance to tell you himself that he'd screwed up at work. He was probably embarrassed about it.'

I take a deep breath before replying, trying to calm myself so I don't fly off the handle at Caroline. 'So this photo of you and Ian, that was you asking him about this work for your client?'

Caro nods.

'What did he say?'

She sighs and rolls her eyes. 'Exactly what you'd expect from him. That I didn't know what I was talking about, that I was stupid and shouldn't be wasting my time trying to interfere in other people's lives. He said some unpleasant things.'

I bite my lip and think. It's not something I would have predicted, but it is also plausible.

'Look, this is why I'm so keen to help you,' she continues, leaning forward, and I can see she's anxious. 'I've seen exactly what he's like. If you're concerned that he might be involved in Jenny's death then I believe you, and I want you and the girls to be safe.'

She leans back again, but she's fiddling with her napkin, and I can tell there's something else she wants to say. A moment later, Caro looks up at me, fear crinkling the edges of her eyes. 'Bella, do you think Ian could be dangerous?'

I think for a moment, then I shrug. 'I honestly don't know. I don't *think* he'd hurt me. He certainly would never hurt the girls. He knows that if he laid a hand on me, I'd be straight out of the door. He's got a temper, but he's learnt how to keep it in check. It comes out as words now, snide comments. But not physical violence.'

She chews her lip for a moment. 'That's not exactly what I meant.'

Realisation dawns and I swallow hard. Is she suggesting what I think she's suggesting?

'Do you think Ian might have something to do with Jenny's death?' she asks quietly. She maintains eye contact when she asks the question, and it's all I can do not to look away.

'Caro, are you really asking me that question?' I can't process it. Why does she think he could be involved? Unless there's something else she's not telling me?

She nods, but doesn't say anything else, still watching me.

302

I shake my head firmly. 'No. With any luck we're wrong and this has nothing to do with my family. You just said that the police are linking her death to that of this homeless woman, which surely suggests it's just a random attack? Some psycho who gets their kicks from hurting women. Jenny was in the wrong place at the wrong time.'

I look down at my food and start attacking it with gusto, hoping to avoid any more questions, but a few moments later, Caroline is still looking at me.

'What?'

'What if Ian killed both of them?' Her voice is so quiet I can barely hear her, but the words hit home. She's asking me to believe that my husband could have killed two people in cold blood, and I have no idea how to respond. The worst thing is that part of me leaps on the idea: if Ian goes to prison for murder, I don't have to worry about the past any more. By the time he would be released, the girls would be grown up and long gone; I could move and have a whole new life far away from him. Even if he found me, after something like that I'm sure I could get a restraining order.

No, I can't think like that. Not right now, not yet. My pulse is racing, and Caroline is still waiting for an answer to her question.

'Why? Why would he have done that?'

My friend picks up her glass of wine and drains it, then looks back at me. 'There are some things I've done that I'm not proud of,' she begins, and I feel anxiety starting to flutter as I wonder what she's going to say next. 'I kept some things from you that I shouldn't have

303

done. But please, Bella, please understand that I did it to try and protect you.'

'What are you talking about? What have you done?'

'I knew who Jenny was, before you told me. Before she was killed.'

I stare at her. How could she have known? And if she knows who Jenny was, what else does she know? This is too much. I can't take it any more, the secrets, the lies, the arguments. I've had enough, so I do the only thing I can think of: I stand up, grab my bag and walk out of the restaurant.

I'm only a few metres up the road when Caroline catches up with me. She grabs my arm but I shake her off.

'Bella, please. You have to listen to me. I know about Jenny, and I know about you. About who you were before, who Ian was.'

'Leave me alone,' I growl at her through clenched teeth. 'You were the one person I thought I could still trust, you know that? Through all this, I thought you were my friend, that I could rely on you. And now it turns out you've been lying to me too.'

'I know, and I'm sorry. Please, let me tell you everything.'

IZZY

Chapter 37

'Bella, please. Come back to the restaurant.'

I have to convince her to listen to me, or the nine months of our friendship has been in vain.

'Caro,' she begins, shaking her head. 'You need to leave it.'

Every time she calls me by that name I feel like I become more her, and less Izzy. I even found myself signing off a work email as Caroline the other day, as if it's Isabella that's the made-up name. I feel like this is the person I was supposed to be, like my old identity was holding me back from reaching my true potential. Now I need to use this to keep Bella on my side.

'I can't.'

There's a heavy pause and I'm convinced she's going to turn round again and keep walking away, but she sighs and nods. We return to our booth, getting a few strange looks from some of the staff, probably because we haven't paid yet and it looked like we were doing a runner.

When I asked her to come here today, I didn't know what I was going to say, but I'm already regretting my lie about why I was talking to Ian in that photo. It was from the day I waited outside his office to speak to him, when I thought he'd been having an affair with Jenny. I remember at the time thinking I saw Jenny over the road, watching us, but she vanished so quickly I thought I'd imagined it. Obviously not, and she'd been taking photos of me and Ian.

I order us another bottle of wine, which probably isn't wise, but then nothing I've done in the last few weeks – hell, the last year – could be called a smart move. Things came to a head when Jenny died, though.

Remembering that night, I shudder. I set off to meet her to try and find out more about her brother, Ryan Beckley, going early in order to check out her house first. But it got to eleven, and the house was still dark. Nobody had come or gone in the two hours after I arrived, and when I rang the bell there was no answer. I considered sending her a text to ask where she was, but I decided against it.

By midnight, I knew I needed to do something. I couldn't hang around outside her house all night, waiting for her to appear. In the end I gave up, and set off home. When I neared the end of the street, I passed an alley. It ran behind the houses that sat at right angles to the row where Jenny lived, and something made me glance down there. There was a large shape on the ground, about three metres into the alley, so I pulled out my phone to use the torch and get a better look. I don't know what I was expecting, but what I found was Jenny's lifeless body, lying in pooling blood.

It was pretty clear she was dead, and probably had been for a while, but I checked her pulse anyway. The blood was coming from a wound in her stomach, but I turned my face away and didn't look too closely. What had happened? Had Jenny genuinely intended to meet me and then been attacked on her way home? I didn't know, but I wasn't hanging around in case whoever killed her was still there waiting for me.

I don't know how I avoided having a panic attack, and I barely remember getting home. It was a long walk in the early hours of the morning, probably a good thing that very few people were around because it was only when I got back to my flat that I discovered I had Jenny's blood on me. I scrubbed myself like Lady Macbeth, taking off a layer of skin before I was happy that I'd left no trace.

That was when I knew I needed to do more to protect Bella. There's no way this was a coincidence, Jenny being murdered just as I was about to meet her to ask about her brother. Because she wasn't really Jenny Holdsworth; as the police told Bella a couple of days later. Her name was Jenny Beckley, sister of Ryan Beckley. I didn't get the information I wanted, but I've pieced most of it together myself along the way. The question now is how much do I tell Bella?

We sit in silence until the bottle of wine arrives, and the bill comes with it. I'm not surprised; they want to make sure we don't run off again. I quickly pay for both of our meals and our drinks, then sit back and look at my friend across the table. How I wish it hadn't come to this. But I do genuinely think she's in danger.

Reaching into my bag, I pull out the photos of Jenny and Ian. I need to at least tell Bella the truth about why I was speaking to Ian that day.

'I'm sorry. I lied to you just now, when you asked me about why I was speaking to Ian in those photos.'

Bella looks down at the photos, spreading them out on the table in front of her. I've included the one I took through the window, even though it's very unclear. If you didn't know the two people, they could have been just about anyone.

'What is this? So he *was* having an affair with Jenny?' Bella rubs a hand across her face. 'I'm so confused. First I thought he'd been sleeping with her, then I thought you had something to do with it, and now you tell me I was right the first time?'

I choose my words carefully before I continue to explain. 'I followed Jenny one day. She went into a restaurant, and a few minutes later, Ian followed her. I didn't get a decent photo,' I say, indicating the blurry one, 'but they were sitting together at a table. When they left, they deliberately left a minute or so apart. These are what I showed him when we were together in the photos. I waited for him outside his office and confronted him, but he denied everything.'

I see something close to a wry smile cross Bella's face, because I assume she knows he's a good liar. She definitely believes that part of my story.

310

'They could have just been talking, though,' Bella says, but it's half-hearted. 'You didn't know for certain that they were having an affair.'

'No, that's why I went to speak to him. I suppose I should have known he would brush it off, but I thought I should try.' I sigh. 'Okay, I'm a coward. I could have come straight to you, shown you the photos, but I didn't want to be the one to do that to you. Does that make sense? I thought I could make him feel guilty, get him to own up, then I wouldn't have to be the one bringing all this shit to your door.'

She looks like she's sizing me up for a moment, but then she nods slowly. 'Okay, I understand. But Caroline, why were you following Jenny in the first place?'

As I think about Bella's question I can feel some of my old anxieties returning. What do I say? How much should I reveal?

I take a slow sip of wine, enjoying the sensation of the cool liquid slipping down my throat. I've had too much to drink, even though I've eaten, and I can feel it going to my head now. I can't let it affect my judgement, so I take a moment to think.

'I suspected she was up to something, ever since she showed up at the book club. There were a few times I caught her looking at you in a strange way, as if she hated you, but she was always quick to be nice to your face. I know I encouraged you to spend more time with her, but I thought it would soon become obvious what the problem was. I didn't think she'd manage to keep up the act for as long as she did.'

'Why the hell didn't you tell me any of this? How long have you known about her and Ian?'

'Not long,' I tell her. 'I was going to tell you, but I didn't know how.' I know I sound like I'm pleading with her, but I can't help it.

'There's something else,' I add, knowing I need to tell her some of the things I've discovered. 'I know what Ian did. In the past.'

She frowns at me. 'What do you mean?' I can see real fear in her eyes now.

'I know about the child who died. I know Ian used to be a doctor, and that you both changed your names after what happened. That's why you don't have any friends who've known you for more than a couple of years. You had to make new lives after what he did, and he's dragged you down with him.'

Bella is breathing quickly, and she reaches for her handbag. I put my hand over hers to stop her leaving, but she pulls it away.

'No, Caro. I can't. I need to be on my own. Don't follow me.'

She stands up and leaves for the second time, but this time I don't chase after her. I know she needs to process this. I just hope she still trusts me enough to let me help her, because there's still something she needs to know.

It was a chance conversation with Tony that helped me find out the truth about Ryan Beckley. About who he was. I could never have seen it coming. I'd never have known I was connected to him like this.

We were on the phone, having another conversation about Dr Palmeri, and I was feeling frustrated.

'I can't find anything about Palmeri, I can't find anything about Ryan Beckley, the internet is so full of junk I can't find anything useful!'

'Why are you looking up Ryan Beckley?' he asked me.

I'd never told him about what happened, but maybe now was the right time.

'He attacked me one day, outside my flat. It was ages ago now, last year. Anyway, then he died, but I was trying to find out more about him.'

There was a long pause, then Tony told me something that suddenly brought the whole jigsaw together. Ryan Beckley had been holding a grudge: three years ago, his daughter died because of a medical error, and he blamed her doctor. Dr Palmeri – the exact same person my brother Tony wanted me to look for.

This is the thing Bella's been hiding from me, the thing that she and Ian have been keeping concealed. They didn't move too far, just from further south in Lincolnshire into the city of Lincoln itself, but they changed their names and managed to scrub all records of Dr Palmeri from the internet. I don't know how they did that, but I don't really care. I need Bella to know that I don't blame her, in all of this. She isn't responsible for what her husband has done.

Because that's what I found in Ian's filing cabinet that day, files referencing Dr Palmeri, and some handwritten notes from the day the girl died. It wasn't what I'd been looking for – at no point had I connected the person my brother was searching for with the man who had attacked me, or with my friend's husband. But suddenly, with that one file, everything slid into place. I'd been hoping to get some clarification out of Jenny on the night she died, but someone got to her first.

Ryan must have found out that the Palmeris changed their name to Butterworth. After his first mistake – coming to my flat looking for the wrong Isabella Butterworth – he must have found them, but I don't know exactly what happened next. Did Ian arrange to meet him to talk about what happened, to make more excuses about his involvement in what happened to Ryan's daughter? Was Ryan's death an accident, or did Ian deliberately throw him over the railing? Did Jenny then take up where Ryan failed, getting to know the family and hoping to make Ian pay for what he did? Whatever happened, she underestimated him, and now she's dead too.

I don't want to tell Bella all of this until I have some more answers. I don't have any evidence of this, or I would have told the police; it's all supposition, but I know deep down it's true. Until I can prove it, I need to do my best to protect her and her children, before Ian kills someone else.

Chapter 38

The next day, I walk round to Bella's house. I've barely slept, because I spent all night tossing and turning, wondering if I've done the right thing. Did I tell her too much? Not enough? But if I told her any more, I would risk revealing who I really am.

Standing in the park opposite, I watch the house. There is movement behind a couple of the windows, and both cars are on the drive, so I don't approach. I definitely can't talk to Bella while Ian is there, or the girls. I shouldn't have come so early, but I didn't have anything else to do.

Finding a bench, I sit down to wait. I don't have anything else to do this morning, so I can sit here until I know Bella is in the house alone. Last night, I typed and deleted so many messages to her, but in the end I didn't send anything. How could I know what was the right thing to say? I need to talk to her in person, to find out what she's thinking now.

It's funny, before I knew who Ryan Beckley was, I was relieved that he was dead. Now I only feel pity for him. His story is one I've been familiar with for a few years without even realising it, and if he'd felt able to come to court then maybe I would have recognised him when he attacked me. Maybe then things would be different, and he and his sister would still be alive.

The day it happened, Tony arrived at my flat in tears. It took me forever to calm him down so he could tell me what was wrong. I'd seen him upset after losing patients before, but never like that. I could tell something was different that day, something terrible.

'A little girl died, Iz. She was only five. She died, and it's my fault.'

I still remember those words, and the horror of them as they sank in. He looked haunted. He'd been called to a school in the morning, to see a small child who was having seizures. The staff had been trained on administering her epilepsy medication, and had followed all the right procedures. He was sent in a car to get there and assess the situation as quickly as possible, while they waited for an ambulance to attend. The child was in critical condition, nothing seemed to be working, so he put an IV in and called to confirm they needed an ambulance as quickly as possible.

The girl's mum arrived at the school, so Tony talked to her to work out the best approach to help stop the seizures. She called Dr Palmeri, her daughter's specialist, then handed the phone over to Tony. On the doctor's advice, Tony gave the child IV diazepam, and the seizures gradually subsided.

Here's where it went wrong for him. He told me that he should have checked the child's blood sugar, but he didn't. It was human error, nothing more, but he sat there on my sofa going over and over it. Why hadn't he done it? He should have done it. Round and round in circles, before he could even get the rest of the story out.

'I thought we'd got there, Iz,' he sobbed. 'I thought she was going to be okay.'

The ambulance arrived, and the girl was whisked away to hospital, but by the time she arrived something was drastically wrong. The dose of diazepam Tony had given her made her blood sugar drop so low, she sustained brain damage and died shortly afterwards.

'It's my fault. I didn't check the sugar. After giving the diazepam I should have monitored her blood sugar.'

'Surely someone else should have thought about it, too?' I asked, horrified by the whole situation but equally wanting to save my brother some of the pain he was clearly experiencing. 'What about the doctor?'

He shook his head. 'Nobody mentioned it. I should have remembered though; it's standard procedure. I'd just had such a long day. I should have been home by then, but someone called in sick so they asked me to stay a few more hours.' He scrubbed his face with his hands. 'I've barely slept in the last couple of days, I've been working so hard. I know it's no excuse but . . .' He burst into tears again.

I knew then that it was serious, but I hadn't understood just how bad it could get. Part of me knew that Tony would lose his job. I hadn't expected him to go to prison, though, but it was ruled as gross negligence manslaughter, a criminal offence.

The worst part is how Dr Palmeri screwed him over. The doctor should have asked Tony about the blood sugar, but didn't. No matter what happened later, what anyone said, if the doctor had mentioned it, Tony would have done it. But when the inquiry into the child's death spoke to the doctor, his notes stated that the child's glucose was in the normal range. How could he have known this when he'd never asked Tony, never considered that factor himself? Tony maintained that the doctor must have altered the medical report somehow, and added that information in at a later date when it became clear he could be held partially accountable.

When it came down to it, it was Tony's word against Palmeri's. Palmeri insisted he asked about the glucose and wrote down what Tony told him. Despite the fact that Tony admitted responsibility, the inquiry ruled that he'd lied in order to try and cover up his mistake. It made no sense to me, but they had their scapegoat, someone who could be held up as an example. Someone whose name could be released to the press, for them to say here, this is the person to blame for a child's death. Never mind the failing system that put Tony under so much pressure he was barely functioning that day. Never mind the fact that there were other people involved in the chain who could, and should, have spotted the error. When it came down to it, Tony was alone, with nobody to back him up. My brother was broken.

At first I thought his vendetta against Palmeri wouldn't last because it wouldn't really make much difference to his situation. His sentence might be shortened if they believed he hadn't lied about his conversation with the doctor, but that wasn't guaranteed. Tony wouldn't get his job back. But eventually I realised it wasn't about that, it was the principle of the thing. He'd been honest enough to admit to his mistake, and I know the little girl's death will haunt him for the rest of his life. But the doctor did everything he could to hide his mistake. He certainly didn't ask Tony about the blood sugar, so that reference in his notes must have been added later, after the child died. If that's not a sign of guilt, I don't know what is.

Now I've met Ian, none of it surprises me. He's an arrogant bastard, and I expect he doesn't give a shit about anyone else. I'm just glad he's not practising medicine any more, probably handed a nice well-earning IT job in the insurance firm by one of his friends after he decided to lie low. The fact that the family have changed their names shows they're hiding from something; why hide if you're not guilty?

I haven't told Tony that I've found Palmeri yet, because I don't want to get his hopes up. I mean, what do we do now? Just because I've found him doesn't mean we'll be able to get him to admit to anything. The best I can do is try to record him saying something incriminating, but that's highly unlikely. No, what I need is to find the proof that he killed Ryan and Jenny Beckley, and Lucy too, and make sure he's locked up for a long time. It might not be paying for what he did to Tony, but at least he'll have lost his liberty.

While I've been sitting on this bench, I haven't been paying attention to my surroundings, and time has moved on. I look up at Bella's house, and neither of the cars are in the driveway. Ian will have gone to work, and she's taken the girls to school. Well, when she gets back I'll go and see if she's willing to talk to me, now that she's had some time to think about what I said.

A few minutes later, I'm aware of someone approaching me. A police officer, one in uniform this time, a man I haven't seen before.

'Excuse me,' he says, stopping right in front of me.

'Yes?' The sun is behind him, so I have to squint when I look up at him.

'Can I ask what you're doing here?'

I look around me. 'I'm sitting on a bench in a public park. Is there something wrong with that?'

He clears his throat, obviously not amused by my sarcasm. 'We've received a complaint from a local resident.'

'About me sitting on a bench?' I reply, trying to keep my voice light. I haven't caused a nuisance to anyone, so it must have been Ian. If he spotted me on his way out of the house, would he have gone as far as calling the police?

'It's a harassment complaint,' the PC says sternly. 'We've had a report that you've been watching one of the families in the area, and that you've been making yourself unwelcome.'

He doesn't go into detail, but I can just imagine the sort of things he's been told. I swallow down my anger.

'Fine. If me sitting on a bench is deemed "unwelcome", I'll leave.' I can walk around until the PC leaves, then come back when Bella's home and speak to her then. Hopefully this will help my cause, if Ian has called the police on me.

'Wait a moment,' he says as I stand. 'Can I see some ID, please?'

I pause, wondering if I can refuse. Does he have the right to search me? Could he arrest me for something if I don't show him some sort of identification? I don't know, and it's not something I want to risk right now.

Digging in my bag, I find my purse and pull out my provisional driving licence. I've never passed my test, but this is useful to have as photo ID.

The PC looks at my licence, then frowns at me to check the photo is definitely of me. Next, he pulls out a note-book and checks something then puts it away.

'Are you wasting my time?'

'No,' I tell him, puzzled. 'What do you mean?'

'According to what I was told, you're the one who made the complaint.'

My heart sinks. Bella's the one who called the police? Not Ian? I understand why she might still be upset with me, but this feels a bit drastic. I glance back over at the house, and see that her BMW is just pulling into the driveway, and I sigh. I can't lie to the police, whatever else I've done.

'No, I didn't make the complaint. She and I have the same name,' I say, nodding over the road to where Bella is getting out of her car. 'It's just a coincidence.'

I watch her, and as she turns to enter the house she glances over to the park. For a moment our eyes meet, and I wish I knew what she was thinking. The PC hands my licence back and pulls out his notebook to write something down, then once again tells me to leave. I do as he says, glancing back over my shoulder a moment later. He's crossing the park, heading toward Bella's house, and I feel a wave of desperation and fear wash over me. He's going to tell her what my name is. My secret will be out, and I'll never be able to help her, because she won't trust me any more.

Chapter 39

It takes me several days to find the courage to get in touch with Bella again. In those days I barely sleep, I completely ignore the work that's fast becoming overdue, and I live on takeaways and alcohol. Every time I hear a sound outside, I think it must be the police arriving to arrest me. I'm not sure what for, but I can understand how my behaviour could be seen as sinister.

In that time I type and delete numerous texts, alternating between begging for Bella's forgiveness and pleading with her to get out of that house, no matter what she thinks about me. What am I supposed to do? I know I've gone about everything completely the wrong way, but the fact remains that I'm sure her husband is guilty of murder. Not just one, but possibly three – Jenny, Ryan Beckley, and Lucy the homeless woman who was in the wrong place at the wrong time. I feel like Lucy's death is still partly my responsibility, though. Until I went and spoke to her, I don't think Ian knew she'd been there. He's the sort of man who wouldn't notice a homeless person, because they'd be too unimportant in his world view for him to take into consideration.

By the time I emerge from my haze of self-pity, I've come up with a plan. Yes, Izzy is exactly the sort of person who would curl up in a ball and hide from this situation, but I haven't really been Izzy for months now. I'm Caroline, and Caroline is stronger than that. I text Bella, sending it before I have a chance to second-guess my decision.

We need to talk.

It's half an hour before I get a response, which is as short and to the point as mine.

2 p.m., at the castle.

I don't know why she's chosen the castle, possibly because it's neutral territory and will be busy, no opportunity for me to do anything to her. It shames me that she might even think that about me, that I could ever mean her harm, but I understand it might be difficult for her to see things from my point of view.

It takes me a while to plan what I'm going to wear. I want to look strong and in control, but I have no idea what sort of outfit gives off that message, so in the end I settle for something comfortable, do my make-up and head into the city centre. The castle grounds aren't huge, and they're surrounded by walls, so it won't take me long to find Bella.

When I arrive, I walk round for a little while to look for her, but when I can't see her I choose a bench at the side of the main path, somewhere obvious so she'll see me when she gets here. It's only once I'm sitting down that I wonder if she's definitely coming. After all, she did tell me she thought Ian had access to her phone. Could this be a set up?

My heart races as I look around me, but I don't see anyone familiar. Bella is already ten minutes late, which isn't like her. She hasn't messaged me to tell me she's been held up. I bite my lip and wonder what to do. If I leave, and Bella is on her way, will we ever be able to talk about this, or will I have missed my chance? I decide not to risk losing the opportunity to make things right with her.

A moment later I jump as someone sits down at the other end of the bench. It's Bella. I let out a sigh of relief and smile at her, but it isn't returned.

'What do you want to talk about?' she says straight away. Okay, we're going right in, no small talk.

'Where do you think we should start?' I ask.

She turns away from me and looks up at the main building of the castle. 'Who are you? I mean, who are you really?'

This is something I had expected. 'My name, my real name, is Isabella Butterworth. The same as yours. Pretty much everything else about me you already know. I work from home as a freelance virtual assistant. All of my likes and dislikes are real. My family background, as much as I've told you, is all real. The only thing I lied about was my name.'

Bella turns to look at me now, incomprehension written all over her face. 'But why would you do that? It's just a coincidence. Why wouldn't you tell me your real name when we met?'

I think about this question for a moment. I can't tell her the truth, that I was so desperate to change my life, myself, that I became a different person just to make friends with her. But what should I say?

'I thought you'd be suspicious of me if I told you my real name. Ryan Beckley was looking for you, presumably to get to Ian, and he found me first. I thought he might hurt you.'

'Wait, so why didn't you just tell me about him?'

I pause and wonder how I'm going to answer that question, then I think the truth is best.

'By the time we met, he was already dead. I knew he wasn't a threat to you any more.'

She stares at me for a moment. 'We've been friends for, what, nine months now? And all this time you've been lying to me. We didn't meet by chance, did we? You came to the book club deliberately to get to know me.'

I nod.

'But why? If he was already dead?'

'I still wanted to know why he was looking for you, what he wanted. I didn't think I could find out without being part of your life, and I didn't think you'd trust me if I told you my real name. Caroline is my middle name, and Devlin was my mother's surname.'

'How did you find me?' Her tone is sharp, and I know I need to continue being honest if I'm going to win her trust back, however much she's going to dislike what I have to say.

'Over the last couple of years I've received some emails intended for you,' I tell her. 'Before the Beckley thing even happened. I used those to track you down when I realised he must have had the wrong person.'

'So you stalked me and my family,' she spits.

I wince. 'Don't put it like that. It wasn't stalking. Anyway, Beckley's family wasn't the only one damaged in all of this.'

Bella frowns at me. 'What are you talking about?'

'My brother is Anthony Barnes, the paramedic who went to jail for the death of Ryan Beckley's daughter.'

There is a long pause as Bella takes this in. At no point has she denied knowing the story of what happened to the girl, so I know she knows who I'm talking about.

'When I got to know you, I didn't have any idea the two things were connected,' I tell her, wanting to impress upon her the fact that I always meant well. 'It was only when I found a reference to Dr I Palmeri that I put everything together. Now Beckley is dead, and so is the person who witnessed him being killed, along with his sister, who I expect was getting to know you and Ian to try and find evidence of his guilt.' I pause, wondering if I should say what I want to say next, that Ian needs to pay for his part in the death of the child. That even though my brother won't get any of his life back, he shouldn't be the only one shouldering the blame.

I decide against it, however. Even though I know Bella is sick of her home situation, enough to consider leaving Ian, I don't know if she's ready to expose him. She must have been complicit in their hiding – they've changed their last name, he's changed jobs, they moved house. Bella had to leave her old life behind when her husband made his colossal mistake, and now she's paying the price for what he did.

'If you work with me now, you and the girls can escape from him, for good,' I say quietly, not looking at her.

'How can I trust you, after all of this?' she snaps. 'I thought you were my friend.'

'I am your friend. I wish I could go back and change things, actually introduce myself using my real name, then we could laugh about the coincidence before getting to know each other. I was wrong, and I freely admit that. But now that you know, now that I've been completely honest with you, will you let me help you?'

'What's in it for you?' she asks eventually.

'I help my brother. He's going mad with the idea that he was screwed over, that someone shares the responsibility for the child's death but managed to get away with it. He always admitted his part in it, and he knew that his career would be over as soon as he did it, but he was honest regardless. Now he's fixated on Ian. When I talk to him, all he wants me to do is find Palmeri. I've been trying for over two years, and to be honest I'd given up. I know it won't give Tony his career back, or change anything that happened, but it will give him peace of mind, and right now that's worth everything to me.'

I don't tell her that I also want to see justice done for Lucy, because I don't know if Bella would understand that side, my feelings of responsibility for her death. Still, I've made my case, so I sit back on the bench and look up at the tree that leans over us, waiting for her to respond.

It takes so long, I have to look over to check she hasn't got up and left while I've been thinking, but she's still there, staring at the entrance to the castle.

'Okay. I'll at least talk with you about it,' she says, her voice low. 'I can't guarantee I'll agree to anything, but at least we can work through what you've got, what you know and what we can prove.'

I feel like a weight has been lifted from my heart, but I try not to seem too jubilant. After all, we're talking about putting her murdering husband in jail; it's a terrifying prospect.

'Thank you,' is all I say.

'Where do we start?'

I talk her through everything I suspect, from Beckley's death through to my conversation with Lucy, how he could easily have seen the two of us that day and discovered he might have left a witness. I tell her about the homeless man I spoke to who said Lucy had witnessed a murder then was killed, and then I get round to Jenny. As I tell her the story of going to meet her at the house that night, Bella's eyes widen.

'You were actually there? You saw her body?'

I nod. 'It was horrible.'

'Did you call the police?'

This is something I'm not proud of, and I shake my head. 'No, I was too scared they'd think I had something to do with it, and scared that whoever killed her would find out I'd been there and suspect I might have seen them. I didn't, or I would have gone straight to the police, but if Ian killed her he might not be willing to take any chances. I didn't want him to find out I'd been there.'

Bella wraps her arms around herself as she sits there in silence for a few moments. 'This is serious, Caro . . . wait, what should I call you now?' she asks with an annoyed glance at me.

'Izzy,' I reply. 'That's what people usually call me. Though it might be easiest to keep calling me Caroline for now, especially if we don't want Ian to get suspicious of what we're doing.'

She considers this for a moment. 'Fine, we'll stick with Caroline, then I'm less likely to make a mistake. Anyway, I don't know what we can do. You don't have a lot of concrete evidence here.'

'I know. That's why I think we should confront Ian with it, try to catch him out.'

Her laugh is more like a bark and startles me. 'Seriously? I thought you'd got to know him. I thought you under-stood what he's like. There's no way that plan will work. If you present all this to Ian he'll laugh in your face, tell you everything is wrong and make you think you're going mad. It's what he does best. That strategy isn't going to work.'

I sigh, but keep my thoughts to myself. She knows Ian better than I do, so I can't really argue with her, but I also don't see what other options we have. As we continue talking, we discuss other ways of getting evidence, but in the back of my mind I know exactly what I need to do next.

Chapter 40

I wait for Ian outside his office again, but this time I take pains to find a more secluded place to sit. No good him spotting me out of the window again. I want to take him by surprise, if I can, and not give him any time to think about why I might be here. Bella insisted that she hasn't told him my real name, or my connection to Ryan Beckley, but I don't know if I can trust her completely. Even if I can, could Ian have found out by himself?

It's colder today, and I pull my coat and scarf a little tighter as I wait for him to emerge from his office. I know he hasn't left yet, but I hope it's not too long until he does. If I get too cold I think my courage will start to dissipate with my body heat.

After another half an hour, the front door opens and three men spill out onto the pavement. They're chatting and laughing, and I feel a sinking sensation when I see that one of them is Ian. Now I'll have to try and get him on his own. Before I approach him, I slip my hand into the interior pocket of my coat and set my phone recording. I'm not going to risk this conversation without getting some sort of evidence.

'Ian,' I call, but my voice is lost beneath their chatter. I hurry to catch up with them, and take him by the elbow.

'Ian,' I repeat, and this time I have his attention. He turns, the smile on his face dropping to an expression of confusion, with a flash of anger in his eyes that he quickly masks.

'Caroline,' he says, his voice smooth, and suddenly everything about him oozes charm. The performance is something he's putting on for his colleagues, I know instantly. He's saying look, women are chasing me down on the street.

'What can I do for you?' he asks, his smile lurking somewhere between snide and predatory. He stops, and his colleagues stop as well. Ian glances at them, then back at me. I don't say anything, but I'm sure the look on my face tells him this isn't something he wants to talk about with an audience.

'You guys go ahead, I'll see you in there,' he says casually, cocking one of his eyebrows to make them chuckle before he turns back to me. Good to see he's surrounded himself with like-minded people.

As his colleagues move away, Ian grips my arm just above the elbow and steers me across the road in the direction of the cathedral. There aren't many people around at this time of night, and I have to hope he isn't going to deliberately lead me into a dark corner. Thankfully he releases me when he sees an older couple walking toward us, smiles at them as they pass, then steers me toward the cathedral itself. We stand in its shadow for a moment, not speaking, and size each other up.

'What is it this time?' he asks eventually, his voice low and threatening. 'Because I've had enough of you harassing me and my family. Bella isn't happy with you either.'

'We had a good chat yesterday,' I tell him. 'I wanted you to know that I know about Ryan Beckley and the death of his daughter.'

Ian takes a step back and cocks his head to one side; this clearly isn't what he expected.

'I thought this was about Jenny,' he says carefully.

'Jenny Beckley, you mean? His sister?'

'Well, aren't you clever? But I don't know what the hell you think you're going to gain by knowing all of this. The pair of them were hounding us. I'm sorry they're dead, but I have to admit it makes life a lot easier for my family.' He flashes me a wolfish grin again, with no trace of humour in it.

'They're not the only people who died, though, are they?'

'What the fuck is that supposed to mean?' His charm is starting to slip now.

'There was a homeless woman. She saw Beckley go over the railway bridge.'

'He committed suicide,' he said, and I have to give him credit for his acting skills, because he looks completely convinced.

'Bollocks,' I reply, and he looks surprised at the

vehemence of my response. 'He was murdered, and she saw who killed him. So that's why they came back and killed her.'

For a moment he just stares at me, then he shakes his head. 'I don't know who you think you are, but you don't know what the fuck you're talking about.'

'I talked to her, before she died. The homeless woman. She's the one who told me about Jenny leaving the flowers for Ryan every week. The day that I followed Jenny, when she met you in that restaurant, that's how I knew who she was.'

He's shaking his head. 'You're unbelievable. You've known my wife for what, less than a year? You have no idea what we've been through, and now you're sticking your nose where it doesn't belong. If I were you, I'd back off.'

'What are you going to do when the police start asking questions about the night Jenny died?'

Ian's eyes narrow. 'What are you suggesting?'

'You know exactly what I'm suggesting. I told you, I know everything, including about your previous life as Dr Palmeri.'

There is a long pause before Ian lets out a low chuckle. 'Oh, I see. You know everything, do you? So you know that I was away for a work meeting in Oxford on the night Jenny was killed? I was in the bar with my colleagues until nearly two in the morning – kind of hard for me to also be in Lincoln murdering someone. And as for Dr Palmeri, well . . . you should stop making such wild assumptions.' He gives me an appraising look. 'I can

334

promise you, Caroline, I have never been a doctor. I've worked for the same company for fifteen years, and I'd be happy to let you talk to our HR manager tomorrow, if you really want to be convinced.' He pauses and smiles slowly, 'I wonder, when you found reference to Dr I Palmeri, did it ever occur to you that I'm not the only person in our household whose first initial is I?'

He takes a couple of paces back, already turning away from me.

'For someone who claims to know everything, you've got some pretty major facts wrong here. I don't know what happened to Jenny, but it has nothing to do with me. Maybe you should consider your sources before you go any further, yeah?'

With that, he turns and walks away, leaving me speechless.

I don't remember getting back to my flat. I need to talk to Tony, but I can't, and that fact drives me mad. Thankfully, he should be calling me tomorrow. How could he have told me Dr Palmeri was a man, if she was actually a woman? Bella's voice might be a bit deeper than average, but not to the extent that you could mistake her for a man. I know Tony never met the doctor in person, and Palmeri had been completely cleared by the point of Tony's hearing, but surely he still would have known?

But no, I remember him telling me that the inquiry insisted there should be no contact between them at all, and that if they did communicate it would look bad for him, so he will have stuck to that. He's not stupid, he knew they were going to rule the child's death as his fault, and he didn't want to make it any worse for himself. Of course, he didn't count on the doctor lying.

Bella, though . . . really? All this time, she was Dr Palmeri? Now I think about it, it all makes sense. She's the one who isn't working, presumably because she doesn't want anyone to connect her with the case, so is keeping a low profile. Butterworth is probably Ian's name, and she kept her own name until it suited her to change it in order to hide, unless they both changed their names completely.

If I've got this crucial piece of information wrong, what else have I been wrong about? Could Bella really be the one who killed all three of these people, in order to protect herself? The more I think about it, the more the pieces begin to fall into place: Ryan Beckley threatened me, or rather the woman who shares my name, not her husband. He'd met Bella plenty of times in her professional capacity because of his daughter's condition, so he knew I wasn't her. He must have discovered her new name, found a flat registered in that name, and gone looking for her that way. It was her he was after all along. I thought he had latched onto her as a way of getting to Ian, but she was the one he blamed for his child's death.

Beckley must have found her in the end, so she pushed him over the edge of the bridge, whether intentionally or not. Then, when she realised Lucy was a witness, she had to kill her too. Jenny must have threatened her, told her that just because her brother was dead, it didn't mean Bella had got away with what she did.

I pace around my flat for a long time, trying to get the story straight in my head. There's no way I can sleep, I'm sure, but in the end I crash out around four in the morning, then wake a few hours later with a pounding headache. Time seems to drag until my phone rings, but finally I hear my brother's voice.

'Palmeri is a woman. Isabella Palmeri,' I tell him.

There's a long silence. 'Shit. Really?'

'How could you have got that wrong, Tony?' I try to keep my voice even but the pitch climbs as I speak, and I find it hard to hold back my emotions. 'All this time I've been looking for a man, and she's a bloody woman!'

'Shit,' he says again. 'I'm sorry, Iz. I barely remember anything about that day, and I was so focused on the kid I didn't spare a thought for the person on the end of the phone. It's not uncommon with paramedics. We get this sort of tunnel vision, so we're in the zone and don't notice what's going on around us. One of my colleagues didn't notice a fight going on just a few metres away from him, once. The police asked him for a witness statement and he was completely oblivious, couldn't tell them a single thing.'

I sigh and rub my face, feeling tears well up behind my eyes. I'm scared I've messed the whole thing up by telling Bella everything I know, and I'll never be able to get justice for Lucy, Ryan and Jenny, or get Tony the closure he deserves.

Can she really have killed three people in cold blood? This is the point I keep coming back to, the one thing I'm finding hard to believe. Ian seemed like such an obvious suspect, with his shitty attitude towards his wife. Though it makes sense in a way – Bella's true identity is what Ian knows, his hold over her, and his weapon if she ever tries to take the children away from him. I wouldn't be surprised if he knows she changed her report, if she told him when she was stressed and didn't know what to do. Of course, he works in IT – he could have helped her to falsify the report. If he did that, it would make sense why they're still together even though they seem so miserable. They each have the power to ruin the other if they leave.

The main question now is whether or not Ian will have told Bella that I spoke to him last night, and that he corrected my mistake about which of them is Dr Palmeri. I'm hoping he hasn't, because he has to be wondering himself if his wife could be a murderer. But if he has, that's it, all our cards are on the table. There's a good chance I could be her next victim.

Chapter 41

I've avoided contacting Bella for several days, while I decide what to do, but I can't put it off any longer. What the hell do I say, though? If I knew exactly how much Ian had shared with her, then I'd have a better idea of how to approach her, but I can't exactly ask him.

In the end, she calls me. When I see her name pop up on my phone screen, fear churns in my stomach.

'Hello?' My voice sounds a little strangled, so I try to clear my throat quietly.

'We need to talk,' Bella says, and there's an edge to her voice. Is she scared?

'Sure, what's up?'

'No, in person. Are you free this afternoon?'

I have work to be catching up with, but I can stay up later if necessary. It's not like I'm sleeping well at the moment anyway. I agree to meet her in one of our usual coffee shops, and I take that as a good sign.

When I arrive, she's already there, and a look of relief crosses her face when I walk in. It's unlike her to be early, so she really must have been keen to see me.

'What's wrong?' I ask the moment I sit down.

'I need to leave. We need to get it sorted as soon as we can. Do you still have those holiday cottages you were looking at?'

So Ian hasn't told her what I know. I swallow, and decide I have to go along with the charade a little longer. Reaching across the table, I squeeze her hand.

'Of course. I'll help you with whatever you need, you just have to tell me what I can do.'

She nods, then looks down at the table for a moment. When she looks up again, there are tears in her eyes.

'I can't put the girls through this any more. I was thinking about our conversation the other day, all the things we think he's done. What if he turns violent one night? What if he does something to me? I can't bear to think about what would happen to the girls. Even if he went to jail, if I wasn't around then they'd go into care. We don't have any family who'd take them in.'

'What about Ian's mum?'

Bella lets out a harsh laugh. 'God no. She'd never put herself out like that.'

I take a deep breath, wondering where to steer the conversation next.

'What are you going to do?'

'Like we said, you book us somewhere, print out the details and give them to me. No email trail, nothing digital that he can use to find me. Then once we're there, I can look for something else. I'll pack during the day, pick the girls up from school, then just leave. Ian has been working late every night recently, so that gives us plenty of time.'

'When?'

She looks me in the eyes. 'As soon as possible. As soon as you can get something booked.'

At first I wonder why she's still keeping up this story, now I know Ian isn't the dangerous one, then it hits me. She's not trying to hide from Ian; she's trying to run from what she's done, because she knows it won't be long until she's caught. And she's using me to do it. I'll book one place for her, thinking that's where she's hiding, then by the time anyone realises she isn't there, she'll be long gone.

'I can probably find something for tomorrow night, as long as you don't mind where you go,' I tell her, wondering if there's a way I can stall her. If I sound positive and proactive, then hopefully she'll believe me when things take a bit longer, so I can delay her.

How can I let her leave now I know the truth? We sit in silence for a moment, and I take the time to really look at her. She seems so scared, so innocent, but she isn't. She can't be.

I need to go to the police. That's the only option I have. I need to go and see them, explain everything I know – and suspect – and tell them that Bella is planning on leaving as soon as possible. She claims she's escaping Ian, but now she knows about me and my attempts to find out the truth about these murders, she's doing what she can to avoid being caught.

Is it possible she's just going to run and leave the girls behind? Whatever I think of Bella, I still believe she loves her daughters, but she'll be much easier to find with two children in tow.

'There's something else,' she says, looking up at me and interrupting my train of thought. 'I've found something.'

She looks around us, as if gauging whether anyone else in the coffee shop can overhear us. It's not busy, but there's a couple at the next table.

'What did you find?' I keep my voice low, hoping she'll feel secure enough to go on.

Bella presses her lips together so tightly the skin around them goes almost white, then shakes her head. 'I can't.'

'Tell me, please. I can help you, but you need to be honest with me. Once you've gone, and the girls are safely a long way away from him, then I can go to the police with all of this. If there's something else I can tell them, I need to know what it is.'

She shakes her head. 'You can't go to the police. He'll find out it was you, and he'll kill you too.'

I shiver at the sincerity in her voice, knowing she wants to keep me away from the police in order to protect herself, not me. She's so believable, it's frightening. I wait, knowing the value in silence, in giving people the time to say the things they really want to say but are scared to. It feels like it stretches out forever, but eventually she murmurs something I don't quite catch.

'Tell me again.'

'A knife. I found a knife.'

342

I feel myself go cold. 'A knife? What sort of knife?'

'It's like a kitchen knife. Not one from our kitchen though; I would have noticed if it had gone missing.'

'Where did you find it?'

She swallows. 'He has a filing cabinet in his study. I never use it, but I thought I should look for things for the girls, their birth certificates, so I have them safe. It was wrapped in a plastic bag and shoved at the back of a drawer.'

I sit for a moment and try to take this in. If she's telling the truth, that there's a knife in one of those drawers, then it's been put there since I was last in their house. Obviously, I can't tell her that, can't ask her why I didn't find it myself.

'Why has he hidden a knife?' I ask, wanting to draw her out and get her to say what I know she's implying.

'There's something on it. Blood. It must be what he used to . . .' She gesticulates, but doesn't finish the sentence.

I sit back in my seat and look up at the ceiling, thinking. Assuming I'm right, that Bella is the one who killed all of these people, there are two possible scenarios here. One is that she kept the knife, and has planted it in Ian's filing cabinet in order to frame him. If this is the case, then she must have wiped it clean of her own prints, maybe even used a bag he'd already touched in order to try and fake more evidence against him.

Or there is no knife. I have to accept that Bella might know I'm onto her, that I know she's really Dr Palmeri and so has the best motive and opportunity for carrying out these killings. If she knows, then this is a trap. She wants me to try and get hold of the knife, because she knows I won't be able to resist getting my hands on the best piece of solid evidence I could have against her.

So what do I do? She's looking at me, an anxious frown on her face.

'What do I do?' she whispers, echoing my thoughts. 'What the hell do I do?'

'Take it to the police,' I tell her. 'Tell them what we know.'

'They won't believe me.'

'They will, especially if they can match that to the two people he stabbed.'

It feels so harsh, saying it out loud like that, but I want to be harsh, I want to get a reaction out of her. There's something so frightening about the vulnerability on her face because it seems so real. For a moment I even question myself, wondering if I've got it wrong yet again, but I know I haven't. She's that good an actor.

Bella nods slowly. 'Okay. I need to think about this. I need to figure out what the best thing to do for me and my girls is.'

I squeeze her hand again. 'You can do this.'

She gives me a wan smile. 'Come on, we haven't even ordered anything yet, they're going to throw us out soon.'

I laugh, and attract a waiter's attention.

For the next fifteen minutes we drink coffee and eat cake, attempting stilted small talk, but we keep lapsing back into silence. Eventually she checks her watch, then stands up, announcing she needs to collect the girls from school. Before she leaves, she gives me a rare hug.

'Thank you for being such a good friend.'

I smile, watching her walk out of the coffee shop, and I wonder if she thinks I believe a word she just said.

What do I do about the knife? Should I try to get hold of it, then I can take it to the police without letting Bella know? Or should I turn up at her house tomorrow, insist on seeing it and force her to go with me to the police station? The latter would be a risky strategy, but it might be the best way to call her bluff and discover whether the knife really exists.

Since I got home, I've been trying to remember if I saw a knife when I found Jenny's body. It's such a blur, a horrific memory that I've been trying to blot out, that I can't remember clearly one way or the other. If there was a knife at the scene, then surely the police have it now? Unless Bella went back for it, but that seems unlikely. And if the police have it, then she must be lying to me, and I think she might be doing that just to lure me back into the house. She suspects I've been through their things, that I've been digging into their lives even more than I've let on, and she's trying to catch me out.

But I need to see if it really exists, and if it does then I need to take it to the police.

I lie awake all night, wondering if I should go into the house under cover of darkness, but I don't want to risk someone waking up and finding me there. Maybe it's safer to go in the day like I have done before.

The next morning, I plan. My vantage point in the park is no use now, not since Bella spotted me, so I'm going to have to try something else. A disguise would just be comical, and she'd still know it was me, so I need to make sure she's out of the house without being there to see her leave.

She should be back from the school run by half nine, so I wait in a neighbouring street and send her a text message.

Meet me at the castle, urgent.

Give me fifteen minutes, comes the almost instant reply.

I wait for ten, then walk round to her house. Her car has gone, and there's no sign of life, but I ring the doorbell anyway. No good sneaking into her house if there's actually someone in.

A few moments later, when there's no answer, I think I'm safe, and walk casually around the back, letting myself in. I go straight for the filing cabinet, using the same trick with the metal nail file as I used last time. Sure enough, there's a plastic bag at the back of one of the drawers, exactly as Bella described. Once I have it in my hand, I whip around, expecting her to be standing there waiting for me, but the house is still empty. I can't see anything in this room that might be a security camera, but that doesn't mean she isn't watching me.

I feel my breath coming in ragged gasps as I look down at the knife in my hand. I know she's been manipulating me, but right now I don't know what her endgame is. All I know is that I have to take this to the police.

346

Chapter 42

I feel like the knife is burning a hole in my bag as I walk away from Bella's house. It's all I can do not to run, but I don't want to draw too much attention to myself. Keeping my head down, I try to maintain a measured pace as I go down her street, turn the corner and cross the road. I just need to get away from there as quickly as I can, before anything happens. What might happen, I don't know, but I'm scared anyway.

If Bella left the knife there, I think she did it because she intends to frame Ian and is using me. Maybe she wouldn't have even thought about it if I hadn't latched onto him as my main suspect, so I need to fix this before it gets any worse. I briefly consider that she might be setting me up, but what could she possibly gain by doing that? No, I'm sure Ian is the one she's got in the frame.

No time to go home; I need to take this straight to a police station. If only I knew who had been dealing with

Jenny's murder, I could take it straight to them, but I don't even know where the nearest police station is. I pull out my phone and look it up. There's one in the city centre, so that seems like my best bet.

It takes me fifteen minutes to walk there, and all the time I'm looking over my shoulder. I've already had a message and a couple of calls from Bella, asking where I am, but I ignore them. I could reply and make some excuses, but I don't want to waste any time.

When I arrive at the police station, there are a couple of people waiting, so I stand in a queue and shift nervously from foot to foot until it's my turn to speak to the woman on the desk.

'I have some information about a crime,' I tell her, not really wanting to say the word 'murder' out loud in a public space.

'What sort of crime?' the woman asks me.

'A death,' I say, still reluctant. The woman frowns and asks for some more details, so I give her Jenny's name and wait while she goes to speak to someone.

'An officer will come and speak to you soon, if you'd like to take a seat,' she tells me smoothly when she returns. Hopefully they'll take me seriously.

It's not a long wait, thankfully, because I feel like I can't sit still. I'm pacing when a tall woman in plain clothes comes through and calls my name. When I walk toward her she looks confused, then checks my name again, but when I confirm she simply holds the door open for me.

'Follow me,' she says pleasantly, then leads me to a

small interview room, where another detective is already seated.

'I'm sorry, I thought you were someone else when they told me your name, that's why I had to double-check,' the first detective explains.

'I know,' I reply. 'She's the person I want to talk to you about.'

The two women both lean forward slightly. 'Okay, what information do you have that you can share with us?'

I put my bag on the table between us. 'There's a knife in there, in a plastic bag. I found it in Bella's house – that is, Isabella Butterworth's house. She used to be Isabella Palmeri. I think that knife was used to kill Jenny Beckley, and maybe a homeless woman called Lucy, too.'

There's a long pause.

'You say there's a knife in your bag?' the first detective asks. 'We'd like to see that. I'm going to ask you to take it out, place it on the table, then sit back.'

I do as she asks, making sure I don't move too suddenly. It's important they realise I'm here to help them, to give them information, not to do anything threatening.

Once I've done that, the detective puts on some gloves and picks up the knife in its bag, transferring it to another bag.

'Can you tell us how you came to be in possession of this knife, and why you think it might have been used in the commission of a crime?' the second detective asks smoothly.

I think for a moment. 'I don't know where to start. I

think this is connected to the death of Jenny's brother Ryan, too. Do you know that Isabella Palmeri, or Butterworth as she is now, was partly responsible for the death of Ryan Beckley's daughter – Jenny's niece? I think we have to start there.'

Both of the detectives have raised eyebrows, and I wonder how much of the story they've connected up. Maybe nothing I tell them will be new information, but I know I need to try.

I begin with the girl's death, telling them about my brother and his part in it all. I try to make it clear that he accepted responsibility, and that we're not looking to overturn his conviction. He just wants Dr Palmeri to be held responsible for her part in the tragedy. Working through the story, I pause occasionally to make sure I'm getting everything in the right order. The first detective has made some notes as I've talked, but mostly she's just been listening. Eventually, I reach the point where I tell them about the knife.

'I think she latched onto my theory that her husband was the one who killed those people, and decided she would use me to try and frame him. So I took the knife, and brought it to you.'

'How did you get it?'

I wince. 'I have a spare key to her house. I let myself in and found it in the filing cabinet.' There are a few things I've omitted from my story, including anything about how I came to be in possession of a key to the house. I've done some things I'm not proud of, but they've got me to the truth, which is all that matters now. I just need the police to listen to my story and use their resources to fill in all the gaps.

'Okay, that's a very comprehensive story,' the first detective says once I've finished. 'As you've handled the knife, or at least the bag it's in, I'd like to ask you to give us a sample of your fingerprints and your DNA, then we can eliminate you from the enquiry when we send the knife to forensics.'

I agree; anything to make sure this is finally over. The two detectives get up and leave, asking me to wait in the interview room, and I sit back in the chair feeling deflated. I don't know what I expected, but this feels like a huge anticlimax. I've told my story, I've given them as much as I can, so what happens next?

I wait for what feels like ages before a different woman enters the room. She explains the process of taking my fingerprints and DNA, which I agree to for a second time. After she's finished, I stand up, but she shakes her head.

'The detectives want you to wait here. I think they've got a couple more questions.'

'Okay,' I say, sitting down again slowly. Maybe they just want to check a few details.

It's another half hour until they come back, and by this time I'm starting to worry. Has something happened? They smile at me when they walk in, which puts my mind at ease, though I'm still nervous.

'We just wanted to double-check a couple of details, if that's okay,' the first one says brightly. 'You mentioned that you've been using a different mobile to contact Isabella. Is that the number you gave us? If we want to look at her correspondence we need to have both numbers.'

'Oh, I can give you that one,' I say, relief washing over me. They're ensuring they have everything they need to arrest and charge her, without her wriggling out of it. I reel off my other phone number, then answer a couple more questions before they tell me I can leave.

When I get home, I see more texts and calls from Bella, so I spend some time trying to work out what I can say to her.

I'm so sorry. Something urgent came up, and I wasn't in a position to call. I'll explain everything next time I see you.

I send it, then wait a few moments before following it up.
Let me know if you need anything.

Regardless of what I've done, I still want her to think I'm helping her. How long will it be until the police arrest her? I know they'll need to carry out tests on the knife, compare it to the wounds as well as test it for prints and DNA, but how long will that take? On the TV it would be a couple of hours, but I know in real life it could be a lot longer. Can I keep up the pretence for much longer, even though I'll be waiting every day for the news that Bella has been arrested?

I stay inside my flat the following day to avoid bumping into her anywhere, and she doesn't get in touch. The lack of communication worries me, but I don't think she will have made a run for it just yet. She needs me to book something that isn't traceable, and if she still thinks I'm her friend and believe Ian to be the murderer, I'm sure she'll take advantage of that. Then when she does run, she'll tell me to delete everything, but I won't. If she manages to get away before she's arrested, I'll need to be able to tell the police exactly where she's gone.

Will I be in trouble if I help her? If she disappears before she can be arrested for these murders, and I've booked somewhere for her, will that make me an accessory of some sort? No, surely not. I've already told the police that she's seriously thinking about leaving Ian and taking the girls with her, so they know she's a flight risk. If I've warned them about it beforehand, that will exonerate me, surely?

These thoughts go round in my head for hours, all while I'm wondering when Bella will get in touch. Eventually I start to wonder if she's already been arrested. Scouring the internet for related stories, I can't find any new reference to Jenny's murder, or to Bella herself, but does that mean they haven't made a move yet, or that they're keeping it out of the news? I'm going mad wondering what the hell is going on, but I still can't bring myself to call Bella or ask her if she wants to meet. Now that I've handed over the knife and collected my thirty pieces of silver, I don't think I can face her in case she sees right through me and instantly knows what I've done.

It's Saturday morning when there's a knock on my door, and I look out of the window to see the two detectives standing on the front path. I go downstairs to let them in, then lead them up to my flat, hoping they're here to give me news about Bella and their investigation.

'How's it going?' I ask, once we're inside and out of the way of prying neighbours.

'The investigation is progressing,' one of them says, glancing sideways at her colleague. 'We wanted to talk to you about something.'

'Okay,' I say, sinking down onto the sofa. This might not be the good news I was hoping for.

'The phone number you gave us, can you confirm it please?'

I do, and the detective nods. 'Thanks, we just wanted to double-check. Now, on the night of Jenny Beckley's death, there are some text messages between her phone and the number you gave us. Can you confirm that you arranged to meet her?'

My heart sinks. I didn't tell them that part when I went through my story at the police station. I'd completely forgotten about the messages that would lead back to me from her phone, despite the fact that I've deleted them from mine.

'Er, yes. I wanted to talk to her about her brother. But she suggested such a strange place and time to meet, I didn't go.'

'You didn't go?'

Why did I say that? I should have admitted that I went, but didn't see her.

'Er . . . well, I set off. But I didn't meet her.' I hold out my hands, palms up. 'If I'm honest, I was scared. It was late at night and she wanted to meet me at her house, on the opposite side of the city. It didn't feel right.'

The detective nods. 'So you didn't meet up with her that night?'

'No.'

'In which case, can you explain why your DNA was found at the scene of her murder? Specifically, on her body?'

I freeze. I touched her. I checked her pulse, despite the fact she was clearly dead. If I tell the truth now, it will only sound like I'm lying, make me more suspicious.

For a moment, I stand there with my mouth open, unable to think of what to say. After a few beats, the detective steps forward and puts her hand on my arm.

'Isabella Butterworth, I am arresting you for the murder of Jennifer Beckley. You do not have to say anything, but it may harm your defence . . .'

BELLA

Epilogue

It's a three-hour drive to Sussex, where Caroline is in prison. I suppose I should stop thinking of her as that. She's Isabella, the same as me. Yet nothing like me. As I drive, I think back on our friendship and find myself feeling a pang of regret. I know she lied to me, but she was still a great friend to me, for a while.

I never intended for it to end like this. When I told her about the knife I expected her to call the police and tell them where to find it, not break into our house and take it herself. The whole plan had been to frame Ian, but I misjudged her.

In court it came out that she'd been letting herself into our house whenever she felt like it. All of the little things that made me think I was going mad, items being moved, my emails having been read, even when I thought Ian moved my car seat, all of those were her. She was obsessed with me, the prosecution said, and I can't deny that's exactly how it looked. Perhaps things have worked out for the best.

Everything spiralled after Beckley found me. I thought changing my name would be enough, but he was determined. When we met that night, I didn't go with the intention of pushing him, it just happened. If he hadn't threatened me, mentioned my children and how I should lose them the way he'd lost his daughter . . . Anyway, after that I intended for it to end there.

When Beckley's daughter died, it was an honest mistake on my part, but I couldn't risk going to prison. I had a family to think about, more than that paramedic had. I'm sorry he got a longer sentence, but that was hardly my fault. It was his mistake in the first place. I just didn't think to ask him about something that should have been part of his job.

After it happened, I told Ian everything. He loved me, so I knew he would do anything for me. He was the one who hacked into the system to change the date and time on the report I'd filed, so it looked like the note about the girl's blood sugar had always been there. He was also the one who managed to get rid of my name and photo from every hospital or professional website, and assured me that nobody would be able to find me. It was only afterwards, when he discovered that someone else was going to be held accountable for the girl's death, that he realised what he'd done. He's never looked at me the same since.

Ian and I talked about separating, not long after the girl died, because the stress of it was tearing us apart. In the end, we agreed to stay together for the children, but also because we each had something we didn't want the world knowing – I didn't want to be known as Dr Isabella Palmeri, whose mistake killed a girl and sent a man to prison, and he didn't want anyone to find out he'd been complicit in my lie. We were at a stalemate, but I think he'd got to the point of not caring. He still loves me, I know he does, because if he didn't love me he wouldn't want to hurt me. Otherwise he simply wouldn't care.

After Isabella was arrested, I asked him again about the photos she'd taken of him with Jenny and he admitted there'd been some flirtation, that they'd met for drinks a couple of times, but that it hadn't gone any further than that. His heart wasn't in it, he said, and he only did it because Jenny herself instigated it. After her brother died, she decided to carry on where he left off, blaming me for her niece's death. By seducing my husband, she was trying to ruin my life. If only she'd known I might have been quite glad to be rid of him.

It's become clear in the last six months that I can't be around him any more. We're destroying each other. But as long as we agree to keep each other's secrets we might manage an amicable separation. The girls are the only sticking point because I don't want to let go of them. That's why I decided to frame him for the murders – the perfect way to get him out of our lives. Of course, the girls would have been upset for a while, but I could have given them a much better life without him.

But in the end, Izzy was too easily convicted of killing Jenny; after all, she was obsessed with me, jealous of me getting close to another friend. I played up that angle in my testimony. The knife matched the wounds of the homeless woman as well, whatever her name was, but the Crown Prosecution Service decided to only focus on Jenny, because they couldn't find a clear motive for her to kill the other woman.

It's pure coincidence that Izzy saw her not long before I did. If I'd known she'd spoken to someone else about seeing me push Beckley over the barrier, I would have silenced both of them. As it was, I was crossing the foot-bridge of my own accord when I bumped into the homeless woman. She stared at me, and I could just see it in her eyes. She was scared of me, and she knew. I stopped to talk to her, hoping I'd imagined it, but she wouldn't speak to me, glancing furtively between me and the barrier. I came back the following night and slipped the knife between her ribs before she even had the chance to move. I was a doctor, I have no problem with blades.

Jenny was trickier, though. After I pushed her yet again on why she wouldn't give me any personal information or really let me know anything about her at all – given we were supposed to be friends – she snapped and told me everything. She told me who her brother was, and that she hated me for what I'd done to her family, causing her niece's death then driving her brother to suicide. At least she didn't realise I'd pushed him. Still, I thought it best if she was out of the way, too, not least because I felt like she'd humiliated me, pretending to be my friend for months. And because she knew who I was, when I'd tried so hard to be someone else . . .

I followed her home one evening, after she'd been to a class at the gym. She never told me where she lived, so I took matters into my own hands. Then I went back the following night and waited in that alley, knowing she would walk past. There was no hesitation on my part when it came to killing her; that's something I'm proud of. I left as quickly as I arrived, and I think I was just lucky that Izzy didn't see me.

As it is, she found out everything in the end anyway, thanks to Ian and his big mouth.

When I arrive at the prison, I sit in my car for ten minutes, steeling myself. I've dressed well today, understated but still in a way that shows my privilege. It won't hurt to demonstrate the power I have over her. Several times her defence tried to introduce me as a potential suspect, but the prosecution skilfully shot them down every time. I expect she's not very happy with me about that.

I'm shown to a table where I wait for her to be led into the room. A moment later, there she is, and I swallow down my shock at how much she's changed in such a short time.

'Isabella,' I say once she's sitting down opposite me. I've decided to use her real name now. Caroline has gone, the friend I confided in, the one who was going to help me escape from my miserable marriage. I'm still annoyed I didn't manage to get that part of my plan completed before she was arrested. The girls and I could be living hundreds of miles away by now.

'Isabella,' she replies, with a slight nod of her head.

We sit there for a moment, watching each other. Glancing surreptitiously at the other prisoners, I wonder what life must be like for her in here. She always struck me as a confident woman, though that part of her seemed to shrivel and die when she was in court. Has she toughened up now, or is she being eaten alive by the other women in here?

'Why are you here?' she asks eventually, unable to keep the snap from her voice.

'I wanted to see how you're doing,' I say, and she laughs, an actual genuine laugh. She's right, it doesn't sound plausible, and even I can't fully articulate my real reasons for being there. Part of me still cares about the version of her who was a good friend to me; part of me feels slightly guilty that she's in here for a crime she didn't commit, even though I know she tried her best to make sure I was there in her place. There's also a part of me that wants to draw a line under everything that happened, and tell her to let it go, accept her fate and let me move on with my life. The expression on her face tells me that won't be happening any time soon.

The one thing I still have to worry about is Ryan Beckley's death. The Crown Prosecution Service couldn't find enough evidence that he was murdered so his death is still officially a suicide. But if something were ever to be found, or if someone started to believe Izzy's story, they could still come for me. I can't guarantee I didn't leave another transient witness.

Izzy sits back in her chair and folds her arms. I think she's enjoying watching me, and I feel myself start to squirm under her gaze. We're the only two people who know the absolute truth about this situation, and she knows it. Maybe I don't have as much power as I assumed, and that thought terrifies me.

'What the hell do you expect me to say?' She glares at me as she speaks, never dropping eye contact, which makes me more uncomfortable. 'Everything's wonderful, I've never been happier?'

She glances over her shoulder at one of the guards, and I realise she's about to go back to her cell. I can't let her leave just yet. This meeting was supposed to be on my terms, not hers.

'Wait,' I say, and reach out to take her hand. I remember all the times she did the same to me – when she was reassuring me, comforting her friend, advising me on how to get away from Ian. I hope it'll make her think we still have a connection, that I'm concerned for her, but she shoots me a look of disgust.

'No physical contact,' she snaps, pulling herself out of my reach. I take a deep breath, wondering what to do now. This wasn't what I expected. She was obsessed with me, wasn't she? I know she thinks this is all my fault, but if she hadn't broken into my house, my plan to frame Ian would have worked. She only has herself to blame. I thought she'd see that, and be happy to see me.

'Look, just say what you want to say then get out. I don't want to see you.'

I sigh and shake my head. 'I don't know. I don't know what I wanted to say.'

'Leave.'

'I'm sorry. I know you probably never want to see me again.' I try to soften my expression, but she laughs bitterly.

'Don't try pulling your woe-is-me face. I know it's just an act designed to make people feel sorry for you. You used it well in court, I have to give you that.' She leans forward and lowers her voice. 'You should remember just how often I've seen it, and how it won't have any effect on me now. And after I get out, I'll see you again. Don't you worry about that.'

Izzy signals to the guard that we've finished and she wants to leave, and I stand up so quickly I catch the back of my calves on the chair, forgetting that it's bolted down and won't slide backwards. I ignore the sharp pain that shoots through my legs, trying to maintain my composure.

'I never meant . . .' I begin, but she glares at me with such venom that I fall silent. She turns away and follows the guard out of the room, not looking back. I don't know what she meant about seeing me again, but my mind is already racing. It'll be a long time before she gets out, but I need to make sure she can't find me.

And if she does, maybe she'll end up having an accident of her own . . .

Acknowledgements

Every time I sit down to write acknowledgements, I panic because I'm sure I'm going to miss someone. Writing a book isn't as simple as getting the words on a page, because there are so many people around you who help to make it happen, whether that's in the practical aspects of turning those words into a physical book, or through support, in the many forms that can take.

Huge thanks as always to my wonderful agent, Juliet Mushens, who is always the perfect balance between supportive and no-nonsense.

Thank you to my editor at Avon, Lucy Frederick, for trusting me when I had no idea what this book was going to be about, and for helping to shape it into something readable!

Also at Avon: Elisha Lundin, Becci Mansell, Ella Young, Maddie Dunne Kirby, Sammy Luton, Hannah Avery,

Charlotte Brown, Georgina Ugen and Emily Chan. Thanks to Claire Ward and Sarah Whittaker for cover design and Mayada Ibrahim for copy-editing.

I'm extremely grateful to John McKenzie for devising the scenario that led to Tony's imprisonment – any mistakes or flights of fancy with medical details and/or procedure are mine entirely. Also thanks to Amy McKenzie for putting up with me turning up at the house to ask about plot points!

As always, I'm thrilled to have the support of Nick and Mel Webb at The Rabbit Hole, Brigg, a wonderful independent bookshop that does loads for its community.

Thank you to all of the booksellers who have helped to champion my books, and to those who have invited me to take part in events – I'm always up for meeting readers and chatting about my books!

To my little writing group, Emma, Amy, Mel, Lorraine and Donna – thanks for always making me feel like a local celebrity, and not calling me out on how little I actually write when we meet!

To friends and family, both near and far, thank you for all your support – Will, Michelle, Hannah, Jen, Mette, Kate, Faye, Monica, Kay, Lizzie, Becky, Morna, Shane, Kirsty, Vicki, Sam, Suzy, and anyone else I might have forgotten!

Family have been a constant and invaluable support in the last year: my parents, Glynis and Mark; Gary, Edna, Julia and Patrick. Thanks for being on hand when help was needed!

And, most importantly, to Stuart, Bertie and Bea – thanks for putting up with the days I don't emerge from the office, and my strange plot conversations over meals. I know you wouldn't have me any other way.

If someone was in your house, you'd know . . .
Wouldn't you?

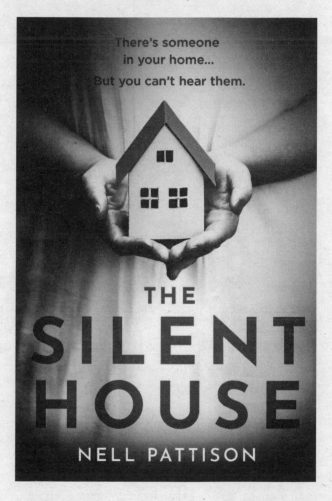

There's someone
in your home...
But you can't hear them.

THE
SILENT
HOUSE

NELL PATTISON

The first gripping Paige Northwood mystery.
Available in paperback, eBook and audio now.

What happened while they were
sleeping . . .?

No one
saw them.

No one
heard them.

No one can find them...

SILENT
NIGHT

NELL PATTISON
USA TODAY BESTSELLING AUTHOR

The second in the unmissable Paige Northwood series.
Available in paperback, eBook and audio now.

On a quiet street, one house is burning to
the ground . . .

THE
SILENT
SUSPECT

Only he
knows the
truth.

Only I
can save
him.

NELL PATTISON
THE *USA TODAY* BESTSELLING AUTHOR

The third heart-pounding Paige Northwood installment.
Available in paperback, eBook and audio now.

Seven friends. One killer. You can run,
but you can't . . .

'Guaranteed to give you shivers'
T. M. Logan

Available in paperback, eBook and audio now.